Finding the NANCY LYNN

By

DL Havlin

ISBN: 978-1-933678-33-7

Front Cover photograph provided by the author from the public domain.

Palm Pen Press, LLC.

Bokeelia, Florida 33922

www.DLHavlin.com

Dedication

I reserve my largest, most heart-felt thank you for my loving wife, partner, do everything assistant, *Jeanelle*. Without her support, encouragement, understanding and tolerance I would have abandoned writing long ago.

Acknowledgements

I used to read acknowledgements with little or no appreciation and with less feeling for the author and those cited. No more! After my writing journey of the last 20 plus years, I truly know the value of those who vitally contribute to the success of any author on their quest to produce a worthwhile work.

My first major debt is to Babs Brown and Robert Fulton, Ph.D., my patient, skillful, editors, and to authors Bev Browning and Mary Ann Evans, both mentors whose efforts have immeasurably improved my craft.

Chapter 1

"Are you sure you want one of these?" Trotter scanned the first large boat I'd look at with the intent of buying. I didn't answer him. I wasn't sure how much I wanted one. I stood on a dock in St. Petersburg because I knew how much my new girlfriend did. We waited for the boat broker to join us. Trotter, my business associate, and friend tried to keep me from making mistakes.

I changed the subject. "You could fish off this one." Some of the craft we'd walked by were built like streamlined bullets. A person only had a few feet at the transom to wet a line. This boat had an open area, one not encased with fiberglass and covered with fancy built-in seats. I shook my head to clear it. For the first time in my life, I wasn't buying a boat to go fishing.

"It's a Grady-White. That's a good boat maker," Trotter walked to the rear of the boat and said, "She's called, *The Hard Ass.* Her home port is Ocean City, New Jersey. She's for sale a long way from home. Want to get on her? I'm sure the person trying to sell her wouldn't mind."

I looked at the Marina and saw a salty looking lady step on to the dock. She smiled at us. From her nautical clothes, I believed our sales lady approached. She sized us up as she walked the dock. Her white Bermuda shorts, a white 'sailor's blouse' with a bit of blue rope decoration, and a captain's hat covered a tanned body, a body past its prime, but one cared for intensely. When she was ten feet from us, she said, "Gentlemen, you must be interested in the Grady. I'm Sal, you are?" "SJ Harrell," I said and extended my hand.

"Ken Bass," Trotter followed my lead.

Sal reached in her shirt pocket and removed a business card. She handed it to me.

"You're the one interested, correct?"

I nodded and said, "Yes."

"First big boat?"

I wondered if I was dealing with a mind reader. "Yes. How did you know?"

Sal laughed, "You look petrified and confused. I been doing this a lot of years. You're no different than 80% of first-time buyers. The remaining 20% are too stupid to be scared. Believe me, you're better off being apprehensive." Her deck shoes barely made a whisper when she hopped into the boat. Her knees acted as a shock absorber and she was as stable as a mountain goat on a slope. "Come aboard."

~ ~ ~ ~ ~ ~

"Well, what did you think?" Sal asked.

"It looks like it's been well maintained...for a boat built in 1991. There's wear and tear that you'd expect in a boat that old and one that appears had lots of use." I nodded to the kitchen and head. "A lot of fixtures and appliances need replacing."

"They do." She hesitated for a few seconds before asking, "Truthfully, what attracted you to this boat?"

I shrugged my shoulders, "The price." It was a hundred thousand less than comparable boats for sale.

She grinned, "This boat is actually overpriced. I take it that neither you nor your friend, are shipwrights. If you bought this boat, that's what you'd need to be." Sal patted the hull and said, "As far as I know, the hull is in good shape and I can't swear to that, other than that the '*Hard Ass*' is a money shredder."

"This boat hasn't had the whiskers, that's barnacles, removed in over a year. You don't know what's under them, that's the true hull condition, until they're off. Everything on this boat is original, and for the most part, it's been well maintained. That's fine, but the motors have 2,700 more hours than their recommended replacement point. Don't know if you noticed, but the bilge pump runs almost continuously. I happen to know why.

There's no leak in the hull. The water is seeping past the propeller driveshaft packing. That's on both shafts. They need replacing. The problem with that is: What is causing them to fail? If it's old age, it's not horrible. If the shafts are bent, major problem and major expense. There's a boat two berths up the dock, that's five years younger, four feet longer, that's recently been repowered, that's price is $110,000 more. Buying it will cost you $40,000 less, that's a minimum figure, than to put this vessel in reliable condition. Remember, you can't call AAA fifty miles out in the Gulf."

I was silent for several seconds, I'm sure my eyes were wide, and my chin was a tiny bit ajar. Trotter had that, 'I told you so,' look on his face.

"I didn't tell you that to scare you. Hell, I want to sell you a boat. But...I want to sell you the right boat." Sal leaned forward. "This might sound too elementary, but have you really thought about what you want out of your boat?"

The second I realized I had to search for an answer, I realized I had no idea what I wanted. It would be nice to be able to catch some grouper and snapper from it, but my primary intent was making Dennia Hays happy. I admitted, "Past being able to fish some off it, I don't even know the questions to ask myself."

Sal nodded, "You just past the first big hurdle. That's realizing you haven't given enough thought to what you want. Owning a boat, a big one like this, can be one of the greatest experiences in life. Get the wrong one, and it can be hell, and I don't want you pissed at me because you spent a few hundred thou on an anchor around your neck. You married?"

"Not yet." I wanted to be.

"Okay, you got something to write on?" Sal asked.

"I have an I-pad. I can just record them." I answered.

"Good, ready?"

In a few seconds, I nodded.

"First thing you want to ask yourself is: Do I want to take extended trips? Are you going to go out and be back to the dock the same day most of the time? You buy different boats depending.... Second, how many guests are you normally going to take with you? That changes the size and configuration. What are your activities? Cruise? Fish? Sunbath? Shack-up? Dive? Third thing makes a lot of differences. Are you going to do coastal cruising or deep-water boating? That determines things like hull design and cabin configuration. How fast do I want to get from point 'A' to point 'B'? It determines what equipment you need, tank capacities, even defense weapons."

"Weapons?" I asked.

Sal looked at me for a few seconds before answering. "You heard right, weapons. If you stay in US waters, you're relatively safe from modern-day pirates. But, they do exist.

Drug cartels seize boats. Terrorists seize boats. Human traffickers seize boats. They've all been known to stop a boat, kill its occupants, and use it to ferry drugs or whatever." Sal saw the doubt in my features. "Sound far-fetched?"

"A little," I answered.

"Think about how easy a boat like the ones you're looking at makes their lives. There are no customs waiting at a public boat ramp or a private dock. No way for a sex slave to escape or scream for help...it's a big ocean. No need for a mule who could talk.

Terrorists can smuggle weapons, bombs, and agents with a minimum fear of detection. They can even live on the boat and store death until they want to unleash it. Why do it at sea? Why not just steal a boat from a dock. There's a hell of lot less chance of getting caught. People are around marinas and they usually know who should and shouldn't be there. A boat missing from a dock is likely to be reported in a few days. At sea, there's no one around; there's no better place to dispose of evidence...bodies. It usually takes a week to a month to realize the owners are missing. Is that going to happen to you? It isn't if you stick to staying close in US waters. If you venture deep into the Caribbean, go to Mexico, even the Bahamas have a few incidents, you have a chance to become a victim. Not a great one, but a chance."

I nodded my head, "I can see that. Makes taking a cruise on Royal Caribbean make more sense." I stood and extended my hand toward Sal. "I have a lot of homework to do before I pull out my checkbook. You have my complete confidence. When it comes to buying, I'll be back."

She smiled, shook my hand, and stood. “Two more suggestions, if I may. First, you said, ‘not yet’ when I asked you about being married. If that means you intend to take a wife, make her input part of the decision. People have gotten divorced over boats. Second, once you think you know what you want, find one as close to your ideal as you can, then rent one, borrow one, wiggle an invitation as a guest...do something to spend time on a boat like you want to buy before you pull out your checkbook.”

# # # # #

Chapter 2

“I might know someone.” Riaffort clasped his hands behind his head and leaned back in his chair.

“I’ll owe you big time, buddy,” I said. My initial investigation into renting a big boat found rentals were scarce as hen’s teeth, and *very, very* expensive. I’m, by nature, cheap.

“Actually, you won’t. You’ll be helping me out with a client’s request.” Riaffort Richards gazed out the window of his beach view, legal office. “You and Dennia would have to pass muster. “I handled Marvin Hellmann’s legal affairs for twelve years before he died, and I’ve handled his wife Melanie’s for ten, afterward. In those twenty-two years, I haven’t had a client who has been a greater source of revenue or contributed more to this.” He pointed to his white hair.

“You don’t make this sound good. Maybe I should go ahead and rent the cruiser I found in Ft. Lauderdale.” His words raised a caution flag. Riaffort was a master of understatement.

“Don’t run so quickly. Let me explain something to you.” Riaffort put on his friendly smile. I instinctively reached to protect my billfold, as a funny. He laughed and continued, "Melanie owns the perfect boat for you and Dennia to take a trial cruise on. The boat is named the *Nancy Lynn*. It's a bit more than you're looking for, but it is close.

Forty-two feet, sleeps six comfortably...eight if you're friendly, has all the bells and whistles of home, twin screws, diesel engines, and I've caught everything from grouper to marlin off it."

"So, what's the problem?" I asked.

"Melanie Hellmann is a sweet lady. She's not old, fifty-two, but she can be as tedious as dealing with an eighty-year-old. Pure fuddy-duddy." I'm sure I didn't look convinced. He took a deep breath and said, "Cards on the table time. Melanie wants me to be a chaperone of sorts for her daughter...who really doesn't need one."

"How does that affect me?"

"I want you to be my stand-in. Her daughter is named Margo. Margo is a free spirit. She's asked if she can borrow the boat for a month to sail around the Bahamas with her boyfriend and two other couples. Melanie's arranged a four-day trial run of sorts. Margo and friend and one of the other couples are to go along on a maintenance run. Melanie hasn't said it in so many words, but I'm on board to see if Margo interferes with Captain

Springer's running the ship."

"Captain Springer? Is there a professional skipper she hires to run her rig?"

"Yes. She pays him 365, whether he's running the boat or not. He's a good fellow. And a good sailor. You'll like him." Riaffort shook his head. "This is one of those mother-daughter feuds. Margo is thirty and is Melanie's stepdaughter. The girl was spoiled rotten and she hasn't grown up. Margo thinks everybody died and left her boss."

"Riaffort, the last thing I want is to get involved in is a family pissing match. I want to take Dennia out to sea and find out if we really want to buy a cruiser. I don't want to worry about being a referee in a smackdown."

"If I can work out a *separate trip* for you and Dennia, will you do this for me. It's a four-day trip for the annual hull exam and to get the bottom painted with an anti-fouling coating. You'll learn a lot. Dennia can go or not, it's up to you. I'll get the second trip setup with Melanie. Your trip will be five days to wherever you and Dennia want to go."

The proposition was an interesting one. "You said Melanie wants to meet me. Okay, I want to meet Margo and her boyfriend, so I know what I'm getting into...before I say yes."

"Deal!"

"Hey friend, I did not say yes." I cautioned him I might back out if Margo and company were a nightmare. "One question. Why doesn't Melanie ride along to observe?"

Riaffort sighed. "Melanie hates the boat. She seldom goes out and when she does, it's only for a day. Besides, I think she believes Margo would be on her best behavior if she went. She wants to know what the girl will do when the cat isn't there."

"If Mrs. Hellmann hates the boat, why does she keep it?"

"Marvin, that's her late husband, made her promise she'd keep it...on his death bed. Look, Melanie is a nice woman, who has a hundred times more money than brains.

She is stubborn; Margo gets more than a little from the environment she lives in. But......You'll like Melanie. Let me set up the meeting."

"Alright." I looked out at the sands of Vero Beach and the blue Atlantic beyond. The waters beckoned me. What could go wrong? Even if I have a miserable time on the Margo monitoring trip, it would be over and done with after those four days. *I thought*.

# # # # #

Chapter 3

"The GPS and Riaffort's instructions don't match." I looked at the notes my lawyer had scribbled on a sheet of paper. According to the screen in Dennia's Lincoln, the road we drove on, ended.

"I'd depend on Mr. Richards' instructions more than the electronic system." Dennia steered the curves that undulated with the contour of a branch of the Indian River estuary. She turned onto a road that didn't exist on the screen. "It's probably a private road, Sly," Heavy vegetation surrounded the drive. Cabbage palms, low coastal oaks, palmettoes, and Spanish Bayonet restricted vision to a few yards on either side.

Two hundred yards down the road, a large iron gate blocked the blacktop. It swung open at our approach. Ten-foot-high white brick columns supported the wrought-iron gate and an arch over the drive that featured the name of the estate, "*Hells Acres*," centered on it. Dennia said, "The name must come from Hellmann. The grounds and house are beautiful."

Indeed, they were. The sprawling three-story mansion was situated on a point where a tidal creek joined with the Intercoastal Waterway. A structure much larger than most peoples' homes sat over the water. Royal Palms lined the drive to an elaborate entrance. Gleaming white paint covered everything man had made. Bougainville and Hibiscus added bright colors to the area on both sides of the front door.

I recognized the man waiting for us at the stairs leading to the porch. He was dressed in a tan suit, jacket off and over the shoulder, with tennis shoes: Riaffort's version of casual. It was the first opportunity I'd had to introduce Dennia to my lawyer.

~ ~ ~ ~ ~ ~

"Did you have problems finding the place?" Riaffort asked.

"None. Your instructions were clear." We walked a path around the house with a profusion of flowers and ornamentals lining it. "Sorry, I'm late," I added.

"Five minutes is not late. Besides, if things operate like normal around here, we won't see Margo and her man for another half-hour. Melanie and Captain Springer are on the lanai. You'll get a chance to get acquainted." Riaffort turned his head to Dennia. "Mrs. Hays, Sly said you were beautiful. It is one of the few times I've known him to understate a fact."

"Thank you, Riaffort. And...please...call me Dennia."

The beautiful lady beside me was dressed as I had expected at our first meeting, not in 'ranch duds.' The designer dress, high heels, and auburn hair piled high with loose curls cascading looked the part of a celebrity.

Breathtaking was not hyperbole. We rounded the corner of the mansion and the screened lanai came into view. Tennis courts and a basketball backboard were behind it; a pool occupied space between the lanai and the boathouse.

Seated on the porch were Melanie Hellmann and an older gentleman who I assumed was Captain Springer. She smiled, waved, and welcomed us with, "Please, please, ya'all come in!"

~ ~ ~ ~ ~ ~

Awkward silence wasn't a problem. Melanie Hellmann was an interesting character, capable of asking a question, answering it, and venturing an opinion without the interruption of others. Our cordial introduction and good chemistry started from the first touch of our handshake. Melanie reminded me of my good friend and associate, Russ Foxx. I imagined a non-stop conversation between the two and wondered if that would even be possible.

Captain Springer...Captain Adrian Springer, that was another matter. *Entirely*. I guessed the man's age as sixty, plus or minus a few. He was a small man, no more than 5'6" in the thick heeled boots he wore. A thin, wiry body emphasized his lack of size. I sensed his character overshadowed any other shortcoming. From the firmness of his handshake, to piercing eyes that emanated strength, the sense that Captain Springer was a trustworthy, honorable man was clearly stated.

An interesting contrast existed between Dennia and Melanie. The differences between their ages were chronologically minimal, the visual and behavioral black and white widened the eye. Though only seven years difference in age, Dennia looked and acted a dozen years younger. Melanie presented the appearance of a mid-seventies matron, from a layer of extra padding, to a pompous, self-righteous manner she tried to control without total success. Dennia strived to improve her appearance, the calendar be damned. Melanie had succumbed to the nebulousness called age.

When Melania stopped to get her breath, Captain Springer asked, "Mrs. Hellmann, while we're waiting for Margo, could I take our guests aboard the *Nancy Lynn*. Mr. Richards assures me they're very interested."

"Why, of course." Melanie brimmed. "That will give me a chance to become a proper host. I don't know where Rosita is with our mint-juleps and the canape tray. I'll check on Margo, too. She is a wonderful girl, but she doesn't check the clock frequently enough."

~ ~ ~ ~ ~ ~

My first look at the *Nancy Lynn* was impressive, even contained inside the confines of the boathouse. From the flying bridge to the stern to the bow the boat was immaculate. No scuffed-up varnish on the normal wear points where wooden plates were used to board the boat or act as a coaming on the transom, existed.

The white fiberglass shined for its entire 52′ length and its 15′ beam. We stood on an elevated platform even in height with the flying bridge. Every instrument, control, and panel gleamed from polish.

Captain Springer stepped onto the bridge and welcomed us to what we found out was 'his baby.' "Welcome aboard the *Nancy Lynn*. She's a lovely lady. Lonesome since Marv passed."

Dennia stepped into the boat, whistled, and said, "This is cleaner than my maid keeps my kitchen."

"Who details her?" I asked.

"I do. Actually, she should be perfect. Keeping her spotless is most of what I do." Captain Springer pulled a rag from his pants pocket, waved it in the air, and said, "I use this more than the radar. Ferrying you around will be a treat for me. The *Nancy Lynn* only sees blue waters five or six times a year. She makes three or four trips up and down the Intercostal and a couple of maintenance trips. That's about it. All told, she's out and about less than thirty days a year."

"If I had a boat like this, you would have to pry me off of it!" Dennia rubbed the captain's seat.

"Back in the day, if you wanted to find Marv, this is where you'd go."

"What does she draw?" I asked.

"Thirty-seven inches. Mr. Hellmann had the hull custom made. It draws nine inches less than the standard model. The change in design slows her a little, but Marv didn't care about speed. It doesn't sound like a great deal, but he used to go down to Florida Bay and the Keys a lot. It makes a difference there. She hasn't been that far since Mr. Hellmann died."

"How fast does she run?" I asked.

Springer laughed, "She'll do 34 mph, but you need to pull a fuel barge behind for the diesel you burn with those engines wide open. Cruising speed is around 26 mph. That's the best mileage speed. She's got twin screws with extra capacity for fuel. Mr. Hellmann had the idea he wanted to take her through the Panama Canal. Never got the chance." The Captain sighed and nodded his head. "That man dearly loved this boat." He pointed to a stairway. "Let's go look at what the ladies want to see; what's down below."

~ ~ ~ ~ ~ ~

Three luxurious cabins, a completely equipped kitchen, a polished mahogany wood bar, completely stocked, a head with a larger than normal shower, and padded plush everywhere summed up the *Nancy Lynn's* interior. In spite of being used to living in 'high tone' surroundings a lot more than me, Dennia was wide-eyed at the opulence. She shook her head and said, "This is a bit much, Sly. I'd be worried I'd damage something every time we used it."

We stood in the rear cockpit, talking to Captain Springer, when a buzzer scared us all. The Captain said, "Someday, I'll rip that thing off the wall. Melanie is signaling that we need to go back to the lanai. The Golden Girl has arrived. You met Margo?"

"No, that's what we're here for," I said.

He smiled as he climbed the stairs to the flying bridge and stepped onto the dock.

I asked him, "It's not that bad, is it?"

"You be the judge."

"If you're going to be stuck on the boat with her for a month...that's tough duty," I said.

"Sweating in a foxhole in Desert Storm was tough duty for an old marine. Margo isn't much to worry about." Captain Springer chuckled a little. "I'll handle it the way I will this meeting we're going to. I'll disappear. You'd be surprised, you can do that even on a boat the size of the *Nancy Lynn*. Anyway, I doubt we'll be out more than two weeks. Margo is like a cat I had once. She drags trash home, plays with it a week or two, then can't get far enough away from it. That's the way she's always treated her boy toys. She won't change."

"Really," Dennia said. "That the reason you don't like being around her?"

Springer laughed heartily and said, "Ma'am, I was born on a dairy farm. A man shouldn't have to be exposed to shit but so much in a lifetime."

# # # # #

Chapter 4

We hadn't settled in our chairs when Captain Springer expedited his exit. "If you all will excuse me, I have to make sure everything is shut down on the boat. I may have left some lights on."

We got our first exposure to Margo's style and character. She frowned and squeaked in a falsetto voice, "Bye, Captain S." She shot a bird at him as he left the lanai.

"Margo, please!" Melanie said in a disgusted manner.

"Why don't you fire the old fart?" Margo asked. Her miniskirt exposed more than it should have...on purpose. She looked at me out of the corner of her eye. Trying to be as sultry as an over-weight, over made-up girl of thirty could be, she failed, miserably. "You know the only reason you keep the old bastard around here is because he was Daddy's drinking bud."

"That is not true. Adrian Springer is a fine boat captain and one who has been unfailingly loyal to your father and me." Melanie was incensed.

"It's my fault the Captain left. I asked him to turn on some systems on the boat and talked enough to distract him." I smiled and asked the boyfriend, Gino Razze, "Have you seen the boat? It's quite a craft."

"Yes." His answer was bored and dismissive.

"What do you two do for a living?" Margo demanded center stage.

I looked at Dennia and she said, "You first."

"I have a ranch in the center of the state. Raise cattle mostly. And, I have a business doing contract recovery work."

Margo's eyes brightened, "Oh, like finding sunken ships?"

"Something like that."

"What do you do?" Margo asked Dennia.

"I have a ranch near LaBelle. We raise cattle and horses. I own a couple of small businesses."

"That's nice. If you have to work, you might as well be your own boss." Margo looked at Dennia with distaste. She had a superiority complex and saw no one as her equal. She'd fired a verbal shot across Dennia's bow.

"That's true," Dennia said. The twinkle in her eye as she spoke to Mrs. Hellmann dismissed Margo from the conversation. "Melanie, I love your shoes! Would you mind telling me where you got them?"

"Alexander's in West Palm. He specializes in shoes and accessories," Melanie beamed as she spoke.

Margo wouldn't be left out. "Sure you didn't get them at Pay Less?"

Dennia came to Melanie's defense and crushed Margo at the same time, "Yes Margo, I can see that you're familiar with that store, by what you're wearing. My maid says they have a great bargain rack."

Melanie laughed to make Margo's humiliation complete, and added, "Dennia would you like directions on how to get to Alexander's?"

"I certainly would," Dennia said.

While Melanie and Dennia began a long conversation on the virtue of buying quality shoes, I watched Margo's reaction and her boyfriend's lack of any interest in...anything. Margo knew she'd been figuratively thrown out of the conversational bar. After being left out and ignored in the first few sentence exchanges, Margo announced, "I need a fucking drink," got up from her chair in a manner to expose what wasn't already visible under her skirt, and flounced out of the room in a huff.

Since Gino expressed no desire to talk, I spent my time observing him. He was olive-skinned, with black hair, and dark brown eyes. His name sounded Italian, but his look was more middle east. Margo's reason for the attraction was obvious...his George Clooney level of good looks. Average sized, his well-conditioned body, made the time he spent in the weight room visible. His face was an expressionless mask. Coldness seeped from his pupils, a frigidity that gave him a strange, zombie-like effect. He showed no interest in anything transpiring around him. I guessed him at thirty-five, though he had one of those timeless faces that defy accurate results. If I was to be stuck on a boat with him,

I wanted to know a little more.

I asked, “Gino, you live around here?”

“Ft. Lauderdale.”

“You work down there?”

“Some.” He shrugged his shoulders. “I make pizzas.”

“You own the pizza place?”

“No.”

“Oh, you like to fish or anything?”

“No.”

“You live in Ft Lauderdale? Last time I drove through there the traffic was horrible,” I’d decided to make one last try.

“I live with Margo in Delray Beach, okay? She keeps me fed; I keep her happy.

Know what I mean?” Gino’s frown told me how futile further discussion would be. “Yes, I do.”

~ ~ ~ ~ ~ ~

“Before you ask, I have your answers. I will pass up the four-day trip with that Gino ghoul and Queen Slutsky. If you think you can face that, go ahead. Question two, it would be wonderful to spend time on the *Nancy Lynn* with just you and the captain. That was what Riaffort promised, right?” Dennia spoke as we drove through the front gates of Hell’s Acres.

"It's only four days. I'll have Captain Springer for company. I can spend all my time with him learning some seamanship." I was trying to convince myself, not Dennia.

"At least, her boyfriend keeps to himself. Margo...what a piece of work." Dennia shook her head. "We'd end up, pulling hair, scratching eyes, and rolling on the deck, if I went."

"Yep, I'm more concerned about being trapped on the boat with her than dying of boredom from Gino."

Dennia chuckled, "Want to make a bet?"

"On what?"

"At least once, while you're on the trip, Margo will make an appearance, buck naked, offering you her fat ass as a freebie. I'll give odds, say five to one."

"Nope. I won't take that one." I smiled. "She doesn't like Captain Springer. If I stay in his vision at all times, maybe—"

"Wouldn't work. She's the type to do two to get the one she wants."

I whistled and said, "You're probably right. I need some varmint repellent. Any ideas?"

"None."

"I think there a couple of skunks in one of the cypress heads on my ranch. I could catch one of them and put it in my cabin."

Dennia laughed and said, "I've never met a young woman who was as well off with so little class."

# # # # #

Chapter 5

I didn't see them until two hours after the *Nancy Lynn* left the boathouse. Margo's friends failed to make an appearance. It made me curious but not enough to seek them out.

We'd made the turn to port and had entered the St. Lucie Canal a half-hour ago.

The south fork of the St. Lucie River became the canal that connected the Atlantic to Lake Okeechobee. We passed under the I-95 bridge. Sitting next to Captain Springer on the flying bridge gave me a great opportunity to learn. Focused on his handling of the *Nancy Lynn*, it was the Captain who called my attention to the couple at the transom.

"I don't much care for *them*," Springer said. He nodded his head toward the man and woman leaning on the transom.

All I could see were rears. The woman wore a flowered dress...large red and pink hibiscus on a solid black background. The man...jeans and brown shirt. Neither wore hats, so I could see their shiny black straight hair. I thought, *Oh, well, I have four days to see them and enjoy or be sick of the experience*.

"Damned nuts!" The Captain refocused my attention on the canal ahead. "See the wake that asshole is throwing? In a canal like this, the wave action plays hell with the banks. Pulls the sand into the canal."

I looked back at the couple, but they had vanished. "Margo's guests. What's the deal with them?"

"You mean why did I take a dislike to them so quick?" He snuck a glance at me and quickly returned his eyes to the canal. After several seconds, he said, "I have to admit to being prejudice. I don't like people talking in front of me in a language I can't understand."

"What language were they speaking?"

"Hell, I don't know. That's why I don't like it." He shook his head. "Leave it to Margo to bring home strange fruit. She went to college up north until she flunked out of most of them. Brown. Columbia. NYU. Iona. And, a bunch more. She used to bring home some of the weirdest collection of street sweepings I ever saw. It like to drove poor Melanie crazy. Now she brings home a new boyfriend every six months. She wears them out and goes on to the next. Margo's due for a new one."

"Wears them out?" I needed confirmation.

"You're no choir boy. Figure it out."

Confirmed.

~ ~ ~ ~ ~ ~

The turbid waters of Lake Okeechobee curled away from the bow of the *Nancy Lynn*. I was in the captain's seat for the first time and thoroughly enjoyed it. When we cleared the confines of the St. Lucie Canal and entered the lake, Captain Springer offered me the chance to take the helm and I snatched it. The channel markers that would safely guide us through shallows as we approached the south shore and the rim canal were in view. That canal would connect us with the Caloosahatchee River.

Springer tapped me on the shoulder, and said, "Okay, Sly, I take the wheel here. It gets tricky in spots."

I moved out of the captain's seat and Springer slid in. "You did good. Handled her like a pro. Most folks are nervous at the helm the first time they run a big boat like the *Nancy Lynn*. You were calm...didn't over-steer...no panicked adjustments that weren't needed."

"Thanks." If I looked calm, it wasn't because I was calm inside.

The Captain removed his Polaroids, cleaned them, and propped them back on his nose. He looked up at me and asked, "It's almost one. How about going to the galley and fixing a couple of sandwiches and bringing them up here? I'm hungry. I like salami and Swiss. Bread's in the locker on the left of the stove. There's soft drinks and water in the fridge."

"Sure." I'd been up and down the stairs and in and out of the cabin enough to move freely. The sound of voices came from inside the cabin. When I could see in, Margo, Gino, and the mystery couple were lounging on the couches. They were engaged in serious conversation until they saw me enter the room. It became quiet, instantly.

I said, "Hi folks," as I entered and opened the refrigerator. They smiled.

Margo said, "Hello, Sly," and tried to look sexy.

Gino nodded at me and said, "Hi." Then he spoke to the others, "Iyon ang sinabi ko sa iyo."

I recognized the language from one of my assignments with the government. The translation of his words was *this is the one I told you about*. Tagalog is a Filipino dialect. I smiled and said, "Magandang umaga," or good morning in English. I expected one of two reactions: A profusion of conversation at finding someone with whom they could talk or silence if the use of the language was to remain secretive. Those on the couches exchanged glances. No one spoke. My anxiety level rose immediately.

As I was fixing sandwiches, Margo got up and walked to me. After watching me slap mayonnaise on bread slices, she said, "My, Sly, you are looking *good* this morning." "Thank you," I purposely didn't smile. My gut began telling me something. Problems were possible and I didn't need Margo's over-active libido creating complications.

"Where did you learn Tagalog?" she asked.

"In the Philippines," I answered and asked, "Do your friends speak English?"

"Yes, we do," The dark-haired man stood up and joined Margo and me at the cabinet top where I was finished the sandwiches. He offered his hand and a wide smile. "My name is Galang Marcos. I am *not* related to the former dictator. The woman on the couch is, Dalisay, my wife. My family moved to the States when I was a baby. Dalisay is from north of Manila near where the old US base, Clark Field, is located. And, you are *our new friend* Mr. Sly Harrell, correct?" There was a hint of Bostonian in his pronunciations.

Smiling, I nodded a response.

"Hello, Mr. Harrell," Dalisay stood, spoke, and returned to the couch.

"Don't you want to know where I learned to speak Tagalog?" Margo was feeling left out.

"Where," I tried to sound as uninterested as possible.

"At NYU. Gino and I have been together five months. He speaks it and my friends do. Gino taught it to me in bed. Well, not the Runnells. Diane and Hall, that's the other couple going on the cruise, we met in engineering classes at Tandon. They're working. That's why they aren't here. A company is finishing up diving subs Hall designed we're going to use in the Bahamas."

I asked Gino, "Are you Filipino?"

"My grandmother is from Cebu. I've been there on vacation. I'm from Brockton."

While we spoke, I had a good opportunity to observe the Marcos couple. Both were younger...early to mid-twenties. Galang was a cookie-cutter clone of the hundreds of men I'd met in Manila. Stocky at 5'6", his emblematic black hair spoke of his melting-pot heritage. The hint of some oriental blood shown in the eyes and their set. Those intelligent eyes presented a false warmth and friendliness I felt masked hostility. But, toward who or what? Many Filipinos don't view Americans kindly.

Dalisay, typical of ladies I'd met in the Philippines, warmed the cool cabin with a submerged friendliness. She was smart, observant, and trained to remain a silent fixture in the background. Her pleasant features ran more to her rural Tagalog ancestors. Short, barely over 5' and sexually full-bodied, she dressed to obscure rather accentuate her figure. Impossible to miss, the sharp mind hid behind equally sharp pupils.

Our small talk turned to engineering subjects. Margo was surprisingly well versed in the topics being discussed. However, when I gathered up the sandwiches to take to the flying bridge, something happened that raised my caution flags to the top of their masts.

I paid Margo a casual compliment regarding her knowledge of hydraulics. Her answer, "See, I'm smart, good looking, and the best fuck in fifty states."

Her gross, uncalled for language didn't shock me; the looks of disdain and disgust on all three of her companions did! You don't spend a month isolated on a boat with someone you appear to loathe. Not unless you have an ulterior motive! That concerned me.

~ ~ ~ ~ ~ ~

I loitered outside the cabin entrance before I mounted the stairs to the bridge...and listened. My intuition was rewarded with one sentence from Galang. "Gino, you did a terrible job of finding out what kind of a person we would be with on this trip." I was now sure of who was in charge.

~ ~ ~ ~ ~ ~

"We're going to lose twenty minutes here," Captain Springer said as he maneuvered the *Nancy Lynn* alongside buttressed pilings designed to moor boats waiting for the locks to operate. We were stalled at one of the three water control damns on the Caloosahatchee that operated between Lake Okeechobee and the Gulf of Mexico. Galang sat on the bridge with us. He'd been asking about the damn, their purpose, and what would happen if they were removed.

I asked, "Do either of you know about this area's history? It's interesting."

"Can't say I do," Springer answered.

"This area is part of Florida's pioneer heritage. It's cattle country. Just a couple miles from here, as the crow flies, is the cemetery where Billy Bowlegs III is buried. He was a famous Seminole Indian leader. There's a monument to him there."

"Would you like to see it?" Galang inquired.

"How you going to do that?" Springer asked.

"I'll show you," Galang went down the bridge stairs and disappeared into the cabin. Within three minutes he reappeared. He held a drone and a laptop in his hands. "Which direction?"

I pointed toward the north-northeast. "I'd guess two miles plus or minus."

Excited to have an opportunity to display his skills, he had the drone airborne and the camera returning pictures to the laptop screen in a few minutes. The TV broadcast an oak wooded area with houses scattered through it. The drone was elevated enough to see Florida Highway 78. I told Galang, "Get over that road and follow it to the right." He complied. In less than a minute the cemetery came into view. Another half-minute and the large marker-memorial to the old Indian chief was in sight.

"I'm going to take a few still pictures," Galang said. A couple of flashes confirmed his intent.

"We're close to being able to go through the lock. You need to get that thing back here, so you don't lose it," the Captain said.

"Don't worry about that. I'm as good as there is with drone guidance systems."

~ ~ ~ ~ ~ ~

At the last lock we had to pass through, I was holding one of the ropes used to keep the boat stable as water poured through the gates allowing the boat to drop to a lower elevation. As I held on, I felt something drop on my shirt. I looked down, then up! An anhinga deposited a large white smear of guano on me. Cursing, I couldn't change my shirt until the boat was on its way downriver.

Captain Springer got us underway, the couples headed for the bow, and I headed for my cabin, and pulled a clean shirt from my luggage. Footsteps in the hall drew no attention other than the knowledge someone passed my door. I carefully stripped off my shirt, folded it, and found a plastic back to store it in.

I had my clean shirt over my head when the click of the door latch told me someone was entering. Hastily, I spun around and got my head through the shirt's opening.

"Oh! I'm sorry. Wrong cabin." Margo stood in the doorway, naked except for a towel draped over her shoulder. The only other thing she wore was her most available smile. My two thoughts were that I was glad I hadn't taken the bet with Dennia and it was difficult to look at chopped liver when you were used to fillet mignon. I turned away and said as coldly as I could, "Not a problem."

~ ~ ~ ~ ~ ~

Our trip took longer than anticipated, the locks causing a major time loss. We arrived at the Owl Creek Boat Yard a half-hour late. Captain Springer anchored the *Nancy Lynn* in an oxbow bend that had been cut off by the canal the Army Corp of Engineers dug. It was a quiet evening with one additional disconcerting observation...both Galang and Gino had added hidden knives in sheaths located in the small of their backs, beneath their clothes. The day had been instructive. My knowledge of the function and control of a large cruiser was increasing exponentially. My concerns about Melanie Hellmann's plan to loan her boat to stepdaughter and friends were growing as fast. I wondered what I would learn tomorrow.

# # # # #

Chapter 6

I woke up to Thump! Thump, Thump! “Ahhhh, that hurts!” The noise and scream came from the cabin next to me, the one belonging to Margo and Gino. After that, I heard low groans and Margo crying. There is little way to hide what goes on in a 52’ boat. Making the decision if I should knock on the door and ask if they were ‘alright,’ was almost made when sounds ended.

I was in the first twilight of sleep when the sound of angry male voices snatched me back to full consciousness. There was a brief scuffle followed by the slamming of the cabin’s door. My adrenalin was pumping. Sleep was unobtainable. A long period of time elapsed. Noises began to seep through the thin wall that’s soundproofing was inadequate. This time...no pain. Margo’s words were full of passion, urging on her partner. I’d had enough. As silently as I could, I slipped my clothes on, climbed the stairs to the flying bridge where Captain Springer chose to sleep. Mosquito netting kept the little beasts at bay. Lifting it as carefully as I could, I ducked inside, curled up on the vacant couch, and tried to get to sleep.

When I found a comfortable position, Springer said in a low voice, "Disgusting. I'm facing a month of that shit." It was the last thing I remember as sleep reclaimed me.

~ ~ ~ ~ ~ ~

"Sirs." A gentle sounding voice eased me from sleep's clutches.

"Sirs." It repeated. I squinted at a face that only partially blocked the strong first rays of the risen sun. Springer's couch squeaked as he rolled over. He blinked at the girl peering at us through the mosquito netting.

"Magandang umaga, Dalisay," wishing her good morning, as I swung my legs off the couch and sat up.

Seeing the dismay in the Captain's countenance, Dalisay said, in English, "Good morning sirs, I am making breakfasts for us. Galang asks if you wish to join us. I am making a Philippine breakfast. Garlic fried rice, Eggs...sunnyside up, and longganisa. I think you will like it. Will you join us?"

"Thanks, I will," accepting her offer that sounded good to me.

Springer nodded and said, "Sure, thanks." She disappeared as silently as she came.

As we slipped shoes on, before heading downstairs, Springer asked, "Eggs and rice are great. What the hell is longganisa? I don't want to eat no bull's balls or any of that crazy stuff."

I laughed and started down the stairs, "Sausage."

~ ~ ~ ~ ~ ~

The sober mood, limited conversation, and visible results of what transpired in Margo and Gino's cabin, made for an air of uneasiness. At times, outright tension.

Purple bruises were on Margo's thighs, arms, and were on one cheek. She sat on a cushion confirming a suspicion. Despite the obvious, she was as close to Gino as she could force her body. She clung to his elbow.

Gino had his own battle marks. A big bruise on his throat, redness spreading from one cheek to and across his swollen nose, and a bandaged forearm were evidence of the violence that occurred last night. Galang's knuckles and hand were discolored and a bandaid covered a cut.

The frown and expression on Captain Springer's face were as indicting as a 200word speech. I believe the spectacle froze his vocal cords. He'd already expressed his dismay at being required to endure a month at sea with our "company." The remaining two plus days of the trip I doubt he spoke a hundred words to Marcos, Gino, and Margo.

I did my best to appear unaffected by the violence I audibly witnessed. Communications between the Marcos and me were uneasy but existed. Hiding my feelings isn't a strong point of mine. The result was the complete end of communication between Gino and me. The longer the trip lasted, the more animosity built.

Whether on purpose or accident, an incident occurred on the last day of the sail back across the state.

I started down the cabin stairs at the same time Gino started up. We ended up staring at each other with less than two feet between our noses. Our eyes locked in a test of wills. He inched forward. I didn't budge. Hate fired his eyes. I'm sure mine reciprocated. His fists balled and raised. "If you want to live, I'd forget what you're thinking, Gino," I said. His teeth bared, and he trembled slightly—not in fear—in pure rage. My eyes stayed locked on his and I stood rock still. Finally, I won the test of wills...he retreated off the stairs and allowed me through. I knew one thing. There was unfinished business between us that must come to a conclusion. It would mean unpleasantness for one or both of us. I thought, *bring it on*!

My negative opinions dropped even lower when I witnessed something that added to the disturbing events that had occurred. I made a trip to the cooler for a bottle of water and saw Gino and Margo hunched over a table, straws in hand, sniffing lines of white powder. Drugs were the last figurative straw. I had to try to convince Melanie Hellmann to cancel her stepdaughter's trip.

# # # # #

Chapter 7

Mercifully, the trip came to an end. I sat next to Adrian Springer as he piloted the boat through the last few miles of the Intercoastal before berthing the *Nancy Lynn* in its familiar boathouse. He'd been quiet, so quiet that I feared I added to his predicament in some manner.

He sighed, breaking his silence, and talked while he stared at the channel markers ahead. "I've worked for the Hellman's thirty-four years. In all that time, I've never told them, *no I won't do that*. I might have to. I can't see myself babysitting that crew for one month."

I patted him on the shoulder, "You'd do Melanie a favor if you refused."

"What are you going to tell her?" he asked.

"What do you mean?"

Springer laughed, "You know she's going to ask you what you think."

"If she asks me, I'll tell her she should cancel the trip." I tapped my fingers on my thigh. "No...I'll tell her she's crazy if she doesn't."

"I hope she listens to you." Springer set his jaw. "I know one thing. I'm not running that boat to wherever that crews tells me. If I have to go, I want a float plan, and I want it stuck to!"

I nodded, "That's reasonable. You might want to agree to have regular communications. Like Tuesday and Friday cell phone calls at noon."

"That sounds good except for two facts. Melanie forgets her ass if she doesn't stick it with a pin to remind her it's there. And, most places they're talking about going don't have cell service. I do have a telefax radio sender on board so I can send written messages."

"If you end up giving in and going, send me a copy of what you send Melanie. I'll be your security blanket." I hesitated a few seconds then added, "Captain, think long and hard before you go."

He nodded. "Come find us if we get in trouble."

"I will." I said casually.

Captain Springer spun the wheel to the right to make the sharp turn into the channel leading to Hells Acres. The boathouse was in sight.

"If we get stranded on an island, I'll make a signal fire and send you smoke signals in Morse Code." Springer laughed. "Do you understand it?"

I grinned and nodded, saying, "That I do matey, that I do."

# # # # #

Chapter 8

"You really aren't looking forward to this," Clareen said. My office manager/personal assistant knows me so well, honesty is the only policy. I didn't know how Melanie Hellman would react to what I would tell her. People aren't usually pleased to receive unpleasant information about family members. Being the bearer of bad news has never been one of my favorite tasks, and I'm sure my face registered those feelings.

"What time did Riaffort say they'd be here?" I asked.

"You've got another fifteen to wait," Clareen looked at my coffee cup and said, "You're on empty. Go fill your cup. It will give you something to do."

"It's that obvious?"

Yes, you look like you have a meeting scheduled with the chief torturer for the Spanish Inquisition." Clareen frowned, "I'll get your damned coffee, go ahead and stew."

We played tug-of-war with the cup, as I rose to get my own when the front door buzzer sounded. Clareen said, "They're early. Sit down. I'll let them in and get coffee for everybody." She disappeared out the conference room door.

It had been two weeks since I'd made my voyage on the *Nancy Lynn*. I tried to figure a way to present the facts without being harsh. I hadn't found one. Even though she'd requested an honest evaluation, individuals don't always respond well to cold negatives. How do you tell someone that their daughter has the morals of a hound-dog in heat, that her guests tended to be violent, and cocaine was their possible priority? I tried to smile as Riaffort and Melanie entered my conference room.

Clareen stopped in the doorway. "You need me in here? If not, I'll be at my desk." "Call you if I need you," I said to her back.

Riaffort looked uncomfortable as we said our hellos and got seated at the table. That bothered me. Things rarely had any effect on my lawyer. Not one to evade issues, Riaffort said, "Melanie, I'd suggest you hear what Mr. Harrell says before you make your proposal."

Melanie's pout was an answer-in-itself, but she muttered, "I'm sure you know best, but I really wanted Mr. Harrell to know how much I value his judgment and how much I hold him in esteem."

Her words alarmed me. I knew what I had to say. I knew what she wanted from me. They weren't going to match.

Riaffort had a, *let's get this over* expression on his face, and his posture told me he'd rather not be where he was. He said, "I'm sure Melanie would like your opinion about lending the *Nancy Lynn* to Margo and her friends. What do you think? Yes or no." Riaffort was hoping to spare me going into details. I'd already told him the maintenance trip wasn't a pleasant one.

I tried, "No."

Melanie's eyes moistened, "Oh, Mr. Harrell, I hoped you would have a different answer."

"I'm sorry, Mrs. Hellmann. I have to be honest. I don't believe it's to your best interest, or Margo's to loan the boat to her and her friends." I dreaded the question I knew she'd ask next.

"Why?"

Hesitating, I hoped she'd see my reluctance and retract her question. No luck. She repeated, "Why?"

"I have concerns about the people's characters that will be on the boat. There is also a matter of trust." I stopped, hopeful that my general statement would be enough.

"Are you worried they'll trash the boat?" she asked.

"Yes," I answered.

"Captain Springer said they didn't do any permanent damage, they just were a little piggish about cleaning up." Melanie looked desperate when she asked, "Did you observe them abusing anything?"

"I can't say I saw them doing deliberate damage. I can say they didn't use care using the onboard facilities. Do I think they'd do damage on a longer trip with less observation?

Definitely, yes!"

Melanie asked, “Don’t you believe Margo can manage them?”

Hoping silence would answer her, I remained mute for a minute, but finally realized there was no avoiding a full explanation. I gave her one. “Mrs. Hellmann, I don’t believe Margo can manage herself, let alone manage strong personalities like Gino and the Marcos. That’s without seeing and evaluating the couple who didn’t go with us but will be on the month-long trip. I saw evidence that Gino and the Marcos man could be violent. They carried weapons. Margo and Gino were doing lines of cocaine, so I doubt she’d be in condition to keep things under control. Honestly, Margo has a problem keeping her clothes on…I’ll stop there.” I paused for a few seconds then asked, “Have you consulted with Captain Springer?”

Her answer was a flat, dead toned, “Yes.”

“What was his opinion?”

“He doesn’t like Gino. Margo and he hate each other.” Mrs. Hellmann’s eyes concentrated on her hands resting on the table.

“Did you talk to him about what transpired on our trip?” I wanted to know how much she knew.

“Yes, Adrian was very complete in his description of Margo’s actions. Too explicit. I know she occasionally is into taking drugs. That’s why—” Riaffort shook his head and she stopped speaking.

I asked, “Has Captain Springer agreed to go on the trip?”

Melanie looked desperate, "No, not unless you go." She glanced at Riaffort but spoke before he could react. "I need you to go on the trip, Mr. Harrell. I'll pay you $25,000 for the month if you will."

I shook my head and said, "I'm sorry, but—"

Melanie interrupted, "If I make it $50,000?"

I took a breath, hesitated, and said, "Mrs. Hellmann, you can make it $500,000 and I still wouldn't do it. I see too much potential for real danger and problems. Take my advice. Cancel the trip and get Margo some psychiatric help." I wanted to say to put the girl in a kennel but that was too harsh.

# # # # #

Chapter 9

"Anything I can do?" Trotter asked.

I thought then shook my head, "Nothing pressing." I pointed to my office bookshelves. "Find something to read."

He nodded and wandered to the shelves. He asked, "How long?"

I looked at the stack of paperwork on my desk. Was there any more? I called Clareen in the outer office, "You have anything that I need to look at besides what's on my desk?"

Her muffled response was, "You got it all."

I thumbed through it, and estimated, "Three hours plus or minus a half."

Trotter nodded and sighed.

"What's your problem? You'd be working your butt off if you were at the ranch."

"I don't like ass time." He pulled a copy of *The Hunt for Red October* from a shelf and said, "I've read this enough times that the print will just be a reminder."

"You didn't have to come along," I waved toward the door. "Take the Jeep and drive down to Vero. Your girlfriend's birthday is next week."

"I already bought it," Trotter spoke over the sound of the office phone ringing.

I looked at the first paper on the stack, signed the check, and laid it aside. "What did you get her?"

"None of your business."

Clareen interrupted us. "Sly, there's a man asking to talk to you. His name is Adrian

Springer. Want to talk to him?"

"Sure. I'll pick up in here."

As my hand reached the phone, Trotter asked, "Who's Adrian Springer?"

"He's the captain of the boat I was supposed to borrow from Riaffort's client." I picked up the handset and said, "Hey, Captain Springer it's good to talk to you."

The captain sounded cheery. "Same to you. Say, when we took the *Nancy Lynn* to the boatyard, remember talking about what was required to get your captain's license? I found some books on the requirements and sample questions that appear on the test. You interested in reading them. I have some notes you might find helpful."

"Hell, yes."

"I called your ranch and they told me you were in your Wabasso office. I'm en route to Vero Beach on board the *Nancy Lynn*. Her electronics are going to be checked out, radar, and such. Meet me at the Atlantic and Bay Marina's dock. I have the books with me."

"I'll be there. What time?"

Springer hesitated a few seconds then said, "I should be dockside between 1:30 and 2:00. Any time after that. In fact, I'll be here overnight, so if today isn't good……"

"No, no. That's fine! See you this afternoon. I owe you one!"

"Well, since you offered, I could use a favor," Springer asked tentatively.

My hair stood up. I almost yelled into the phone, *There's no way I'll go on the trip with Margo and company*, but I said, "What do you want?" and waited for his response.

Something in my tone must have transmitted my thought because he chuckled before he said, "I'm not going to ask for you to take another cruise with Margo and the monkey crew. I'd like that but I know you wouldn't go. I need something else from you."

"Captain, did Melanie talk you into taking Margo's gang on that Caribbean cruise?"

"Melanie didn't. The $50,000 she offered did. Unfortunately, I'm suffering from buyer's remorse. Let me explain."

"Go ahead."

"It was my intention to have no part of the whole thing. I told Mrs. Hellmann what I thought about the adventure. Melani told me that you told her the same thing. I thought everything had died. Then she approached me again. She said I could schedule everything after Margo gave me the destinations she wanted to visit. Set up rules that I wanted. Plus, if things got out of hand, I'd have the right to head the *Nancy Lynn* back to Jupiter beach. No unscheduled stops for any reason. I could cancel a port if I foresaw a problem. No additional guests. No weapons on board. I controlled the credit cards for boat-related purchases. Gas, that kind of thing. No drugs. I could limit alcohol consumption. I thought I had things in control." Springer shook his head. "Only conditions I didn't get were three things. I wanted to slip the whole trip back for two weeks. Nope, they had to be at sea the fourth week on April 26th. Doesn't make sense, but I could live with that. I wanted to meet the third couple before setting sail. Turns out they have big jobs and can't get down early. The lady is an interpreter for the UN and her husband is an engineer with a defense contractor. Last thing, the diving subs that the third couple is bringing are being finished in Titusville. I wanted them delivered here, but I ended up agreeing to go there."

"I don't see where I can help on any of that," I said.

"Well, you see..." Springer was struggling. "I want to break one of my own rules without breaking it." The phone went silent for several seconds before he asked the question. "When you come down to pick up those books...and if you were to bring one of those guns you were telling me about...and if you were to leave it in the lockup cabinet on the flying bridge......Hell, I don't trust that bunch, there are six of them and one of me. A voice keeps telling me, I need some kind of insurance."

I hesitated. Springer was a good guy and I believed very trust-worthy, but lending him a firearm without knowing his ability to use it, plus I didn't know him *that well*.

He read my reluctance. "It will stay in the locker unless I have something akin to a mutiny on board."

"Have you ever had any training with an automatic?" I asked.

"I was a deputy sheriff for seven years. Shot expert with a colt .45 every range qualification."

The fact he'd been a deputy was better news than he'd been well trained with sidearms. There was one question I had to ask. "Why did you leave the sheriff's office."

"To be the skipper of Mr. Hellmann's cruiser. And, when I left, the sheriff told me I could get my job back any time I wanted it."

"I have a .45 in a box with three spare clips. I'll lose them on your boat this afternoon."

# # # # #

Chapter 10

"You sure you want to do his?" Trotter loaded the final clip that fit in the gun case.

The Colt stared up at me and asked the same question.

"Captain Springer's a good man. He wouldn't do anything with it I wouldn't approve." The words were to convince me more than Trotter.

"Riaffort's on the phone," Clareen spoke from the front office.

I picked up the phone and greeted my friend, "Morning, Counselor. What's up?"

Riaffort's said, "Hi, Sly. I wondered if you had a chance to look at the valuations on the Sumner artifacts."

"They're probably in this stack of paperwork on my desk. I haven't looked at them.

You need something quick?"

"No, just sometime in the next week."

I asked, "Did it total as much as we thought?"

"No. Almost twice what we estimated. Our client is going to be an even richer old lady, and you're going to have to find a way to minimize taxes on another million-and-a-half."

I whistled, "I'm glad I took your call. Captain Springer is bringing the *Nancy Lynn* up for maintenance and called to tell me he had some books I wanted. When Clareen told me, you were on the line, I thought you might be trying to talk me into going on the cruise with Margo and company."

There was silence, then, "That's not happening, is it?" Riaffort *definitely* wasn't happy.

"Unless something's changed from around ten this morning, it's on," I informed him.

"Damn! I can't believe she changed what we agreed on!" The steam from Riaffort's heated anger was radiating from the phone. "You sure he said he was captaining the trip?"

"Yes."

"When are you going to visit him?" Riaffort was mad.

"I told him I'd see him at 1:30."

"I told her...I call you back. Don't leave until I do."

Click.

# # # # #

Chapter 11

Riaffort's last words from his second call reverberated in my mind, "I doubt Melanie will see the *Nancy Lynn* again."

"I think they'll leave the boat in the water." Trotter motioned at several vacant slips near the office of the huge boatyard. "They shouldn't have to jerk her out of the water for electronics." We passed a number of portable lifts, some with, some without big boats suspended from them.

I parked the Jeep next to the office. "Somebody in there will know if he's here, and if not, where they're going to berth him. You might as well wait here, Trotter."

Trotter was distracted. A young woman dressed in Daisy Dukes and a tee shirt with the sleeves cut off walked by and tossed a smile at my friend. "What?" he mumbled.

"Stay here." I shook my head as I said, "You have a girlfriend."

He replied, "But I'm not dead."

As I walked around the Jeep, Trotter asked, "Isn't the boat we're looking for called the *Nancy Lynn*?"

"Yes."

"That's her backing into that slip over there." He pointed to the sleek lines and gleaming white fiberglass of the cruiser. Captain Springer sat in the flying bridge as he maneuvered the big boat into the slip, stern first. The dockmaster and a rope handler stood by to assist. Captain Springer's skill made their presence unnecessary.

"That's the boat you went out on?" Trotter asked.

"She's the one."

"That's not a boat, that's a freaking yacht." Trotter was on the dock, halfway to the *Nancy Lynn* before I could get the gun case out of the Jeep and follow him.

"Come aboard, Sly," Captain Springer waved us on the boat as a dock worker placed a boarding ladder.

The *Nancy Lynn* was truly impressive. It was forty-two feet of luxury, style, and comfort. The cabin extended eight feet from the bow to six feet from the transom. The windows were more conventionally shaped than some of the newer boats that were tied to the wharf. They featured windows with many unique curves and slants that complimented their streamline design. The *Nancy Lynn* had a narrow walkway on either side of the cabin, a feature omitted on more recent designs. Only a dingy mounted behind the flying bridge broke the *Nancy Lynn's* clean lines. Three cabins, a spacious, opulent salon, a galley, and two heads provided ample living space for long cruises. Aerials, radar scanners, and other high-tech devices dotted the flying bridge. Comfortable, padded chairs framed the after deck, where Captain Springer offered us a seat and a drink.

"I see you beat me," Springer said with a smile and cast his friendly gaze on Trotter.

"Who's your friend, Sly?"

"This is Trotter. Ken Bass is his birth certificate name, but no one calls him that."

Trotter and the Captain shook hands, the Captain introduced himself, and 'pleased to meet you's' were exchanged.

"What would you like to drink? The bar is well stocked," Springer said.

"Bourbon and water," I answered.

"Do you have beer?" Trotter asked and added, "Coors?"

"Yes, and yes," Springer answered and turned toward the cabin entrance.

"Hey, Adrian, put this up somewhere." I extended the gun case carrying the Colt .45.

Captain Springer smiled as he accepted it. "I'll get whatever this is out of sight. This marina has a no firearms policy, but no one adheres to it." His nimble feet took him up the stairs to the flying bridge. Within a minute, he was back in front of us, flashing a key and a smile. He said, "She's stashed in the lockbox and I'm hoping she stays right there for the whole cruise."

Springer disappeared into the cabin to get our drinks.

~ ~ ~ ~ ~ ~

"I think it will go okay." Springer was trying to reassure himself more than us.

"You know Riaffort Richards? Melani's lawyer?" I asked.

The Captain nodded.

"He's my lawyer, too. He and your boss had some serious discussion about the whole Margo trip thing. He believed Melanie had agreed she wouldn't allow the use of the boat. The liability exposure is huge. He was pissed when I told him you were going, and angrier when he called me back to tell me he'd confirmed it with Melanie." I squinted my eyes and asked, "That won't get Melanie mad at you I hope?"

"No. I believe Melanie would like to cancel the whole thing. The Mrs. Hellmann part of her won't let that happen."

My scrunched eyebrows asked my question.

"Sly, Melanie is Mrs. Hellmann *number two*. Margo never has accepted Melanie as part of the family, much less as her mom. That tore my old drinking partner up. Marvin wanted to slide Melanie into their lives as a seamless replacement for Elsie. Elsie was a great gal. She was the disciplinarian. If she hadn't died of cancer, Margo would be one hell of a lot different. In the three years between Elsie's death and Marvin's marriage to Melanie, he spoiled Margo rotten. Didn't deny her anything. After Marvin passed, Melanie continued indulging Margo. Margo loved old

Marvin. She wipes her feet on Melanie. The more Margo does that, the more Melanie gives in. That's why this trip is happening."

"Can you change your mind? Blowing this off might be the best thing for Melanie, Margo, and you."

"I could, Sly. But that wouldn't stop the cruise. Margo was looking for a captain to hire when I said I wouldn't take them. Melanie said she wouldn't allow that, but when the shouting got hot, she'd have caved. That would put the old *Nancy Lynn* in real harm. I can't do that."

Trotter asked, "What are you concerned about? Seems to me that you have the whip in hand. Without you, do they have anybody who can navigate and run the boat?"

Captain Springer took a deep breath, "I don't know because I haven't met them all. Margo can't. Gino couldn't. Hell, Gino would have trouble wiping his rear with toilet paper that didn't have printed instructions on every sheet. Galang and Dalisay Marcos? They could run the boat but couldn't navigate it. The other couple, who knows. It might be a problem; it might be just the opposite. One of them might be able to run a boat and navigate. They have highfalutin sounding jobs. I told you about one working for the UN and the other in national defense. I'm sure folks like that have to have all kinds of background checks done. If they can pass them, I don't figure they can be too slimy. That made me feel better about going. Who knows? It might be that Margo and Gino are the worst."

"Do you have the names of the third couple?" I asked.

"Yes," he said as he reached for a manilla envelope sitting on the seat beside him. Springer handed it to me. "The names are in there along with some other stuff." He looked at me in a way I can't describe. My hair rose.

"What other kinds of stuff?"

"When we went over to Ft. Myers, you told me you'd learn to trust your gut. I do too. A nagging thought gets into the back of my brain and I can't get it out. If that happens, I do something about it." He tapped a finger on the envelope. "That's my doing something about it."

Opening the flap, I removed a small ledger. Folded papers were behind it. I left the thick stack of nautical charts inside. The ledger's first page listed all the names, and some of the addresses, phone numbers, email addresses, and employers of the six that were to be on the cruise. The next pages contained detailed information about the *Nancy Lynn*. Everything from how much water she drew under conditions of load and speed, to details on her electronics and the telefax address was included. Why I'd need capacities of potable water, gray water, diesel fuel, food to be taken, etc., I couldn't imagine.

All information after that, concerned the planned destinations and timetable for reaching them. The chronology for the entire sail, departure to return to Jupiter, was clearly recorded. It filled half of the ledger book. A range of probable arrival and departure dates were given for each port. The names of marina's, supply houses, and port officials composed most of the page dedicated to each of the ports-of-call. Captain Springer demonstrated his knowledge of the destinations by providing the names of business owners and government personnel living at each. It provided contact information...email address, phone numbers, radio call letters and information, and street addresses. Even navigational information for the seaward approach and street directions to use when ashore, had been documented by Springer.

Closing the ledger, I asked, "What do you expect me to do with this?"

"Keep it." Springer thrust his head forward to make eye contact. "This is a copy of what I've given Mrs. Hellmann. Unfortunately, she doesn't take such things seriously. It will be in the garbage in a week. I need someone who has a record of where I'm going, in case there's a problem. I'm hoping you'll be it. I'll be sending out a telefax twice weekly. If it doesn't come, I want you to notify the authorities and turn the envelope over to them."

He raised his eyebrows.

"Yes, I'll do that." I didn't realize the impact my words would have...on me.

# # # # #

Chapter 12

"A boat like you're talking about...I've heard people say it's a hole in the water you throw money in." Clareen took a sip of coffee. "I know why you're doing it. But......... Don't you think you could take Dennia on a cruise every couple of months? You could do that for fifteen years and save a pot load of cash."

Riaffort Richards, Trotter, and I sat around Clareen's desk in my Wabasso office. We drank coffee, munched donuts, and killed time as we waited for a courier.

Trotter answered Clareen's question for me. "Who wants to willingly get stuffed in a can with 5,000 other sardines?"

"There are some upsides to cruising on a liner. Think of the shows and all types of activities going on non-stop. And don't forget the food." Riaffort nodded his head and smiled. "Trotter, your dedication to your digestive track makes you a prime candidate for a Royal Caribbeanesk experience."

"Too many people and too claustrophobic," I said.

"Get a cabin with a balcony," Clareen countered.

I shook my head. "Dennia can go on a liner anytime. That's not what she wants. She wants a cruiser."

"If you're getting this for her, it sounds to me as though you're getting ready to buy the cow, too." Riaffort leaned forward and asked, "Is it time for wedding bells and prenuptial agreements?"

"No! I want the damned boat as much as she does." I was glad there were no lightning bearing storm clouds outside. A bolt would have honed in on my lying tongue.

Riaffort asked, "Have you considered talking to Melanie Hellmann? She liked you. It's been long enough since you turned her offer down. I wouldn't doubt she'd let you rent the *Nancy Lynn*."

"I don't think so, Riaffort. Even if she would, I'd feel so uncomfortable asking, it wouldn't be worth it. I practically told her that Margo was a half-step up from a streetwalker and the group going with her, a modern version of the Wild Bunch."

"So, have you found a cruiser?" Clareen asked.

"Not yet. I'm working on it."

Trotter guffawed, "Ahhh...he's not. He's got Russ and Val Foxx searching for him."

"Damn it, Trotter, I am working. I called Sal, the boat broker in St. Pete, and she's searching for one too."

Trotter smirked, "You're working hard."

Clareen bailed me out by changing the topic. "Have you discussed where you two are going when you find a boat?"

"It depends where I find it. If we find one around here, we'll make a trip to the keys. Maybe we'll try crossing the Steam to the northern Bahamas, that is if the weather looks good for the whole week. Captain Springer left me charts for every island group there. If the boat is on the west coast, we'll cruise down to the Marquesas and Florida Bay."

"Don't you think that's overly ambitious for a green captain and a one-woman crew?" Riaffort asked.

"Yes, it is, and no, I've made plans." I nodded to Trotter. "He's going with me and I'm looking to find an experienced deckhand to help. Besides, I've run smaller boats, rigs up to 22' my whole life."

Riaffort frowned. "Your biggest Carolina skiff and a 35' cruiser are night and day. The last thing you need to do is wreck yourself on a reef."

"I'm going to be very careful. No moving at night. Be sure I'm running at creep speed when I'm in water swallower than ten feet."

"I'll expect you to check in with me every day." Clareen sounded like an overly protective mother cautioning her child.

"I will every day."

"What if you do get your ass in trouble?" Riaffort asked.

"I won't."

"But if you do?"

I disgustedly stared at Riaffort before answering. "First, I'll call the Coast Guard, Second I'll call Captain Springer to come get us on the *Nancy Lynn*, and if those don't work is guess we'll feed the sharks." My bravado was just that. He was right, but I didn't like thinking of how rank an amateur I would be.

"Smartass!" Clareen snorted and turned to Trotter, "You going to take your new girl on the trip?"

"She can't get off work."

"For a trip like that?"

"She gets seasick. Hell, I get seasick and so does he if it gets really rough." Trotter pointed to me.

Clareen looked at me, frowned, and shook her head. "Tell me again, why are you buying a cruiser?"

# # # # #

Chapter 13

Val Foxx poured a cup of coffee for me, while her husband Russ gave me the bad news. “You aren’t going to find a boat like you’re looking for until the summer months. I’ve canvased the Florida coastline. Nothing is available for rent.” He shook his head. “That’s not completely true. I can find you one if you want to pay a high percentage of the damned purchase price.”

It definitely wasn’t what I wanted to hear. I expected it, but that didn’t make the reality any better. I must have frowned.

“Remember what you’re asking. You want a very short-term rental for an item that is typically leased for long periods of time. The owner’s risk is significant. You have a high value item that requires a level of skill to operate...safely. I can find a couple that will lease you a boat for a longer period of time *if* you’ll hire a captain they approve. Ninety days is the minimum length of time.” When Russ Foxx told you something in strong wording, you knew he’d spent the time researching his conclusions.

“Bahamas,” Val reminded. Valerie and Russ Foxx did special projects for me. Technical expertise in computers and electronics of all varieties were skills me and my organization lacked. We had a unique arrangement. The couple spent a large part of the year traveling in their RV. In the winter, the nomads 'pitched their tent' on part of my property. Their skills in finding information, providing inventive ways to use electronics, and hacking into files were exceedingly valuable to me. We sat at a compact table in their RV.

Russ nodded. "I found one situation that would work if you are willing to go to the Bahamas to do it. It won't be cheap, and it will require you to take the boat for six weeks. The owner lives on Abaco Island. He won't require you to have a captain but wants you to hire one of his employees in a first mate capacity. That man knows the boat and knows the northern Bahamian waters. Of course, you have to find a way to get there. You said Dennia has a Cessna. She could fly you to Leonard Thompson International. That's the airport near Marsh Harbor where the boat is."

"When is the boat available?"

"Sunday, March 24th. That means you'd have use of the boat through the first few days of May. It's not a very long flight. You could shuttle back and forth if you wanted." Russ opened his laptop, stroked the keys, and turned the screen to me. "Here are pictures of it."

The squat lines of a sport trawler were a contrast to the streamlined hull and cabin of the *Nancy Lynn*. The aft section of the boat had fighting chairs installed to be used for sport fishing. Outriggers confirmed this. It was painted light gray and its cabin extended forward leaving minimum space between it and the bow. The flying bridge sat above the front edge of the cabin. From what I could see in the photos, it was clean and well maintained. Stenciled on the bow, *El Gato Gordo* identified her by name and appearance.

While I watched, Russ shuttled photos of the boat's exterior and interior. Not plush, but clean. Not modern, but eminently serviceable. "Not bad," I said. "Do you have more info on her?"

"Yes." Russ punched a few more keys and specifications appeared on the screen.

He read them, "Thirty-two feet long. Nine-foot beam. Draws three feet. Top speed 32 mph. Cruises at 24. Seaworthy to seven-foot waves. Sleeps seven. Complete galley. One head. Salon with bar. Has an emergency tow service within fifty miles of Marsh Harbor."

"Know anything about the owner?"

"Yes. He has a small fishing resort. Hurricane Dorian about did in him and everybody else on that island. He needs the money badly or you wouldn't be able to rent it," Val said.

"Book it."

# # # # #

Chapter 14

Thin cirrus clouds created a delicate veil 14,000 feet above. Dennia kept us at 8,000 feet. It would only take an hour and ten minutes to make the flight from Clewiston's airport to Marsh Harbor on Abaco. We'd crossed the coastline near West Palm Beach, and below us, the deep blue waters of the Gulf Stream made their journey to the north. Dennia was as relaxed behind the controls of the Cessna as she was lying next to her pool at her ranch.

"Look straight ahead. See way out there. Those specs are Grand Bahama, and Abaco is the next group," Dennia waved a finger at the islands that were our destination.

Trotter leaned forward between Dennia and me to get a better look. "How far are they?"

"Eighty miles plus or minus."

I asked, "How far can you see from up here?"

"On a clear day like this, you can see to the horizon. At 8,000 feet that's 110 miles. I thought I saw the islands ten minutes ago but wanted to be sure. See how the water changes to a lighter color? That area north of the islands is a bank that's a lot shallower than ocean around it."

"How long before we get there?" Trotter asked.

Dennia checked the flight plan. "Twenty-five minutes. That's if we land right away.

I thought we might want to circle around for a while. I've never been out here before."

"Will that create a problem with the authorities?" I asked.

"I don't think so. I'm flying VFR, but I'll check with the tower at Leonard Thompson when we get closer."

~ ~ ~ ~ ~ ~

"Good God! These poor people. This reminds me of Andrew when it hit Miami. It will take years for these islands to completely recover." I'd seen the results of hurricanes before. The utter devastation that Dorian ravished on Grand Bahama and Abaco met or exceeded the worst damage I'd ever witnessed. Six months had passed, and cleanup wasn't complete. Rebuilding evidence appeared in the form of newly constructed buildings topped with gleaming white rooves. Dennia had reduced our altitude to 2,000 feet as we flew circles around Abaco and its waters.

Man and nature took a horrible beating. The vegetation was damaged severely. Trees, denuded, leaned at an angle as though rubbed in one direction by a human hand. Mangroves on the border of the shallow flats west of the island were bedraggled remnants of their form selves. Big palms were few and the large number of recently planted smaller ones attested to the wind's fury, palms being remarkably resistant to strong winds. Damaged shrubs and bushes colored the landscape an olive color rather than its usual lush green.

The puny attempts man made to stand in the force that struck, dotted the ground below. Foundations stripped bare, sometimes accompanied by a pile of rubbish, sometimes alone, were stark reminders of someone's dreams. Swimming pools were often the only evidence of those elegant homes that once stood next to them. Their symmetrical shapes contrasted with the combination of nature's randomness and chaos of destruction littered around them. Boats sailed in mangrove woods accompanied by cars and trucks aligned in all manner of positions. Huge piles of trash were concentrated in some areas, there being a holding location until final disposition could be made.

The waters weren't exempt. Pilings stood in groups without the wooden walkways that connected them at one time. Parts of buildings, boats, and shadows of undefinable objects lie in gin-clear waters soon to become artificial reefs. Only the white sands and blue and green waters maintained their beauty. All that said, the island's mystic and camouflaged beauty remained.

We were flying over the shallow waters west of Marsh Harbor when I saw them. I told Dennia, "Can you drop the plane down to 500 feet?"

"Sure."

"Circle right here."

Trotter saw what had drawn my interest. "Damn, there must be 200 of them."

Dennia asked, "Two hundred what?"

I answered, "Sharks. Really big sharks." I couldn't help wondering if they were a welcoming omen.

# # # # #

Chapter 15

Our view from the air minimized the damage done by the hurricane. We passed attempts at reconstruction running the gamut from freshly rebuilt to surrender to despair. Our cab driver provided a running commentary about the damage, the recovery effort, and the effect on his countrymen's lives.

"This house is my friend Raymond's." The structure our driver spoke about was a modest home in the process of being re-roofed. Our driver said, "It was one of the 50% of the houses that survived with only moderate damage. A small part of Raymond's roof came off as the storm was leaving. He made a temporary fix and covered it with tarps until now." The cabbie, Ollie, smiled and said, "My friend was lucky. Many of us had nothing left to fix."

As he spoke, we drove by a two-story pink home whose gay color belied its sad condition. The roof and one gable were missing completely. Many windows stared like vacant eye sockets. Others retained the plywood coverings that unsuccessfully tried to prevent the disaster that occurred. Shrubbery and trees were gone except for forlorn stumps and stubble. The yard's cleanup removed most of the debris that Dorian had left. Evidence remained. Bits of wood, someone's furniture, bits of metal, someone's garage door, and bits of fiberglass, someone's boat provided a sprinkling that interrupted the dead-brown coloring of seawater burnt vegetation. A sign on the front door probably said, "condemned."

The same story retold the islands fate over and over. These sad tales were separated by new houses that showed the people's will to rise. Construction in all phases were prayers for the future.

Dennia teared as we made our short trip from the airport to Marsh Harbor. Ollie continued to share his witnessing of the hurricane and its impact. Though describing a litany of horrors, his smile and upbeat comments typified the resiliency of the Bahamians. Dennia marveled at his attitude. She asked, "Ollie, with all the suffering we're seeing here, how do you keep such a great attitude?"

"Oh, maum, it is so much better now than it was. Some things return where there was nothing. A frown won't nail a board as fast as a smile will."

~ ~ ~ ~ ~ ~

The Sleepy Dolphin. A battered sign that had been salvaged from the heaps of rubble in the neighborhood, marked the location of the fishing resort. Nailed to a palm that withstood Dorian's onslaught, its slight slant, and the trees lean, robbed the resort of its feel of permanence provided by an archway that previously rose above the drive to the home and motel units. A mailbox was hanging above it. The sign's lettering included the Bay Street address and the promise that the establishment was, "The best rest for the fisherman."

As I expected, being on the water meant that it was in the center of the worst destruction on the island. *The Sleepy Dolphin*, damaged as it was, fared better than its neighbors. Property owners and contractors were busy trying to put lives back together. Construction trucks, piles of building supplies, the noise of many hammers, and other sights and sounds of building were everywhere.

A swarm of carpenters and other workmen clustered around *The Sleepy Dolphin*. The resort consisted of a large home containing a couple of rental rooms, and what had been five small cottages along the waterfront behind the house. Any salvable material from the carpet of wreckage around the home after the storm left, formed organized piles for retrieval and use in the rebuild.

From this group of men, a large smiling man emerged and made his way toward us. His greeting was, "Welcome to *The Sleepy Dolphin*! My name is Shepard Coloton." His round black face exuded friendliness. Coloton's bull chest was encased in a Columbia fishing shirt that dripped with perspiration. "You must be the Harrell party. Please excuse our mess.

I'll get you back to the *El Gordo Gato*." He called to one of the workmen. "Sallar, come help our guests with their baggage."

~ ~ ~ ~ ~ ~

My first look at the trawler that was to be our home for a week, made me wonder if we might have made a trip to the Bahamas that would only last the day. The trawler was recognizable from the pictures...pictures were taken before the storm.

The radar aerial was missing. Dings and scratches decorated the boat's hull and cabin. Two of the cabin windows had plywood replacing the glass. Three deck cleats had obviously been ripped from the gunwales during the storm. That quick visual made me wonder what condition the controls and engines were in. The hastily rebuilt dock I stood on swayed a bit adding to my uncertainty.

Her owner saw my reluctance. "Don't you worry. The storm gave her the measles. Everything but the radar is in top shape. That will be running by tomorrow at noon if you're willing to wait." He patted the hull with a huge hand. "Any boat that made it through what she did won't let you down.

I stepped into the boat followed by Dennia and Trotter. Trotter sported his biggest shit-eating grin.

"Everything will be fine dear," Dennia said as she passed me and entered the cabin.

Within a few seconds, she emerged, smiling. "Everything is alright inside."

Two sighs of relief, one from me and one from Shepard, were our response to Dennia's okay.

"I would like to invite you to have dinner with my wife and me this evening if you don't plan on leaving this afternoon. Now, this is the truth; my wife's conch chowder is the best dish on the island of Abaco." Shepard's good humor was infectious.

"Thank you! We'd be pleased to accept," Dennia said.

~ ~ ~ ~ ~ ~

Our meal was a vivid, pleasant memory and the following conversation enchanting. Shepard Coloton knew Abaco. Born there, he'd never lived anywhere else in his fifty-six years and seldom left the Bahamas for anything. His deep voice reminded me of James Earl Jones as he performed an introduction to his Caribbean paradise that would inspire envy in a Chamber of Commerce official. It was after that, his conversation contained good advice...and warnings.

"Sallar will be going with you. The man is a good pilot. He'll keep you off of the sand. Sallar thinks like a fish and will find any variety you'd like. He knows the waters all the way to Inagua." Shepard held his index finger up as a sign of caution. "But, I would think it wise to not go far south. The area is less populated, and the materials washed into the waters there have not been cleared as well as here. And..." his hesitation was designed to hold my attention, "The farther south you cruise, the more chance of coming in contact with people that can be trouble." Shepard's perpetual smile had faded.

I took a breath and leaned forward. "Trouble? What kind of trouble?"

"The recovery effort has strained our government's resources. That's materials and personnel. Since our islands in the south were not damaged as badly as our area, and since most of our population is in the north, officials, officers, and other government workers have been temporarily relocated to this area. That has created some problems. Burglaries have increased. Assaults. That area of our country is very open. We have many unwanted aliens who sneak onto the islands. Life in Haiti is hard. Many look for a better life here. Unfortunately, some want to take it rather than work for it. There are other problems.

Down by the Ragged Cays, Acklins, and particularly close to Inagua, there are a lot of Cubans. They can be a problem because they see the area as free for their use. They fish there. They steal from the islanders. They have boarded boats and robbed those on them......Some boats have disappeared."

Trotter asked, "Does your government allow that to happen?"

"Oh, no. They vigorously defend the area. The problem is that in normal times there are not boats enough to patrol the area fully. With the hurricane recovery, some have been moved out. Many Cubans who go there. It is only a hundred miles, less in many points. Sometimes Cubans boats go into our waters, some distract our police while others do as they please. You would be a target more than most."

"Why is that?" I asked.

"The Cubans would know you are Americans. Many Cubans hate you."

"How would they know that?" Trotter asked.

"There are few Conchy Joes living in the south. Those that do have boats the Cubans would be familiar with."

"What are Conchy Joes?" I asked.

"Whites. Bahama is a black nation. Ninety percent of us are. You stand out, particularly in that area." His smile returned. "We Bahamians like Americans. Most of our economy is based on your tourist's dollars. You'll be safe where we are."

"Have you ever known of a boat of Americans having trouble there? Like having their boat boarded?" I asked.

"Yes."

"What happened?"

"There were eight people on the yacht. Eight bodies were found. The yacht disappeared." Shepard's smile was gone.

# # # # #

Chapter 16

The clear water turned white by sand and shallow depths disappeared behind the transom. Sallar stood next to me. From the dock to the last marker buoy his total comments wouldn't have filled a postcard. He nodded or shook his head in response to my questions. Unlike his boss, Sallar seldom smiled. He checked the compass as well as the GPS screen. "You will do well, Mr. Harrell. The wind isn't bad. Nine knots from the southwest. Keep on the 110° course for ten more minutes then change to 195. At our current speed, we should see Nassau in two-and-a-half hours." He moved toward the stairs.

My comfort level wasn't 100%. I asked, "Where are you headed?"

"To check the bilge. Mr. Ollie insists on that every trip. Safety first, monn."

"What are you checking for?"

"A wet bilge means we're taking on water. That is not good. Better to head back from ten miles than from fifty." Sallar continued down the flying bridge steps. His errand added to my nervousness.

The low silhouette of Abaco layoff my west beam, the open Atlantic to my east. The sky above was periwinkle blue with wispy clouds scattered in the vastness. More than a thousand feet of water suspended *El Gato Gordo* off the ocean's floor. The limitlessness of the ocean fully registered on my mind for the first time. I'd smugly convinced myself that it didn't make any difference if a boat sank in a twenty-foot-deep lake or in 2,000 feet of sea water...you had to swim. It wouldn't make a difference in my confidence level captaining the boat. I was wrong.

I heard Dennia's excited chattering. "Look... look...look. There are schools of flying fish." The silver fish skittered a few feet above the waves gliding as far as a hundred feet off the *Gato Gordo's* starboard side. She stretched out in a lounge chair on the front deck. Dennia dressed wisely. Her fair complexion was in for six days of exposure from the sun. She wore long pants made from parachute material, a long sleeve UV resistant shirt, and topped her head with a floppy straw hat with a ten-inch brim circling it.

Trotter had been sitting next to her. He'd disappeared. I asked, "Where's Trotter?"

"He went to hunt some Dramamine." She turned her head over her shoulder and exposed a big smile. "Mr. Macho is having one of those humbling moments that come along."

"I'll be fine," Trotter's voice came from the flying bridge stairs behind me.

He'd become frozen on them. When I looked, his pale face had indecision stamped on it. I asked, "You sure you're okay?"

He said, "Yes," so I returned my attention to the instruments and my steering.

"Hey monn, you need to get to the rail," Sallar advised Trotter.

I heard thumping on the stairs as one man came up and the other retreated.

Sallar bent over my shoulder and said, "The bilge does not have any water coming in. If you worried about what I said you can stop."

"Good."

"Your friend has not spent time on the water before?"

I heard cloth rustling and bumping noises on the rear deck.

"No. We fish together. But it's usually on freshwater or inshore."

"He will get over it." Sallar paused, checked on Trotter, and added, "I hope."

I heard Trotter begin his prolonged call for Ralph.

~ ~ ~ ~ ~ ~

My feelings of uneasiness had fled. Each mile dissipated my concerns. The wheel felt like it should be in my hands. We'd made the course change to take us to our destination, the north end of Andros Island. I chose it for our first port-of-call because it was the largest island in the Bahamas and the bonefishing superb. Sallar suggested Morgan's Bluff as our first anchorage.

Now clearly visible, the island greenery grew more defined. It presented a picture from a Michener novel. I decided to depend on one of the charts Captain Springer had included in his 'safety package' to guide the *Gato Gordo* into the bay where Sallar told me we should anchor. I left Sallar with the wheel and went to my cabin to pull the chart from the envelope. As I flipped through them, I saw one for Inagua was included in the pack. That was the place Coloton warned me could be dangerous. Curiosity caused me to pull out the ledger containing Springer's float plan. It called for the *Nancy Lynn* to arrive there at the end of the second week at sea and to stay anchored four days...the longest time in any port during the cruise. I made a mental note to pass along Shepard Coloton's warning to Springer when I returned.

~ ~ ~ ~ ~ ~

The anchor chain rattled its way through the bow guides, followed by the one-inch line that would provide scope keeping the boat in place overnight. Sallar guided us to a cove that protected our anchorage from winds on three sides. I backed the *Gato Gordo* away from the anchor until Sallar pulled his finger across his neck in a cutting motion.

We had enough line to hold us. I shut down the engines.

Joining Sallar and Trotter at the bow, I marveled at the clear water. The anchor and chain appeared to be four or five feet below the surface. I asked Sallar, "How deep is it here?"

"Ten to twelve feet."

Surveying the bay, I noticed it looked deeper toward shore. I asked, "Sallar, why anchor here? It looks deeper closer to shore."

"There are many problems there, monn. This is a better spot."

"Bugs get bad close to shore?" I tried answering my own question.

"Yes, and other pests."

"What other pests?"

Sallar bobbed his head up and down. "Other pests. Ones that can be more troubling than mosquitos and sand flies. People sometimes swim to your boat. Most times they do this for bad reasons. Some, particularly the Haitians, will beg. *Never* give them anything. They will come back with friends. Many friends. If you don't give them something *more,* they will get angry. Sometimes people will come out in boats and try to tie up to the boat or come aboard. Never let them even get close. Many of these people will rob you. Remember there are few police here. Sometimes they must come from far away."

"What do we do if they try to get in the boat after we warn them?"

"Monn, you must protect your people and what is yours. Shoot them in the head."

"Does that mean we need to have a night watch?" I asked.

Sallar nodded, "Exactly, precisely."

~ ~ ~ ~ ~ ~

Supper settled in our stomachs as we sat on the *El Gato Gordo's* front deck. Reds, purples, oranges...they lit the western sky as the red ball dropped behind the western horizon. We sipped our drinks as the colors faded, faded, and disappeared. Light from a quarter-moon, lit wavelets, converting them to moving diamonds. The diamonds below competed with the diamonds above. Stars filled the sky, more visible because no light from civilization was there to dim them. The calm water calmed Trotter's belly and he returned to his confident self.

We were all quiet. The majesty of the setting captured, Dennia, Trotter, and my tongues. Sallar was silent by nature. It was Sallar, however, that broke the silence. "Mr. Harrell, will you take the first watch?"

I nodded.

"Do you want the midnight or the three o'clock shift?" He asked Trotter.

"Three o'clock." Trotter pointed to the flying bridge. "That where we watch from?" Sallar nodded.

"Instead of sleeping in one of the cabins, I plan to sleep on the couch on the bridge or the lounge chair on the bow." Trotter rubbed his gut. "I think this part of me will like sleeping outside better."

"I always sleep on deck, unless it rains," Sallar said. "I have a cot and an air mattress. It's like sleeping on a cloud." He stood, said, "See you at midnight," and disappeared around the cabin.

"I'll stay up for an hour," Dennia wrapped her arm around mine.

"It's time for me to make myself scarce," Trotter got up from his chair, said,

"Night," and followed Sallar's path aft.

I asked her, "What do you think?

"About what?"

"The boat; the Bahamas."

"I love them both."

# # # # #

Chapter 17

After Dennia left, I had difficulty staying awake. A day on the sea has a way of draining you that I can't explain. I had a half-hour of watch left to banish sleep. The irrepressible force wrestled with my eyelids. Even Trotter's loud snores a few feet from me didn't help. Perched in the comfortable captain's seat in the flying bridge aided drowsiness, not my efforts to stay on watch. That was until noises and lights from the shoreline 200 yards away, started my adrenalin pumping.

Winds had died to an occasional zephyr. Sound traveled far and clear in the still, humid conditions. I focused on where the sound came from, and where two flashlights shone. Both their beams pointed directly at our boat. My senses strained to identify what was going on. The scraping sound of metal on metal preceded the thud of something dropped to the ground. More sounds. Very faint. Did I hear an aluminum boat being drug along the sand and the light 'slusshh' it made entering the water? The moonlight wasn't strong enough and the distance too great for me to see.

I considered using the large, powerful spotlight a foot or two from my hand. They knew we were anchored; our white navigation lights were lit for that purpose. Would shining the spotlight on them peeve or provoke them? It shouldn't but it could. Simply waiting and watching seemed the best alternative.

First one, then the second flashlight turned off. Rather than relieving me, it heightened my anxiety. Noises actual or imaged drifted to my ears. I couldn't determine if they were real, much less identify them.

Thoughts crashed into my consciousness, each demanding to be heard. Should I reach out three feet and wake Trotter? Should I wake the others? Should I get my 9mm from my suitcase? Should I illuminate the shoreline to see if there was actual danger?

Should I prepare the boat to get underway? Would leaving the bridge be a mistake?

I blinked my eyes hoping to see better. Was there a small boat silently moving toward us? I couldn't tell if my eyes were sending illusions or real images. I made my decision. "Trotter, wake up," I said as I shook his shoulder.

"Uhhh...what the fuck...Sly, what..." He sat up on the couch, wide-eyed, and confused.

"Keep your voice down. There's activity over on the shore. I think they launched a boat. I can't see for sure."

Trotter spun around and peered into the darkness. "I don't see shit," he said after a minute of concentrating on the shore.

We sat, staring into the darkness, wondering if our senses warned us of danger or if our minds replayed some long-forgotten horror movie. Time passes excruciatingly slow in such situations. The sounds of a drop of condensation and our own breathing registered on our minds, events that would not have without the intense tension the moment brought.

The rattle of an oar in an oarlock and a muffled voice stiffened our bodies. I told Trotter in a half-whisper, "Stay put. I'm going to get my automatic and wake up Sallar." "Not necessary," Sallar's voice came from the stairway. He stood behind us and held something in his hands.

I asked, "Do I need to get my handgun?"

"No, monn. This will discourage them if there is a problem." He displayed a cutoff 12 gauge shotgun. "I think I know what they are about." Sallar rubbed my shoulder to get my attention. He said softly, "I will go down and stand in the bow. When I tell you, turn on the spotlight and point it right down the anchor line." He left, moving as silently as a shadow.

Sallar came into view as he emerged from the side of the cabin. He walked as far forward as he could, assumed a shooting position, aiming the gun toward where our anchor sat on the bottom. He said, "Turn it on."

I pointed the spotlight and flipped the switch. The strong beam illuminated the little bay, send fish leaping in the air, and disclosed two men in an aluminum Jon boat rowing toward us from directly ahead. Their startled faces changed to fear when they saw Sallar had a gun leveled at them. Sallar yelled, "Get out of here!"

The men immediately spun the nose of the boat to shore and rowed vigorously to the place I'd first seen their flashlights. They spoke to each other in excited Creole, a language I recognized but didn't speak. Sallar kept the shotgun trained, and I shined the light on them until they reached the shore and their beat-up truck.

Sallar came up to relieve me still carrying the shotgun. He said, "It is my watch."

Trotter asked, "What was that about?"

"Haitians."

"What were they doing?" I asked.

"They wanted our anchor. Selling it would feed their families or buy drugs. I would bet on the drugs. They go forward of the anchor, come to the boat until they reach the rope, cut it, and pull it up. An anchor from a big boat like this brings good money in these islands."

# # # # #

Chapter 18

Winds were very light as we traveled south. Dennia and Trotter wanted to fish. We paralleled the Andros shore trolling artificial baits behind the boat. Our 4 mph speed meant we'd take a large part of the day to reach our next destination.

The lightly fished waters produced dolphin, mackerel, Allison tuna, and a few barracuda and wahoo. We released what we caught except one nice sized dolphin that would be our supper. Trolling isn't my favorite way to fish. A few hours were enough for me, so I headed for the flying bridge to talk to Sallar. I wanted to ask him about what had happened last night. I took a beer with me as a conversation starter.

"Here you go," I said as I handed him the beer.

He nodded. "Thank you. Though I do not normally drink beer…since you were so kind, I will drink and enjoy it." His smile was one of the few I ever saw.

"I'm not a beer drinker either. Bourbon, if I'm drinking alcohol. The truth is I prefer a cold can of Pepsi to either."

"Tea. I like ice-tea. And I like it so sweet, sugar sits on the bottom of the glass, like sand on the beach." He bobbed his head side-to-side. "It's being around the English influence. My mom kept me full of it when I was little. We could afford that then. And, my family has returned to drinking it since the hurricane past through."

"I saw what tremendous damage that Dorian did. It must have been terrible."

The smile was gone. "Yes, I never want to see another storm like that."

"Did your house survive the hurricane?"

"It was damaged but not destroyed like many of my friends and relatives' houses. It is my mother's home. My wife and I stay there to take care of her. The place is built on high ground and there were woods around it. It helped protect it and caused some damage. The porch roof blew off, shingles came were lost, and there were many leaks. Our garage and tool shed were separate. Both were flattened. But...we were fortunate. We could live in it. My sisters, my aunt and uncle, two friends' families...they were not as lucky. Of course, we opened our house to them. For a time, we had twenty-seven under our roof. We are down to ten now and it seems like heaven."

"What happened to those people who didn't have friends like you?"

"It was hard. People made places to stay from the wreckage, later many got tents, it was desperate for months. Many, many of us still are figuring out how we will live. Last night you saw what people have had to do to survive."

"Stealing?"

"Yes."

"Does the kind of thing that happened to us last night, happen often?"

Sallar took a deep breath. "We are a good people, an honest people. When one is faced with the survival of his family, it happens. After the hurricane, looting was a problem. Now, it has gone away in the northern half of the country. An occasional problem happens like last night. Not often, but yes..."

"Just how safe is it to take a boat and spend a couple weeks floating around the islands."

Sallar tapped his fingers on the steering wheel while carefully considering his answer. He looked at my eyes as though he was evaluating how much he could trust me. He said, "There are two answers. One which the tourist people would have me tell you. One which is not liked by them but is more honest."

"I won't share your answer with anyone."

He nodded his head and explained. "At one time, there was little to no danger to go anywhere in our islands. And, I hope it will return to that. It is that way in most of the north. It is true in places where the government officials have a presence. You must remember we are a nation of small islands. Many of them, no one lives on. They are great places to be alone. To have fun. To do things you do not want others to know. You can swim naked and make love in the sand. You can exchange drugs, hide weapons, and smuggle people. When these two purposes mix..."

"People can get hurt."

"Exactly, precisely."

"Killed?"

"Yes, monn." Sallar held his hand up indicating he had something else to say. "I did not answer your question. I will. People who must, take things to stay alive. They have no wish or need to kill. The problems in Abaco, Grand Bahama, New Providence, Andros are mostly due to this. Inagua and the small islands to the south...they have additional problems. There are more uninhabited places, there are fewer police, there are more close lands that people willing to do bad things come from. The Haitians...they have little to lose. They are desperate. The Bahama officials send them back to Haiti if they catch them. Many would die rather than return. They would certainly kill another to keep from being sent back. Drug people take shipments to these islands, divide them into smaller shipments, and send them to the States in boats that do not go through customs. They are American boats, with American registration numbers, and American crews, that go to private docks. These people smuggle illegals into your country, too. The most dangerous are the terrorists. Everything they do must remain secret. They often leave Cuba for these islands. They get supplies and materials from there. Those ones, they will kill with pleasure to remain hidden." Sallar leaned back in the captain's chair. "If you go south and east of Andros, go to islands that have settlements on them or government stations. Those will be safe. The others, not so."

I thought about the rest of the trip we had planned. Long Island was one port-of call, significantly south. "Would you go as far as Long Island?"

"Only to Clarence Town or one of the resorts," his tone was emphatic. "Monn, there is all you want to see from Andros north. Swimming is as good there. Diving is as good there. Fishing is as good or better there. Lying in the sun is the same. Shopping is better. Stay up there and stay safe."

~ ~ ~ ~ ~ ~

"It is good to see you Sallar," a man wearing a blue shirt with amulets and a beret greeted us at the Drigg's Hill dock. The stripes on the short-sleeve shirt marked him with a sergeant's rank. Tall and slender, the man's smile and twinkling eyes hinted at a good humor and friendly disposition.

I eased the *Gato Gordo* up to the dock and fuel pump, while Sallar caught a rope thrown from the dock by the officer. Trotter grabbed a piling next to the bow. We were soon tied to the wharf and ready to take on fuel.

The officer bent over to speak to Sallar in a low voice. After they'd exchanged a few sentences Sallar introduced us to Walter Dickerson, one of the Central

Andros Island Police assigned to aquatic patrol. He asked no question, our association with Sallar seeming to be a solid recommendation. After some five minutes of chatting, he left in a blue and gray hulled, 25′ open boat, powered by outboards, with a hard cover sporting an array of electronics and lights.

Sallar asked, “Do you want to try some fly fishing for bonefish? Walter told me they are on the flats around Woods Cay in large numbers. I know those waters. It is a short distance from here. It is also a good place to anchor.”

“Sure. Sounds good to me.” I pointed to the fast disappearing police boat and asked, “Was your friend telling you something serious? You two looked that way.”

“Exactly, precisely. Walter is looking for missing persons. Three men from Mars Bay went out two days ago around the south end of the island. None have been seen. The boat was found adrift just south of here. The currents bring items up from the south along the island's edge. They are busy all the time, so they need help. The police can only investigate something they can fix. He asked me to help, to watch for a floater...that is a body.”

# # # # #

Chapter 19

Dennia stirred. I felt her body flex in my arms. Sharing sheets with a lady for an extended period of time proved more of an adjustment than I anticipated. My arm was pinned beneath her, and I wanted to extract it without waking her. Every time I tried to slide it out, she'd mumble, twitch around, and scoot her body back tight against mine. I made zero progress in being able to get out of bed.

Having her curves pressed against my body, was wonderful...most of the time. Dennia slept in an oversized tee shirt. That tee shirt found some way to tangle with my arm no matter how I tried to avoid it. It was an impediment to my getting out of bed in two ways. Pulling the tee-shirt threatened to wake Dennia and the motion caused her tee-shirt to elevate...above her waist. Besides not wanting to wake her the visual made me less willing to leave our bed.

Dennia snored. That beautiful delicate flower sounded like a chain saw when she slept without body to body contact. I quickly discovered I could silence her if I put my arms around, or looped my leg over her. The switch turned off the noise and turned on the furnace.

The heat she generated was remarkable. Heat is good, but I sleep best when refrigerated...there was no air conditioning on the *Gato Gordo*. That magnified other things that kept me from sleeping. The inevitable mosquito that snuck into our cabin that buzzed in my ear. The waves tap-tapping against the hull. The creak of the anchor rope when it pulled tight. Little things that conspired against closed eyelids.

A loud shout from the deck above followed by the sound of a big splash solved my dilemma. Dennia sat up in bed as she swung out her legs. “What was that?” she said in an apprehensive tone.

I crawled out of bed, reach for my shorts, and said, “I’ll find out.”

When I got to the deck, Sallar sat on the transom, with a big smile on his face. He watched Trotter paddle on the surface. Trotter decided to take an early morning swim.

“You finally decide to get up?” Trotter yelled and splashed water against the hull with his cupped hand. The water was so clear it made him appear suspended in the air.

Every shell and bottom detail was visually vivid.

“Yes, seems my alarm clock rang.”

“Your alarm clock says, come on in, the water’s fine.”

“I will,” Dennia pushed by me in a blur, took a couple running steps, and dove into the gin-clear water. When she surfaced, she was sputtering and laughing. She waved her hand at me and yelled, "I've been wanting to do that since I landed my Cessna." Her iridescent green bikini drew attention...make that stares, from Saller.

I said to him, "She is one beautiful woman, isn't she?"

"Exactly, precisely." He smiled. "You are very fortunate."

~ ~ ~ ~ ~ ~

Sallar removed an inflatable raft from a storage locker and we soon had a way to reach the flats and wading water around Wood Cay. After applying a thick coat of sunscreen and sticking extra flies in our hatbands, we loaded our flyrods in the raft and crossed the 200 yards to the knee-deep flats.

As we got close to where we would wade, Dennia said, "I'm going to need some help to get started. I've never fly fished before. I hope I won't be a drag."

"Not a problem. I'll have you pulling them in before we're done fishing this morning," I said. Trotter and Sallar just smiled.

Sallar rowed the raft 150' on to the white and gray sand flat, before telling us, "This is where you get out." He pointed to an area near a small mangrove island. "The fish will be from here to around the end of this cay. Walk slow and cast in front of the fish, not on them. It will be good fishing here for the next three hours. Then the tide will stop coming in and the fish won't bite as well."

Trotter was in the water and stripping line from his reel before Sallar finished. As Dennia and I slipped into the knee-deep water, Sallar added, "You know to look for stingrays?"

"Yes," we said in unison. When we got forty yards away from the raft, I began teaching Dennia to fly fish with words from *A River Runs Through It*. "Casting a flyrod requires a four-count rhythm..."

~ ~ ~ ~ ~ ~

As I suspected she would be, Dennia was a quick learner with excellent coordination. She was casting well enough to catch fish within an hour. She hooked and land her first bonefish after one pull-out. At the end of our morning trip, Dennia wasn't a novice anymore. Sallar called to us at quarter to twelve, "The tide is almost full. Time for lunch. Come to the raft. I will row us back."

Our pursuit of the fish had taken us a half-mile from the point we originally left the raft. We waded toward Sallar as he rowed to us to reduce our walk. It was a wonderful morning and Dennia said, "You know what Sly, I might try to talk you into never going home."

"That might not be hard to do."

Trotter shook his head, "Two bonefish and you're ready to leave LaBelle, Dennia?"

"I'll leave Lily in charge of the ranch and you can run Sly's place for him," she said jokingly. She winked and added, "A girl can dream."

Sallar tugged at the oars while we chattered about the morning's fishing when fifty yards from the *Gato Gordo* our day changed. Dennia saw it first.

"There's something caught on our anchor line."

I looked to where Dennia pointed. A large dark object was folded around the line. I stood up, placing my hands on Dennia's shoulder to keep my balance. The current held what ever it was in place, the trailing portions fluttering in the water's flow. Its dark gray color contrasted with the white-blue of the water. Only a small portion was above the surface; most was submerged. A humped shaped part stuck out of the water. It alternately shined and looked textured. I guessed, "Could be a dead dolphin."

Each stroke of the oars cut the distance and increased what we could see of the mysterious object. "Let me take a look," Trotter said. I sat—he stood. After straining his eyes for several seconds, he ventured his guesses. "Looks like whatever it is, is wrapped in something, Plastic......I bet it's a sack of garbage." Trotter wobbled as he almost toppled into the water. He sat before taking an unwanted swim.

The wind and current worked against our progress. As we reached the edge of the natural channel where we were anchored, Sallar was forced to work hard to make progress. Suddenly, he frowned, stop rowing, and stood up. He looked at the object for several seconds before saying, "Shit!" Sallar sat down and hunched over the idle oars. He muttered, "This is not good."

Dennia asked, "What's wrong?"

"We will not be fishing right after lunch if I am correct." He dipped the oars into the water and pulled. When the raft turned into the wind, I immediately knew. The smell of death crept into my nostrils.

~ ~ ~ ~ ~ ~

Sergeant Walter Dickerson instructed two police officers as they got the human body out of the water and into a body bag. When it was stored aboard the police boat, he scrambled on to the *Gato Gordo* to talk to us.

He asked Sallar, "Can you tell me anything else?"

"No, Walter. When we left the boat to fish at 8:30 it was not there. When we returned at near noon it was as you saw it when you arrived. Do you know who he was?"

"I am not sure. My men found no identification. My guess he is the last of the missing men from Mars Bay. We found the other two. Both were shot, so was he. He meets the description of the man."

I asked, "Were these men tourists or from around here?"

"They were not tourists. All three are well known to us. They have had many arrests. Bad men. Very bad men. And they have business with other very bad men in Matthew Town. Their women told us that is where they were to go. To meet about drugs. All three were involved in smuggling and prostitution, besides drugs. In truth, we are better without them." He shook his head. "I must apologize for this bad thing that has spoiled your day. I can assure you that you will be perfectly safe while you are here at Andros.

Please enjoy yourself without fear. This is a very rare occurrence." He handed me a card. "Anytime you are in the Bahamas and you have a problem or need something, call me. I will be there to help you."

I wondered if the look on my face mirrored the same doubt, I saw in Dennia and Trotter's. The rest of the week went well, but all of us looked over our shoulders more frequently than normal.

# # # # #

Chapter 20

"You have a call from Captain Springer," Clareen leaned into to my office as she spoke, "He said you could call him back if you were busy."

"I'm not involved," I answered.

"He's on line two."

I'd wanted to have a conversation with Adrian since the Bahama trip, but office work kept me busy. The information I'd learned should help him avoid problems on what was already a problematic trip. I said, "You saved me a call Captain. I was going to share some recent intelligence on the islands with you. We made a trip over there to see if we really want a cruiser. Had to go there to rent one. Things are getting back to normal after the hurricane, but they're not right yet."

"I called your ranch last week. A lady named Cindy told me you had taken time off to go to the Bahamas to rent the boat. What kind of boat were you able to get?"

"We ended up with a trawler. I can tell you that *El Gato Gordo* is not the *Nancy Lynn*. It was reliable. The trip gave my girlfriend and me what we wanted. Dennia would have stayed on the boat. It was hard for her to leave. I loved it too."

"Have you figured out what you want? Do you want a cruiser like the *Nancy Lynn* or a trawler like the boat you rented?"

"We don't know yet."

"Before you decide, take a trip with someone or a group. The boat you buy must be able to keep up with the others and go places like the Gulf Stream. You didn't cross it, did you?"

"No. We stayed in the north half of the Bahamas."

"What islands did you visit?"

"Abaco, Andros, and the Exumas. We cruised around Grand Bahama but never went ashore there. By the way, I used some of the charts from the envelope you gave me."

"Good. Are they still accurate? Those were all printed before the hurricane."

"Just a second." I pulled the envelope out of one of my desk drawers and removed the Abaco Island chart. "The two I have the most experience using were the ones for Abaco and Andros. There weren't any changes that I found on the Andros charts. Andros wasn't hit hard by the hurricane. Abaco was. Even so, most of the channels are okay. Moved some a little. There are a few new sandbars. The channels are cleared of debris. The thing you have to be careful of are shallow areas out of the channel. There's all kind of wreckage on the bottom. Parts of houses, boats, refrigerators. One place we drifted over, looked like an appliance store."

"That's good to know. Anything else?"

"Yes. I got warned about cruising in the southern part of the islands. We rented the trawler at Marsh Harbor. The owner is a man named Coloton. He warned me that there was a lot more instability in the southern half of the islands. Coloton furnished us a deckhand – first mate for the trip. He acted as captain until I felt comfortable running the boat. We got the same story from him. But we got those warnings underlined for us. When we were anchored at Andros, a body got caught in our anchor line. The man had been shot and we were told he had dealings with people down at Inagua Island. Isn't that one of the places you are supposed to go?"

There was quiet for several seconds. Then Springer asked, "Did the folks you talked to have any suggestions? That is if you had to go down there?"

"Yes, only put in where there are settlements and resorts."

"Some of those aren't so good."

"Do you think you can get Margo and company to drop the sail down to Inagua?"

"No. They've made a change, but when I asked about cutting out the trip to Matthew Town. It was an absolute no."

"What was the change?"

"Originally, we were going to spend the first four or five days in Andros. That's changed. We're going to Dunmore Town on Eleuthera. Margo's given me coordinates where they want to fish for marlin.

Problem is, there are no marlin there, to speak of. They're more likely to catch a cruise ship than a billfish. I called to tell you what the change in the float plan is. Eleuthera replaces the days at Andros. Then we stop at the south end of Exuma for a day. That replaces Long Island. From there on, the plan remains the same We'll be at Inagua for twelve days. The place we're docked at is called *Boca Bien Marina*. It's new since I was there last. I don't know anything about it. Oh yes, the first place we go is to Melbourne to pick those diving subs. We end the trip by going back to Eleuthera on April 24th and we'll be there until the 27th." He paused. "Don't worry if you didn't get all that. I'm sending you a letter with all the shit in it."

"It sounds like you'd still rather have a root canal a day than go on this trip."

"Yep!"

"Have you met the mystery couple?"

"No. I did talk to the man on the phone. He sounds good. Smart. I don't see what he's doing hanging around with Margo. Hey, Sly……" Captain Springer hesitated for several seconds. When he spoke again, I heard the tension in his voice. "I'm counting on you to get the authorities to come find us if something goes bad. I'll be sending you telefaxes.

Melanie won't act until it's too late."

"You can count on me, Captain. When do you leave?"

"Three to five days, depending on Queen Margo's whim, and the completion of those diving subs up in Melbourne."

"When can I expect to hear from you?"

"I'll call you when we leave Melbourne. If you aren't available, I'll leave a message. Then on, I'll send a telefax every Tuesday and Friday. If you don't get one, you know I'm in some deep shit."

# # # # #

Chapter 21

The smell of fresh-brewed coffee curled up to my nose. It mingled with the sound of Mantovani. They were my self-prescribed medicine for a relaxing morning. No schedule to meet. No pressing issue caused by business or ranch. Just birds wading and flying around the pond outside the ranch window. The luxury of doing and thinking of *nothing* rarely presented itself for my enjoyment.

"Do you want anything else?" Cindy asked. My multi-tasking employee acted as secretary, cook, and domestic staff. She'd removed my breakfast dishes a few minutes earlier. I noticed she had her purse and a paper in one hand and car keys in the other.

"No. Looks like you're going somewhere."

"Tuesday, Sly. It's grocery day. I'm driving up to St. Cloud. You want me to pick up anything for you?"

I thought for a few seconds. "Get me a can of shaving lotion."

"What kind?"

"The cheapest one you can find."

Cindy removed a notebook from her purse and added my shaving lotion to her grocery list. When she finished, she laid a paper in front of me. "This fax came in earlier."

The fax had Captain Adrian Springer's name at its bottom.

As he promised, he'd called me when he got ready to leave Melbourne. Our conversation was brief. His assessment was a good news, bad news evaluation. The couple he'd not met was at the boatyard and marine construction company. He was favorably impressed with them. Friendly. Considerate. They worked hard when loading the boat. Above all, they were smart. The couple was thirtyish. Adrian thought they were affluent but avoided showing it. The negatives...they frequently spoke to the others in Tagalog. Captain Springer was not comfortable with that. The dive subs they loaded onto the boat were a problem. Six units, twelve-foot-long slender devices, he guessed the diameter as fourteen inches. They took space that wasn't available. Storing them below deck wasn't possible. The captain said they ended up lashing them to both fore and aft decks, using blankets to protect the *Nancy Lynn*. Two crates of "spare parts" were stored in compartments below. His last comments summed his feelings, "The couple isn't another Margo and Gino, that's good. But I sure hope we don't run into rough seas before we get to the islands where I can hide from the wind."

What I'd learned from the phone call told me more about Springer's frame of mind than the actual first couple days of the trip. His positive outlook was welcomed. The lack of negativity in his tone and wording surprised me. That was particularly true since I'm sure the diving subs potential to do damage to his sweetheart, the *Nancy Lynn*, must have been traumatic. I perceived his comfort level to have improved significantly. That alone heightened my interest in the telefax. The fax didn't take long to read.

Sly,

This is report number one. Left Melbourne Saturday AM. New couple a plus. Margo behaving. Crossed Stream on Sunday to take advantage of low winds. Couldn't ask for better. Unloaded subs temporarily at Fair Winds Marina while we marlin fish. Hall says there are temporary brackets for the dive subs that won't damage the hull. Can't imagine how that will work but I'll look before I say no. We are in Eleuthera, anchored at Dunmore. Will go fishing today. The location isn't renowned for marlin. Hall is very exact in the location we'll take the Nancy Lynn, 77° plus 10 minutes longitude by 20 minutes north of 25° latitude. It's in the shipping lanes. It's not my cruise. This is where they want things to happen. This crew has electronic gadgets for everything, even an aquatic drone that sends information back to the control unit about where the fish are at, the type, etc.

Going as well as could be expected.

Adrian

One question immediately came to mind. I mumbled, "Who in the hell is Hall?" I figured that it must be the male half of the 'third' couple. The envelope Captain Springer prepared for me sat in my top desk drawer. He'd told me the names of the third couple were recorded in the ledger. Curious, I decided to find out the names of the couple I hadn't met.

Hall S. Runnels. There was an impressive collection of information on him in the ledger. It said he worked as an aerospace engineer for Grumman. I assumed in Falls Church or Baltimore where the company had major offices. Thirty-one years old, three degrees in engineering, and listed as a project manager for 'space initiatives,' his resume was impressive. There were notes about his schooling...MIT...third in graduating class...mechanical...electrical degrees.

Listed below was his 'significant other,' Diane Fanatti-Runnels. Her information grabbed as much attention as her husband. A graduate of both Brown and Columbia, her specialty was languages, nineteen listed as fluent. Thirty-three, she worked for the UN in New York as an interpreter. The address listed for both of them was a street in Princeton New Jersey.

Conspicuously missing, I couldn't find any contact information. No email addresses. No phone numbers. Either professional or personal. I thought that strange. I wondered if it would be worthwhile asking the Foxxes to see if they could come up with a way to contact them.

Then I reasoned, why would I need that. There wouldn't be anyone to contact...both were on the trip.

On the bottom of the page, Springer had scribbled an afterthought note stating,

"Juvenile record of possession of drugs. No detail of what kind. Poor little rich girl? Check...."

The note was never finished.

# # # # #

Chapter 22

Trotter looked at his beer can, hopeful that he'd picked a magic six-pack, one that the last can refilled itself magically. Otherwise, he was out. Temperatures lied about the date. Ninety-two at 10:30 in the morning, those were July, not early April temperatures. He sat down on his seat in my boat and shook his head. The lack of any breeze made comfort-levels tumble further. He cocked his head to one side and said, "The fish aren't biting, it's hotter than hell, and I'm out of beer. Let's go back to the house. One bass and five strikes in four hours...that qualifies as a waste of time."

I hadn't done much better, but I couldn't resist tugging Trotter's leash. "Hmmm, it hasn't been good. I've brought four to the boat and had enough strikes I didn't count them.

That one fish was, what? Five pounds? Want to give it another hour? It might get better. Even you'd have a chance to catch a few."

"Smart-ass," Trotter's smirk said as much as his words. He rested his feet on the boat's side, leaned backward in the seat, pushed his hat over his eyes, and said, "Wake me when you're ready your go in. There's work I need to do at the ranch. I've got a faxed bid coming in for ten White Angus calves......back at the house, you know, where it's cool."

"Don't tell me I'm going to have to buy a boat with a cabin and an AC unit on it. Cowboy up."

Trotter's response was to shoot me a bird.

I started my outboard. While it idled, I asked, "You didn't complain about the heat in the Bahamas."

"If we were wading for bonefish, I wouldn't be bitching now. Far as I know, Lake Marian is still freshwater, and there's no bonefish in it." He sat up and prepared for the high-speed dash back to the dock. "Speaking of the Bahamas, you still have the *Gato Gordo* leased for three-and-a-half weeks. Are we going to go back? If we do, Lily says she wants to go this time."

I eased the motor into gear and let it creep along. "What happened to Lily's seasickness?"

"Dennia told her so many good things about the trip, she's ready."

"What did she say when you told her about the body?"

"We didn't tell her about that."

"A conspiracy? Shame!"

Trotter ignored me, "Are we going back? Tomorrow's Saturday, we have a date, and I know she'll ask."

"Yes," I answered and jammed the accelerator forward.

~ ~ ~ ~ ~ ~

"This was in the fax machine." Trotter spun a sheet of paper the settled on the desk in front of me. I'd forgotten it was Friday. Captain Springer had sent his second telefax. I put it aside for a second and asked Trotter, "Did you get the bid you were expecting?"

"Yes."

His tone and face told me it wasn't good. "That bad?"

"Yes. Told him no deal."

"Did you counter?"

"No."

"Why?"

"This guy thinks he's got you if you try bargaining."

"What did you tell him?"

"We'll keep the cows."

"What if he doesn't come back with a better offer?"

"We'll keep the cows."

"So, our strategy is?"

"Keep the cows. Until someone pays what we want."

I shook my head. Our strategy was to be uncompromisingly stubborn.

Trotter asked, "Have you thought about a date for going to Abaco? Lily will need some time to get off work."

My calendar was open the last week of April. I suggested, "How about April 20th through the 27th?"

"Sounds good. I tell her."

"Make sure she tells her mother about the dates. If Dennia can't make it, we'll have to change something."

Trotter started to leave, spun around, and reminded me, "You need to read the fax from Captain Springer."

I said, "Thanks," and pulled the paper in front of me.

This printing on the telefax almost covered one side of the sheet. Twice, maybe three times longer than his first note to me, the number of words alone told me something had changed. I read the first words and became very confused.

Sly,

This is my second check-in. The trip has been as planned. I have no major problems. Everyone has been helpful. My only concern at this time is the weather. I have to watch it carefully. Everybody on board watches me close. My concern is that I'm missing something. We fished for marlin the last three days and nights. Fished the same five square miles repeatedly. Have seen some fish. No hook-ups until today. I have no idea of what fish are being looked for. The electronics, drones, and radio-controlled aquatic devices are getting the most workout. Marlin are there and also closer to Eleuthera. The weather is strange. The winds are blowing from several directions. Margo has been a model citizen. Gino has not been disruptive. The Marcos are helping. Dalisay is doing most of the cooking. The Runnels are smart. Too smart to play chess or poker with. Hall is an experienced boatman and he likes to run things. I am running the boat most of the time. But not all of the time. When we get into the shallows, I have a concern because I'm not running the boat. The fact that Margo and her friends don't always speak English doesn't bother me much now. Everything is okay, mostly. Sorry about the sticking capital letters. Please. We will leave for Exuma tomorrow, then we go to Inagua and Matthew Town. I'm concerned about the weather we might run into down there. I expect anything from a tropical storm to white powder snow to ski on. That's my not so funny take on things. I will not miss any check-ins, I hope. Gino says to tell you hello. He's here with me.

Adrian

Strange! Very Strange! The rambling wording, the subjects, the obviously false remarks. Springer was telling me something wasn't right. But what? And, how bad?

I read the note several times and tried to glean what I could from his words. Obvious issues included: That he was being surveilled. The fishing trips they were taking were suspicious, but he couldn't figure out their purpose. The communications in Tagalog between cruise members continued to upset him and increase his apprehension. He felt his control and command of the boat had decreased. I believed he was using the weather as a metaphor to communicate that.

The new couple that arrived proved to be a detriment and the driving force in whatever the group planned. Was it diving or something sinister? Captain Springer believed he'd became expendable when the Runnells man stepped on to the *Nancy Lynn*. That put him in danger he did not expect. I could not figure out if his references to technical gadgets had significance or not.

Of all the clues contained in Adrian Springer's telefax, two items stood out. One I caught on my first reading. One of the referrals to weather focused my attention on his comment mentioning, "white powder snow," something I saw as a possible mention of cocaine. That coupled with the focus on going south, caused me to believe he feared the *Nancy Lynn* would become a drug mule. The second item, I almost missed. On my fourth and final reading, Springer taking the time to point out the highly unlikely possibility of a key "sticking" on his telex machine, struck me as odd. After a few minutes of thought, I saw the message he had coded for me. If you extracted all the capital letters from where they did not belong, they spelled, T R O U B L E.

I had to temper my concern. Adrian Springer didn't want to be on the trip, had a hate-hate relationship with Margo, and would over-react to any perceived threat to his lovely lady, the *Nancy Lynn*.

Those people closest to me...Trotter, Clareen, Cindy, Riaffort, and now Dennia...all continually warned me about sticking my nose in places it didn't belong. It had consequences in the past. Figuratively broken several times, my nose did get literally trashed once.

Should I do anything? And if yes, what? Objectively, I evaluated Captain Springer's situation. When finished, my conclusions were:

1) Springer was alive, had nominal control, but felt threatened.

2) At the time of the letter's writing, no illegal activities were being engaged in, but Springer feared they might be in the future.

3) He had more worries regarding his crew than when he set sail.

4) He had some evidence or concern drugs were involved.

5) The message TROUBLE is what he foresaw.

~ ~ ~ ~ ~

How should I respond? Now wasn't the time to call officials and ask them to investigate. Nothing illegal happened I could point to. Making up something would end any effectiveness of such action in the future. A false alarm would cause local officials to blow off any new call for help. If I tried asking questions of Springer and someone else intercepted them, I could precipitate a calamity. What could I do? I decided on one thing that would cause no harm. And in no rush. A thorough check on the backgrounds of all six of the Captain's shipmates might disclose information that would reassure or uncover the reason for serious concern and action

# # # # #

Chapter 23

"Did Lily talk to you about making another trip to Abaco?"

Dennia nodded. "I don't think it will be a problem. Dawn did a good job running the club. If she's willing to manage *The Dancing Dears* for the week, you know I'm dying to go back." She held her palms up in a supplicating manner. "If we could leave on Monday and be back on a Wednesday, that would give us an extra day or two and I'd only have to miss one weekend at the club."

We sat on the edge of Dennia's pool, dangling our feet in the water. Our 'date nights' were Monday, Tuesday, and Wednesday. Her ownership of an exotic dance club forced the reorientation of our social life.

"No problem. There aren't any hot projects right now. Clareen runs the day to day stuff better than I do."

A momentary lull in our conversation ended with Dennia's broad smile. She broke the silence, "How long have we been together?"

"Three months."

"You never have asked how I ended up owning a strip club. That's amazing. You've nibbled around, but you've always given me space on that."

I stared at her in silence for several seconds before saying, "I figured you tell me when you were ready."

"I'd like to tell you it's a simple story, but it's not. My late husband, Larry, had a friend who owned the club back in my husband's bachelor days. When his friend got in serious financial trouble with the wrong people, Larry bailed him out. That's how he ended up owning the club. He did that with the farm supply house, a general store in Goodno, and a citrus packing plant. Larry had a big heart. He couldn't say no to a good friend. When we married, they became my concern, also."

"That tells me how your family came to own it." It was my way of asking the crucial question.

Dennia nodded and said, "I'm getting to it. Most people outside LaBelle think I met Larry as a dancer, particularly since there's twenty-two years difference in our ages. Hell, Sly, you know there aren't many secrets in small towns. The reason I'm accepted in this town is that they know the story. And I have roots here." She swished her feet in the water. Hard. I guessed it wasn't an easy story for her to tell. "My mom grew up in the little community of Goodno just east of LaBelle. She went to Duke and met her husband, my daddy, there. My father was from Farmington, New Hampshire. I grew up a Yankee. When it came time to go to college, Dad saw that I got into Wellesley. I did well, graduated, and was getting my MBA at Warton. The professor I was doing my dissertation for, challenged me to do something unique. I chose the topic of maximizing financial return in the strip club business. I quickly learned that was a no-no. It's exotic dance. That's when I met Larry. His family and my mother's family were friends. He stopped by to visit on his way to Maine. When he learned about my thesis, he invited me to get some first-hand information. I took him up on his offer." She grinned. "Yes, I striped for three months. Made great money three nights a week and spent the rest of the time on the beach. I spent another two months helping him run the office."

"Is that when romance bloomed?" I asked.

"No. I went back. Got my Masters. Larry and I became very good friends. He told me later he was interested past that; I never suspected. He was a perfect gentleman. I wondered about him. He was handsome in a rugged, cowboy way, stood six-five, and weighed two-fifty. I wouldn't have had estrogen if I didn't." Dennia took a deep breath. "A few months after I graduated, my parents died in a car crash. I had no one to turn to. Larry just showed up. He literally did everything from the funeral arrangements to taking care of legalities. Just then, the memories in our house...too strong, too strong. I needed to get away. Larry offered me the job of running the *Dancing Dears*. I accepted." She swished her feet again, but slowly, in a relaxed manner. "After I came back to Ft. Myers, our relationship went from friends to romantic. Larry Hays was a young forty-six. He knew how to make love to a woman. I experienced my first true orgasm with him. He warned me things would get tough when we aged. They never turned bad. We had eighteen great years. He refused to slow down; his heart didn't."

Dennia turned away for a few seconds as she brushed away tears. When she faced me, she said, "I never thought I'd find another man like Larry until I met you." She stood, removed her bikini: first the bottom, then the top. Her hand touched my shoulder. In soft tones, she whispered, "Come with me."

# # # # #

Chapter 24

"Sure. You give me names and some type of a starting point. I'll find out what their backgrounds are." Russ Foxx took a sip of beer. "It may take a while. Val and I have a project with a deadline in four days. Will that be okay?"

"That's fine, I'll get the names and what I know to you this afternoon," I said. We sat on the concrete pad next to his and Val's RV. Watching buzzards ride the wind currents, we'd been discussing his and his wife's upcoming trip to Savanah. The marvel of modern communications meant I would not lose their services for the summer, but it did complicate matters. I wanted the information back on Captain Springer's crew before they left.

"It always helps to know the who's, the why's, and the what's. Can you run some of that by me now, so I have a feel for what's important to you?"

"Sure. Do you remember me talking about that trip I took on the cruiser? The *Nancy Lynn*?"

Russ nodded. "Yep. That was the boat you planned to borrow but didn't for some reason. Friction arose on the trip, something like that."

"Remember I told you about the Captain?"

"Yeh, but I thought you liked him."

"I do. That's why I'm digging into the past of some of the characters he has with him on a trip he's taking to the Bahamas."

Russ's eyes lit up. "When you make one of those trips back down there, see if you can find a way to put Val and me in one of your suitcases. The descriptions you gave sure set a fire in the two of us. Unfortunately, our RV isn't amphibious."

I thought about his request. "If you are willing to postpone your trip to Savannah, maybe we can work something out. I have that boat leased until early in May. Let me think if there is some way to make it happen."

"If you can get us to the islands, consider Savannah cancelled." Russ smiled. "So, give me the who, why, and what's."

"Okay. Captain Springer has been out for a week. He's concerned that his crew might have some ideas about using the trip and the boat to smuggle things back into the US."

"Like drugs?" Russ asked.

"Like drugs," I agreed.

"So, where do you want me to start?"

"Let me think." I eliminated Margo. I thought I knew enough about her but quickly reconsidered. She'd be easy to blackmail. Still, she'd get the last look. I reasoned the UN interpreter and her engineer husband should be at the end also. Serving in those positions, they had to have relatively clean histories. Though Gino could be violent, he was the low intellect in the group...and I judged him to be less a threat. The place to start was the Marcos.

"Okay, Russ, I don't know if this is a who, why, or what. Margo is the daughter of the woman who owns the boat. She set up the cruise, supposedly. It is a group of her friends that went to school at Columbia that is on the sail. They all met in a class. There's a young couple named Marcos. I want you to check them first, mainly because I don't know much about them. Except, he's like you...a genius with electronic gadgets, and she's a good cook. They're Filipino heritage, mid-twenties, past that...... Margo's boyfriend, Gino something-or-other, is the next one. He's a sulky, snarly bastard. He treats Margo like shit, is a self-centered SOB, and if his brains were fertilizer, he'd leave a Gia Pet bald.

I think he has the capacity to be a criminal or violent. Do a quick check on the last couple. Hall Runnells and his wife Diane. He's an engineer with Grumman and she's an interpreter with the UN. They should be fine but give them a quick look. Take a look at Margo.

My primary concern is that somebody is controlling her."

Russ nodded, "You have more information you'll send to me?" He continued nodding praying for more to act as a launching point.

"Yes. Captain Springer left some info. Hopefully, It will be enough to start. I'll make copies and send them to you this afternoon."

Russ finished his beer. As he stood up, he said, "Val's going to want a date." "I'll look at my schedule and send some when's, with the info."

# # # # #

Chapter 25

The last cool front of the season rolled into central Florida that second week of April cooling the air and water a few degrees. To me, that meant one thing; the last chance to catch speckled perch, crappies for you Yankees, before Florida's summer heat gave them lockjaw. Trotter and I drifted across Lake Marian dragging cane poles behind us, waiting for our floats to disappear.

Normally, I prefer fishing with a fly rod or a spinning rod using artificial baits. But occasionally, I like the nostalgia that fishing with a cane pole provides me. Its simplicity transports me back to childhood. I'm sitting next to my father, listening to his stories that were disguised life-lessons and enjoying catching each fish. At those moments I realize that life lived simply, is life lived to its best. What confounds me is how frequently I forget that.

Overcast skies and an occasional light shower, made the oaks and cypress gray and unfriendly and the swampy portions of the shoreline sinister. Lake Marian's tannin stained waters kept secrets all the time, but today the wavelets defied the light's penetration and obscured what was below even more. However, the surroundings didn't depress us; the fish were biting!

Trotter's 'bobber' disappeared straight down into the murky waters. He lifted the pole and it arched over, reacting to the struggles of the fish. It thrashed on the surface for a few seconds before Trotter lifted the twelve-inch Spec into the boat.

I said, "Good Speck. That fish will eat."

"How many we keeping?"

"I'm going to invite the Foxxes over for a fry." There would five for dinner. "Two fish each if they're that size or better. Ten I guess."

Trotter counted those in the bait well and added one. "We're halfway there." He scooped a minnow from the bait bucket, put it on the hook, and was back to fishing. As he settled into his seat, he asked, "Are Russ and Val going to the Bahama's? Russ told me you were working it out." Grinning, he added, "If you can't get away. I have everything in good shape here on the ranch. I can go and keep them out of trouble."

"Then I'd have to go to keep you out of trouble."

"You couldn't go without taking Dennia. Not if you want to keep that lady around."

Trotter pointed to my float which was disappearing.

I lifted my pole and a Speck that probably was the brother of the fish Trotter put into the live well, soon wiggled in my hand. "Number six," I said as I lifted the lid to the well. As I dropped the fish to join his brethren, I added, "The *Gato Gordo* sleeps six and Sallar likes sleeping on the deck. Just saying."

"You saying and, or in place of?"

"And."

"We have to convince Lily and Dennia they can take off work that long."

"Oh, contraire. Don't forget Dennia's Cessna lets them fly back and forth as an alternative."

Trotter thought for a few seconds, "I'll postpone the vet."

"Two weeks late for an annual checkup won't hurt the horses."

Trotter shook his head, "You're forgetting something."

"What?"

"Aren't you playing watchdog for the Captain Springer guy? How you going to do that over at Abaco?"

Keeping tabs on the *Nancy Lynn* slipped my mind. "I'll ask Russ to find some way to do what we need to from the Bahamas. I saw a sign that said they had free wi-fi at the *Sleepy Dolphin*." It occurred to me, "We'd already be there if something did come up."

Trotter grinned, "We can be the cavalry."

It took a couple of seconds, but I grasped Trotter's fun pun. "I'll be John Wayne. You can be Randolph Scott."

"Who is Randolph Scott?"

The generation gap struck once more.

Chapter 26

"You want something to drink?" Cindy asked. Trotter, Russ, Val, and I sat in my living room. We were full of fish, hushpuppies, cheese grits, and green beans. I knew Cindy was anxious to wash dishes and get time to enjoy her number one pastime...reading.

"Pass," Russ and Val said in unison. Trotter shook his head.

"I guess not," I told her. "See you in the morning."

Val was anxious to know the status of the trip. "Have you heard anything from Dennia and her daughter?"

"Not yet, but I'm sure I'll hear something this evening. Relax Val, we'll fly commercial if Dennia can't. There's a flight into Marsh Harbor on the fifteenth." I paused, and turned to Russ, "Have you figured out a way for me to receive messages from Captain Springer?"

"Sure. When the telefax comes into your fax. Cindy sends it on to us at the *Sleepy Dolphin*. I already called the owner. They have a fax and use it all the time. Shepard Coloton said to say hi, and he's looking forward to our coming."

"I guess we're set."

"We might not have to even return to the marina. Coloton is sending me the specification on his boat's short wave. I might be able to rig something to get stuff direct."

"Russ, it has to be a copy of the paper, not just the words."

He nodded and smiled, "We learned that together, didn't we? The grave with greener grass taught us that. Hopefully, this isn't going to get that complicated or dangerous." He bit his lower lip and his demeanor turned serious. "I don't want to be the rain cloud threatening the parade. The telefax thing turned out to be a no-brainer, so I had some spare time. I did a quick check on the Marcos couple. It's not finished...want to hear what I've got?"

"Is it bad?" I asked.

"Ahhhhhhh...not bad. At least, not bad, bad. I guess fishy is a good description."

I looked at Val to see if she agreed. She shook her head, "I haven't touched it yet."

"She hasn't but, she needs to. I got lost in the governmental record keeping. She knows how to find a fly spec in those pepper shaker files. If you want to wait..."

I shook my head, "What have you got?"

"I'm doing this without my notes, so this is big picture...don't hold me to little things. I started with the wife. Okay to start with her?"

A deep breath followed my nod.

"Dalisay, right?"

I nodded again.

"She's twenty-six. Been in the US since she was sixteen. Came with her parents on a guest visa. Her father ended up with a green card. As far as I been able to find out, none of the family has ever applied for citizenship. Her parents started working in San Diego moved to Denver. They moved again. To where I don't have a clue. Her college records are clean, good grades, no trouble. Her social networking that's something else. She has a number of different Facebook and Twitter accounts and some individual ones like Instagram. Very active. Most are normal stuff. Two of them...they're hostile. At least they were, she's not been active for a few years in that crap. She mention's belonging to some radical anarchist groups. INFA, The Anti-Government League. She did make some more recent remarks distancing her from them." He paused. "There's one entry that concerns me, even though it was five years ago, she was inquiring on who to contact about obtaining drugs."

"Shit!" Trotter said. "That definitely isn't good."

That was enough but I asked anyway. "Anything else that jumps out?"

"Not by itself, but she's Moslem. That's nothing until I tell you that her husband's social media has some Al Qaeda propaganda on it, and when he was at Columbia, he was active in one radical group. Active is too strong. He showed a lot of interest. He's hard to figure...some good...some not so good."

"Anything else he was active in?"

"Not in political stuff. Both he and his wife seemed to have lost interest after they married. He is active in all kinds of electronic control related activities. Drones in particular. He's in all kinds of electrically controlled models. Airplanes, boats, cars, anything that moves. The guy must really be good. He's won all kinds of awards for competitions.

Almost all first places. I'd like to meet him. We'd have a lot in common." What about his parents, and other backgrounds?"

"He has a passport, so he's a US citizen. His parents check out. They're both naturalized citizens, spotless history, but that was a quick check. Marcos' grades were excellent. He has a few misdemeanors on his record and three simple assaults. Two are related to his religion at protests. He has a temper problem. I ran out of time before I finished."

Was the couple's history part of their maturation process? I asked, "Would you feel comfortable with inviting them to your home?"

"Based on what I know right now, I would. However, I'd watch the silverware closer than normal." Russ paused for a few seconds. "I'd know better after Val gets into some records I couldn't."

"Do you think you could finish checking those two and the rest of Captain Springer's crew in the next few days? I'd like to leave for the Bahamas early next week. My conscience would be a lot clearer if I had the info before we leave."

"Two days should be enough." Russ glanced at Val and she nodded.

# # # # #

Chapter 27

Winds buffeted the Jeep as I drove the last ten miles to my office. The closer to the Atlantic, the stronger the wind. My route paralleled a canal, a small one, but even in that tiny body of water, winds created problems for boaters. Twice I stopped as fishermen blocked the narrow road with their vehicles. They attempted to load their boats on trailers as howling winds foiled every effort. Captain Springer must be struggling with the Nancy Lynn if winds were anything near as strong in the Bahamas.

By the time I reached the office, I guessed the winds were blowing at 15 to 20 mph. Gusts occasionally had to be reaching thirty.

When I arrived in Wabasso, Clareen met me at the office door. “You have your cell phone turned off?”

“Yes, I can’t hear in the Jeep.”

Clareen tossed one of my favorite football bromides back at me, “Excuses are like assholes, everybody’s got one.”

“So, what did I miss?”

"Riaffort's been calling. Three times in the last hour. He didn't say what he wanted, but it must be important."

"I'll call him right away."

~ ~ ~ ~ ~ ~

"I agree, she shouldn't do that," I said.

"Will you call Melanie, explain to her you're keeping in touch with Springer, and you'll take care of contacting the officials down there if it's necessary?" Riaffort was frustrated.

"Why is all this happening now?" I asked.

"Melanie finally got around to reading the first two telefaxes that Springer sent."

"Why even bother. If something was about to go wrong, waiting that long to do something puts her in the position to pay for the funerals, and that's about it." Though it wasn't a shock, Melanie Hellmann's actions were consistent with her social style. Overreacting would hurt, not help, her daughter's situation if she was in danger.

"I told you when you met her, she and her husband were one of my major sources of income. You see why. One word, Sly, one word. Impulsive." I could visualize Riaffort's scowl. "Please, give her a call."

"Okay, but you owe me one."

After we hung up, I called Clareen on the intercom. "Do you have Melanie Hellmann's phone number? I thought I had it on my cell, but I don't."

"I think I do." There was a brief silence. Then, "I have it, I'll bring it in to you." Clareen wanted to talk to me about something or she would have given it to me over the intercom.

In seconds Clareen laid the phone number in front of me. "What was so critical, Riaffort went into a tizzy?"

"The Hellmann woman was the one I was supposed to borrow the boat from. Remember? Anyway, you know I developed a friendship with the Captain. He's been sending updates to Mrs. Hellmann and me. She hadn't been reading hers and when she caught up, some of it disturbed her. She wanted Riaffort to call the authorities in the Bahamas and check on her daughter and the *Nancy Lynn*. When Riaffort declined, she threatened to call them herself. That wouldn't be good. Riaffort's asked me to call her and calm her down."

"Isn't the daughter the one you said was a bigger disaster than the Titanic? And, didn't you say Dennia got along better with the Hellmann woman than you did?"

"Right on both counts, but Riaffort says she'll listen to me. Anyway, it won't cost me anything."

Wrong!

# # # # #

Chapter 28

"Hello, Melanie, this is Sly Harrell. Riaffort Richards asked me to give you a call and give you an assessment of the cruise Margo's on. He said he explained that Captain Springer is keeping in touch with me too. Do you have some time to discuss this?"

Muffled crying preceded her frantic comments that rolled out like continuous thunder. "Oh, Mr. Harrell, I am so glad to hear from you. I feel so guilty. And, dumb. You tried to warn me, and I was too stupid to listen. When I read Adrian's note's...I've known him so long! He must be terribly upset to write the way he did. It just isn't the way he...thinks. Do you think Margo and Adrian are in danger?"

"No. If I thought they were threatened by some kind of harm, I'd have already taken some action."

"Oh, that does help! But I'm still so upset. I just know something has disturbed Adrian. The dear man is so patient. It really takes a lot to upset him. After reading his notes...well, I realize I don't know *those* people. Margo can be so difficult. I don't know if you noticed, they don't have a friendly relationship.

And...and...and, I don't completely trust that boyfriend of hers. He often just acts...bad!"

"Captain Adrian Springer is a very strong and capable man. You are lucky to have him working for you. If things get to a point where something needs to be done, he'll pull the plug. I'm sure of that. You'll see the *Nancy Lynn* berthed in your boathouse very quickly.

Whether she sensed my fear or not she verbalized it. "What if they take control away from him? Would you call it mutiny? Adrian is not a big man. He doesn't own a gun. There are three of them. Gino can be violent; Margo told me that once. Don't you think we should ask the police, down there, to just check on them?"

"I don't think that would be a good idea right now. Springer is still in control. We wouldn't be getting messages if he wasn't. And think of this. What do we tell the Bahamian police when we call them? We think they should send out a patrol boat, hunt down the *Nancy Lynn*, that will take a day...probably more...based on the fact we don't like the wording in a message? Let's say they go check on her. Then what? If everything is okay, they aren't going to listen to us if there really is a need for them."

Melanie was quiet for several seconds, then asked, "I see what you're saying. You are probably right. But...but...What if those people are controlling what Adrian is saying? It's hard to get that out of my mind."

"That hasn't happened," I lied, for I didn't know that was a fact. "Let me put your mind at ease. I'm doing an investigation...just to be sure the people on the boat with your daughter and Captain Springer are good folks, or at least, not dangerous." I lied again, "I don't think that's necessary, but in an abundance of caution, we'll know."

"Thank you, thank you, thank you, Mr. Harrell. I'm so grateful to you! Will you let me know if you determine there could be a problem?"

"Yes." I thought about how to persuade her *not* to call the Bahamian police. "There's another thing, I'll be traveling to Abaco Island early next week and I'll be there for most of the remaining time the *Nancy Lynn* will be in those waters. Captain Springer's notes will be forwarded to me there. I'll be in a much better position to intervene and work with the police in the remote chance there'd be a problem."

"That is wonderful!"

One problem averted, I thought.

# # # # #

Chapter 29

"Hi. This is the *Dancing Dears*. Would you like a reservation?" It was a standard script the reception ladies used to answer the phone.

I recognized Dawn Worthington's voice. "Sorry, it's Sly. Is Dennia around?"

"Hey Sly. Dennia's out. She went to the supply house to buy some paper products.

I expect her back in a few minutes. Want me to have her call you?" "No, I'll call back."

"Fine. Hey, Dennia tells me you two are headed back to the Bahamas for two weeks.

That sounds great."

"Yes. Evidently, she talked you into running the place while she's away."

Dawn laughed. "She didn't have to do a lot of talking. I enjoy being boss, but my paycheck goes down some. When she told me, she'd make up the difference between what she pays me to manage and what I make in tips...I could take that for a while. Truthfully, I won't miss riding the pole and the vultures crowded around me with their tongues hanging out."

Dawn had answered my question, Dennia was going for two weeks. "I'm glad. Tell Dennia if I don't get her this afternoon, I'll—"

Dawn interrupted, "She's walking in the door now." An unintelligible discussion and laughter came through the receiver before Dennia said, "That's good timing. I was going to call and tell you I'm going for the whole trip. Lily can only get one week, so I'll fly back and pick her up Saturday afternoon the 20th. She chose the second week. I hope that won't mess things up badly."

"No problem. It gives us a chance to bring anything we forgot when Lily comes." I knew Trotter would be unhappy...I wondered, "How did Lily take having to miss one week? Disappointed?"

"Not disappointed, pissed. She threw a fit in her bosses office, I understand, but she calmed down when I told her I'd give her flying lessons for her next birthday."

I laughed, "Bribery works. I'll pass that along to Trotter.......Did she get herself in trouble with her boss?"

"Lily is very, very good at everything she does. Besides, her boss is a forgiving lady. Even though she's in her seventies, she hasn't forgotten what being young and in love is about."

"Good, I wouldn't want to be guilty of being a bad influence and her losing her job,"

I said jokingly.

"Her not being able to come when we fly over, solves part of a problem. There are six bodies to transport and my Cessna seats four. Add the bags, it means two trips. I'll be flying most of the first day."

"It isn't going to be a problem. The Foxxes have a lot of equipment they want to take. All told it weighs 120 pounds and that doesn't include their clothes. I offered to pay for their commercial fares, so they'll actually be flying in on Sunday. They'll be sleeping on the boat before we get there."

"Speaking of sleeping on the boat, are the winds bad where you are? It is terrible here. Lily will toss her toenails if the weather is like this."

"We will stay tied to the dock if it's as windy while we're over there. Remember, I told you a friend was captaining a cruise there. This is supposed to be his last day of marlin fishing. I hope they stayed in port. He's scheduled to move to Exuma tomorrow, which will be a bitch. The wind will be out of the southwest, the worst direction to make that trip."

"Is there a possibility the winds could be like this when we're over there?"

"Dennia, no one can tell you for sure. This time of year, the weather is transitioning. It can be winter winds one day, and summer calm the next. Don't worry. Even if we stay tied to the dock, we'll find a way to have fun." I changed the subject. "Are you going to have enough time to get packed and ready?"

Dennia laughed, "My suitcases are packed and sitting at the front door." She paused and asked in a little girl's voice. "Can you rent scuba gear over there?"

I lied, "We have tanks, masks, flippers, regulators, weights, and whole smear. Have you had training?" I was looking for dive shops to buy what we'd need as I was speaking."

"Yes, I used to go to or three times a year, but it's been a while. I have my own flippers and mask. So does Lily. They're by the door, too."

"Good," I was only half listening.

"Do you think we might run into those people you told me about on Melanie Hellmann's cruiser? Margo's friends." Dennia read my response as a lack of comprehension, not its true meaning of finding words to avoid discussion about them. "The ones on the *Nancy Lynn*? I'd like to try using one of those dive subs you said they have. That would be a blast."

My attention was back on the phone conversation. "I'm pretty sure we won't see them. I can ask Shepard Coloton if he knows if we can rent one on Abaco. He'd know. He might have them at the *Sleepy Dolphin*."

She sighed, "Darling, this is going to be a trip we always remember."

I remember those words and the feeling she spoke them with, for two reasons. First, it was the first time she'd used a 'pet' name for me when we talked. Second, it turned out to be a trip we would never forget!

# # # # #

Chapter 30

"There are only three places it could be. We've been to one and that wasn't it. Another says they only repair fiberglass boats. The one coming up has to be the one" Trotter's eyes flitted between his cell phone screen and the line of waterfront businesses. Marinas, bait stores, and old motels lined the road where we hoped we'd find the company that made the dive subs for the couple now cruising on the *Nancy Lynn*.

"That's all of them?" I asked.

"In Melbourne, yes. I checked Google, the yellow pages, the white pages, the Melbourne Business Directory. I'm pretty sure we have everything listed. The three are the only ones on the water. That's where you said it was located." Trotter's exasperation showed.

We eased along the road allowing my Jeep to creep at 20 mph.

"I see it," Trotter said. "Looks like it, anyway."

The long, high chain-link fence with three strands of barbed wire on top, stretched along 200' of the old crumbling blacktop. When we were even with it, we saw the office, a gray building in need of paint. Surrounding it were new and used machines of a wide variety of uses and conditions. The chain-link angled away from the road, to the building, providing a narrow strip of pavement to park in its front. A sign told us we'd found *"Marine & Military Custom Manufacturing Ltd."* I parked in one of the two spaces marked for 'customers.'

When the engine sounds died, our welcome wasn't a friendly one. Four or five snarling Doberman's raced back and forth behind the fence on either side of the narrow parking strip. They looked hungry.

"Those dogs would like to rip us into tiny pieces," I said as I climbed out of the Jeep.

Trotter had a bad experience with Doberman Pinchers and his comment was harsher.

I walked to the front door of the building that had no windows we could see. The door had two padlocks on it besides the deadbolt. As expected, it was locked. "Push button for service." I did as the sign read. A clanging alarm went off, within a minute it silenced, and the sound of shuffling feet came from inside.

"You have an appointment?" a voice yelled from inside.

"No," I said, "I want to talk to someone."

"What the fuck about?" The unfriendly theme persisted.

"I want to buy a dive sub. I believe you make them here."

There was clicking as the deadbolt and other locks inside were opened. The door cracked a third of the way. A man covered with dirt, and trimmed with grease, filled the opening. He scowled at us leaving no doubt; he didn't want us around.

"Who told you that?"

"A friend of a friend. He said he was picking it up here about a week ago."

"We don't make such things." He was suspicious of us.

"Did you make a dive sub for a man named Hall Runnells?" I couldn't tell if the slight change in his features was a reaction to the name or just impatience.

"We only make custom stuff. You bring us plans. We build it." He hadn't directly answered my question.

"Did you make something for Mr. Runnells?" I persisted.

"I don't know no Runnells, and I don't know if we made something for him. You'll have to ask my boss. He ain't here and won't be for a week or two. I can't help you, so get your assholes out of here." He closed the door and we heard the locks snap.

As we returned to the Jeep, I told Trotter, "That was weird. I'm damned near sure this is the place that built those subs. I sensed a reaction from him. You'd think they'd be real interested in selling more. A job like that has to be a big chunk of business for a small shop like this."

Trotter climbed into the passenger seat. He watched me settle behind the steering wheel and motioned for me not to turn the ignition key. "Could you see past the guy in the door?"

"No, I didn't try."

"I did. There were two 50 caliber Browning air-cooled machine guns sitting on a workbench. That is one hell of a lot of firepower. What do you think they're doing with them?"

I thought for several seconds, "Part of the sign out front, says 'military manufacture.' The owner may have permits. You're always telling me not to poke my nose where it doesn't belong. I'm taking your advice this time."

# # # # #

Chapter 31

I tried my best to stay awake. The insurance contract sitting on my desk was as good as a sleeping pill. I blinked my eyes and stiffened my neck. I was updating the liability insurance on my ranch. Riaffort had already read and approved my signing it but insisted that I read it to familiarize myself with the boilerplate. At least, he stuck 'post-it' notes at the critical points to help. The fine print and weasel wording frustrated me to the point I read it to get it done, not to learn anything. I knew that would bite me someday, I hoped not badly.

My chin rested on my chest, while my eyes closed. At that point, the only purpose my pupils served was to check my lids for pinholes. My golden retriever nudged me with her cold nose, reviving me for several seconds. Soon I traveled back to sandman land.

"Would you like some coffee?" Cindy asked.

I sat up straight, and shook my head violently, to wake up. "Yes. The stronger the better."

"All that legal stuff drives me crazy. The party of the first part agrees to turn summersaults on the first and last of the month, with only one shoe on. That stuff doesn't make any sense to me. I'm glad I don't have to bother with it like you do." She placed a telefax in front of me. "You could read this message from Captain Springer to give you a break."

"It's Friday already, isn't it?"

"All day. I'll be right back with that coffee." Cindy left as silently as she came.

The message covered two-thirds of the sheet. There was something different about it, and it took me a few moments to figure out what. Springer had drawn a line at the top and bottom of the message using periods and hyphens.

--- ... --- ... --- ... --- ... --- ... --- ... --- ... --- ... --- ... --- ... --- ... --- ... --- ... --- ... --- ... ---

Sly,

This is my third progress report. Winds have been strong.. I would not have gone out the last day we trolled for marlin- - We didn't get to fish much- - the waves were so heavy it was dangerous. Almost lost one overboard. Loaded the dive subs that PM. Winds less but not good... I will stop at one of the islands I know in the Exuma chain. It is about threequarters of the way to Georgetown on Great Exuma. – The island isn't inhabited, no one lives within miles, but it has a very protected cove to anchor the Nancy Lynn. Old Dog Cay, remember the name. It is a place to return to. We will shelter there overnight. Winds are supposed to be light tomorrow... I will keep us there if they are not. Wilbur Morris' Cay is twelve miles from it. One of the 'dive subs' broke its lashings and did some minor damage. I can't take the chance. Margo and I have a little more in common? I've learned a lot about drones and electronic guidance systems. You should too. Less tension on board, right now. We are in contact with Matthew Town at Inagua... Runnells knows people there. I expect good traveling as far as Inagua. - I'm not sure of what we'll do, but I've been told- - - lots of diving- . I hope the winds will stay settled but have continuing worries about them. If they stay settled, like now, it will be okay. Wish me fair winds and luck...

Adrian

--- ... --- ... --- ... --- ... --- ... --- ... --- ... --- ... --- ... -
-- ... --- ... --- ... --- ... --- ... --- ... ---

After the Captain's previous note, I examined the fax for hidden or coded messages. I had to assume at least one of his companions was monitoring what was being sent to us. That meant he'd have to exercise caution.

The first, obvious thing, he communicated by his uses of dots and dashes in the lines, and his use of the name Morris Cay were clues he'd use Morse Code to send me messages. It made sense to immediately examine the letter again for its use. There was no need to decipher the top line. The bottom line repeated the code for the letters "O" and "S." Was the Captain sending the SOS message? What was trying to be conveyed? That pushed my alarm button for an instant. After more thought, I realized the Captain would have placed a separation somewhere in the string of codes to isolate that message. I concluded he constructed the last line to confirm his intent.

There had to be code imbedded in the fax. Two obvious places would be in the separation lines and punctuation at the end of sentences. The lines were of no help. It wouldn't take long to check the sentences. I wrote what the code indicated... E, I, M, M, E, E, E, S, E, A, E, E, S, M, E, E, E, ?, E, E, E, S, A, O, N, E, E, S. There were several words like, "I," "me," "sea," "one," and more that could be made from the letters. No matter how I tried stringing them together, I couldn't glean information from them. I deduced it was Captain Springer's way of telling me where to look for future messages.

In the last fax, he'd written his apprehensions into the text, so I reviewed the letter again to see what could be learned.

There was so much reference to weather and waves, I spent a long period of time trying to determine if there was significance in it. References in the first part of the message simply described what happened, as far as I could tell. His mention of winds in the last few sentences I took to as predictions on how the cruise might turn out. It sounded as though his concerns with the intentions of his crew had lessened but had not disappeared. I believed he listed his continuing concerns in the body of the fax. My interpretations were: His shipmates were willing to take unwise risks, the apostrophes around 'dive subs' indicated something, but I didn't have a clue what it might be, he wanted me to know the use of electronics figured in his worries, and he was concerned with Hall Runnells connection with individuals in Inagua. On the plus side, he appeared to believe things weren't as dire as he previously indicated, and he enjoyed improving relations with Margo.

Captain Springer clearly had the *Nancy Lynn* under his control and didn't believe any imminent threat existed. After reading his fax, my major concern was what Melanie Hellmann's thoughts would be after reading the one sent to her. My fear...the mention of damage to the *Nancy Lynn* would cause her to over-react. I picked up the phone to call her, then set it back down. Riaffort would probably be riding herd over her. If I checked with Russ and Val, and they had positive information on the remaining couple, my phone call to her could be reassuring as well as a preventive measure. I decided to talk to Russ before calling Melanie.

# # # # #

Chapter 32

Russ Foxx is the eternal optimist. If he starts a conversation with the words, "You're not going to like what I've got to tell you," you really are not. He sat on the other side of my desk, shaking his head.

"So, what did you find out?"

"It's what I found out about one and what I couldn't find out about two. I have lots of information on that Gino character. The Runnells...I'm having trouble getting into anything that sounds authentic in their backgrounds."

"So, what did you find out?" I repeated.

"Alright...Margo's boyfriend, Gino Razze. He's thirty-two. His father is an Italian restauranteur. Eleven locations in the New York, New Jersey, Pennsylvania areas. The family is very well off. This is interesting—Gino's mother is part Jewish and part Arab. The father lists his religion as Catholic, his momma says she's Muslim. Gino has claimed to be all three. Based on what I can tell, he isn't any of them."

Russ paused to catch his breath. "He had a record in junior high. I can't tell you what that was because that's sealed. Now to high school. I'll just hit the high points; the list of offenses is three plus pages, single-spaced. He tried to burn his school down three times, which was as a freshman. There are two auto thefts that year. That offense repeats annually. Same with assault and battery. Two rapes and four attempts. These are all while he still was in juvenile court. As soon as he made legal age, a judge sent away for two years for assault and attempted rape. Jail time slowed him some. The arrests are less frequent. Lots of dropped charges. I called three victims and found out daddy paid handsomely to get that to happen. He spent four months in Mexico. Ever since he's been involved in drugs, but on the margins. He went to college for the first time at age twenty-six. He got through...that's all. I wouldn't doubt dear old dad helped that too."

Russ glanced at me over his laptop screen. "He has never held a job for more than seven months. Gino even got fired from one of his father's restaurants. Even so, he's always had plenty of money to toss around. Drives a Porche. He's got a half dozen credit cards that get paid to zero monthly. He's been living with Margo for five months and it looks like she's picking up most of his bills. That brings me to his social media accounts."

"Social media? Like Facebook, that kind of thing?" I asked.

"Yes. Exactly. I looked at them to determine what kind of friends he has. They vary all over the place. Some are radicals...left and right. He doesn't show any zeal for any political philosophy. He just likes thugs. The other part of it is his views on sex. You know me, I'm no prude. Damn the stuff he has on two of his accounts...they'd make Larry Flynt blush. If Margo has ever read any of the stuff, he's written about her, and she's within twenty miles of him, she's crazy. It's graphic, detailed, and disgusting. Plus, he mentions what he calls "side trips." Other women. Described in the same way. It's bad."

"I figured he was lower than low. Did you see anything that would lead you to believe he would participate in violence?"

"Oh, yes. He signed up for a skin-head protest that was to hassle a Jewish event. I don't know if he participated, but there were severe injuries according to what I looked up. He was at an INFA event. There's a picture of him urinating on the front door of a bank. That guy is a real piece of work."

"From what you observed, do you think that Gino is capable of participating in seizing the boat?"

"In a New York minute."

"What about killing someone?"

Russ hesitated a second, then said, "Sly, I believe the bastard is perfectly willing to kill...particularly if he thinks there's little chance of anyone finding out."

I took a deep breath, "So tell what you have found out about the Runnells couple."

"Okay, I want to start with the man. Hall Runnells. His age is thirty-four. Born in Ft. Green, Indiana.

Mother, Anabelle Slade-Runnells. Father, James W. Runnells. Signed by a midwife. There was some confusion about that. The Runnells are a prolific bunch. He has four brothers and two sisters. His whole family went off the grid about then. As near as I can determine, he was born, then, turned fourteen. Other than the birth record, there isn't a thing I've been able to find out about him before high school. I tried checking on his parents. The only reference to them is in the high school records where he enrolled. That said they were deceased. His residence was with an aunt, Imogene Fraser, his legal guardian. He must have spent four years studying. He had two B's the rest were straight A's. According to his records, he didn't participate in but one activity, Chess Club. There were comments by his teachers, all glowing. I found that strange because they were so similar. It took some time, but I checked notes his teachers made about other students. Of course, I'm guessing, but some were so different in structure, word use, and length...I swear they could have been written by different people. Last, I decided to look outside the official records. I went to the school yearbook. There's not a single picture of him in the damned books. There were notations in three of four of them, 'Absent for photograph.'

The fourth said, 'Excused on religious grounds.' According to his record, he graduated number 4 in 393. No police record of any kind. No affiliations outside school I could find. This is telling...no driver's license. So ends his high school days."

"Sounds like the invisible student." When working for Justice, I'd been involved in constructing false pasts for people. It sounded like some of those phony records.

"His college records are better. The only picture and description I have that's reliable is his driver's license he got when he was a freshman in college. Long, dark brown hair, brown eyes, thin face. The picture is on the flash drive I made for you. Says he's 5'10" and 178 pounds. His age at the time was nineteen. It's a Pennsylvania license. The grades are outstanding. He had a Facebook account. He never was very active. He only posts something every couple of months, now. He claims he likes to be alone. Interesting is the fact he never talks about anything personal. Not even his wife. The only mention I found of her was when someone inquired if he was married. His total answer, "Yes." Mostly stuff about his classes, disagreements with professors over technical issues. About the three degrees, that's not accurate. He has five. Summarizing the fancy titles, he has bachelors' degrees in mechanical, electrical, and metallurgical engineering, a master's in environmental engineering, all from MIT...and a doctorate in arts from Columbia. He did all that in seven years. Hall couldn't have had time to do much but study."

I said, "It sounds to me like you got a lot on him."

"I have a lot about his accomplishments, nothing about the man. I haven't even got much on those since he went to work for Grumman."

"What do you have?"

"Sly, you have to remember this guy works for one of the biggest and most sensitive defense contractors in the world. Their computer protection software is damned good.

Trying to get into Grumman's files is like trying to get into Ft. Knox with a butter knife. I tried...and within seconds they were backtracing and I got out and stayed out. I found some stuff in Nexus. Press releases mostly. Promotions. Awards. There was one picture of him in a group. His face was shot looking down and to the side. Hall still has his long hair. There was an article about his leading an underwater design team working with Navy Seals. Another was on his theory of sonar homing devices used in conjunction with radio controlled drones. The last...he was a no show as a speaker at an engineering society conference. Now you know what I know."

"Honestly, the whole background is strange. When you started, I thought the information was a fabricated history. Then, as you got into it, it began to sound more like something someone like me hadn't invented. When you checked on his wife, did you find anything about him?"

"A lot...and very little. Diane Fanatti-Runnells. There's lots of verbiage and little meaning. The stuff I'll be relaying to you on the woman sounds more like a series of press releases for someone running for political office. That starts with her parents. They were as much publicity agents as mom and dad. This even goes into the elementary school records. Her mother spent almost as much time at the school as Diane. The girl was another academic wonder. If she received anything but an "A" from a teacher, there was an endless string of conferences and meetings. If I were her teacher, I'd have given her straight "A's" to avoid the hassle. Starting in junior high, she participated in almost every activity possible. The one exception, anything athletic. Drama Club, Honor Society, Spanish Club, Student Government, Future Writers, Culture Club...hell, if they had a Club she'd have belonged. In high school, she played in the band and won prizes for playing the clarinet. She was Homecoming Queen, Band Sweetheart, senior class president. Her social media record starts there. She was in love with a different boy about every six weeks, expressed her intent to be an interpreter for her career, and told about her accomplishments. The lady isn't modest."

"She went to Wellesley for one year, transferred to Rutgers, got an undergrad in languages. Her masters came from Columbia, again in language. Grades were great. You can wade through the lists of awards and honors she accumulated I put on the flash drive. Ninety percent of her Facebook entries start, "I won this award," blankety, blank. She volunteered for two congressional campaigns while she was in college. Both candidates make Bernie Sanders look like a Reagan conservative. One interesting thing. Evidently, she left Wellesley under a cloud."

"That's interesting. Everything so far sounds like she's Mrs. Clean Jeans. What was her problem?"

"She got caught peddling drugs, mostly weed, but some hard stuff thrown in. There was a felony arrest. Lots of lawyers involved. Long story short. Looks like mom and dad got those nasty old police to go away. Charges got dropped...Diane dropped out of Wellesley...the seas calmed...and Diane was in Columbia in two months. The Fanatti's are well connected. After she graduated, she took a job at the UN working for the UAE. Her mother had a connection. A year later, she took a job working directly for the UN as an interpreter. Diane met Hall at this point, I think in the class that is the connection to all six on the cruise. They were married in six months. I found a wedding picture. Margo, Gino, and the Marcos couple weren't in it. Anyway, after that, info on Diane dries up. I found a couple of references in newspaper articles, but she must have adopted Runnells adversity to allowing any information to creep under their front door."

"Did you have any luck getting any contact information...phone numbers...email addresses...snail mail...anything?"

Russ's bitter laugh was answer enough but he elaborated. "That's the real kicker. The best I was able to do, was to get office information. They have cell phones and email addresses, they'd have to. I haven't been able to get a smell. I'd like to learn how they keep them shielded so well. Big one, no credit cards for the last four years. They have Facebook accounts and such but no personal information to speak of."

I sat silently. After Russ completed his compilation, I felt I knew more than when he started, but what was important and what was not? "You said you had contact information for them at where they work?"

"Not exactly. I have Diane's extension number at the UN. If you call it, you get her assistant. The guy is hostile. He wouldn't give me any information. The first words from his mouth were, she did not speak to anybody without an appointment. As far as Hall, I don't even have that much. I have the Grumman Home Office number in Falls Church.

End of story."

"Do you think Val might have better luck with the records?"

"Normally, I'd say yes. In this case, I don't think so. Grumman isn't worth the risk, Sly. She might have some luck with Hall's family or his elementary school days. She'd really good at that." He looked at me and guessed. "I'll have her take a quick look. As far as,

Diane, I don't know where she could look that I haven't."

"I agree on Diane. Do you have that company and UN phone number? And, I'd like the extension number too."

"Sure, got them right here," he said and tapped his laptop's keyboard a few times.

"Got a piece of scrap paper?"

I slid a legal pad to him. He wrote two phone numbers on the pad, one with the extension number following it.

Russ asked, "What's next?"

"I'd hoped to have some glowing information on the Runnells couple to relay to Melanie Hellmann. I want to get her to relax and keep her from interfering and stirring up a hornet's nest. My thought was to parrot what you told me and make it sound like all is well. The trouble is, I don't believe that."

"So, what's next?"

"I haven't the slightest idea?"

# # # # #

Chapter 33

The numbers on the yellow, lined pad, tugged at my mind, even though I'd left them on my desk and went on to other things. I wanted to call the numbers, but realized Russ had done that without accomplishing anything. The trip back to the Bahamas was what I tried to concentrate on...without success. My conscience nagged me. It kept screaming, *'you could be leaving Captain Springer high and dry. Make those calls. Now!'* Halfway through packing, I dropped a pair of underwear in the suitcase, cursed, and went back to my desk. The numbers scribbled on the yellow pad siren's call was too strong to ignore. Feet took me to my desk without protest from my mind.

Staring at them for several minutes didn't help, as I tried to conjure approaches that wouldn't get me a curt dismissal or a hang-up. There was one thing I could do that would get me through the first echelon of phone filters. A friend at the DOJ could empower me by saying I was calling for him and was working on a project. That would be a last resort.

Which should I try first? Over-thinking, over-thinking, over-thinking! I decided to call Grumman. It was the first number listed. As the phone rang, I searched my mind for a creative gimmick to use to get past the reception desk. I decided I'd try a bluff.

"Grumman. How may I direct your call?"

"Hall Runnells," gruff tones were part of my act.

The soft, sweet feminine voice replied, "I'm sorry, I can't put you through directly. If you want to leave a message, I can connect you with his voice mail."

"Tell him SJ Harrell is calling. He should remember me from Justice. I can't leave him the message I have for him in an unsecured environment." I purposely sounded like an arrogant ass, the way the majority of mid-level governmental martinets do.

"Just one moment, please." There was silence. She was checking with Runnells' office.

"Mr. Harrell, did you say Justice?" She asked.

"Yes, as in the Department of Justice."

She responded the way I expected when she returned to the line. "Mr. Runnells isn't available. I can connect you with his assistant."

"Please." There was a series of clicks and the phone rang once.

"Hall Runnells office, Marine Engineering Projects, Elaine Sierra speaking. Is this Mr. Runnells?" The woman on the other end of the conversation sounded professional.

"Yes. I'd like to speak to Hall."

"I'm sorry, Mr. Runnells is out of the office. Can I have him call you?"

I tried to get more information while giving none. "Will he be back next week? I can call him back...otherwise, I can contact someone else."

"I'm sorry Mr. Runnells will—"

"That's okay, I'll get someone else. Thank you." I hung, up avoiding any more questions. The assistant's answers seemed to confirm Hall Runnells was in fact who he said he was and was on the trip.

Did I really need to call his wife? After a few seconds thinking about it, I decided to. It would be better. After confirming Diane Fanatti-Runnells as legitimate, I'd be able to call Melanie Hellmann with a clear conscience.

I dialed the number and got an operator with a heavy New York accent to forward my call. Within a couple of seconds, a lady's cheerful voice answered, "Interpreting services."

Expecting a man's voice, I stammered, "Ahhh, I'm trying to reach Diane Fanatti-Runnells assistant."

"Rod took a late lunch. Might I help you?"

"Yes, ma'am. I'd like to know when Mrs. Fanatti-Runnells will be in the office?"

A cheery laugh preceded, "Why she's here now. I'm Diane. How can I help you?"

# # # # #

Chapter 34

My heart rate changed dramatically. Things turned upside down completely when she said, “I’m Diane.”

“Oh...I thought you were out of the office. At least...someone told me that. Sorry about the assumption.” Talking slowly as I could, I tried organizing my thoughts so I wouldn’t sound like an idiot...and not make her suspicious...I wasn’t sure why.

“Do you want to get something translated or need an interpreter? I’m sorry I didn’t catch your name.” Diane sounded relaxed and wanted to be helpful.

“My name Slydell Harrell. A friend of mine told me you might be able to find someone who can translate some documents for me. I’m from out-of-town, but a friend of mine told me if I was in New York you could recommend someone. She said she knew you. Her name is Margo Hellmann.”

“Margo Hellmann, that sounds very familiar. Margo...Margo...Margo...Oh! I know.

She was in my classes at Columbia. I think she was the one with the Filipino friends. Yes. The big blonde who tended to be expressive. Is that her?”

"That describes her. Particularly if she tended to use too many four-lettered words."

Diane chuckled, "That would be a very good description of her. One of her friends and one of my ex-teaching assistants would be a good person to translate your documents.

If there aren't too many I could—"

"Oh, no, Mrs. Fanaitti-Runnels, there are...sixty, maybe seventy sheets, I can't impose. If you give me your teaching assistant's name?"

"Please, call me Diane. Her name is, Lamisah Asghar. If you wait for a few seconds I can find her phone number?"

"No, that's right. Margo gave me her information and said she was the second person to contact."

"What language?" Diane asked.

"Tagalog."

"She'll be perfect! Can I do anything else for you?"

"I've been wondering. Are you related to Hall Runnells? My brother went to MIT with him."

"Yes! That's my husband. Can you leave me his email? Hall might want to contact him?"

"If you give me Hall's, I'll have my brother contact him."

There was a brief pause. "I am sorry, but my husband is a real coocoo about giving out email or phone numbers."

"That's right. If my brother wants to contact him, I'll give him your phone. Thank you."

We said goodbye. *My thought was, what in the hell is going on*?

I decided to call Grumman again and ask a couple more questions.

"Grumman. How may I direct your call?"

"Hall Runnells, This SJ Harrell, I'm back again," my tone was still gruff, but less unfriendly.

The soft, sweet feminine voice replied, "Oh Mr. Harrell, I can put you through to Miss Sierra."

"That would be fine."

I waited for several seconds before Runnells assistant answered. "Hello, Mr. Harrell. What can I do for you?"

"Yes. My boss wants to know when your boss will be back. He thought it would be in a couple of weeks."

"Oh no! Mr. Runnells will be in the Palau Islands for nine more weeks and will be stopping in San Diego for two more after that. Can I tell Mr. Runnells what subject you want to discuss? And how to contact you?"

"No problem. We can't wait, and this is a face-to-face kind of thing. My boss said he has a friend in DOD that can help. Forget the whole thing."

I took a deep breath and shook my head. I didn't know who two of Captain Springer's shipmates were. I sure and hell knew who they weren't!

# # # # #

Chapter 35

Staring at the calendar and the phone didn't help. They posed questions but offered no answers. Sixteen days. That's how many more the *Nancy Lynn* was scheduled to remain on her cruise. It was time for a hard appraisal...a time to answer tough questions.

Had I created a problem where one did not exist? My commitment to come to the Captain's aid if he found himself in trouble was solid steel. Did that color my view? If my concerns were valid, would Captain Springer retain control of the *Nancy Lynn*? What would happen if he didn't? How could I determine when and if my conjecture became actuality? To the present, no specific criminal activity had occurred.

There was the question the phone sitting in front of me refused to stop asking. Should I call Riaffort to disclose what I'd learned in the last hour? If I did, could I count on him keeping the information confidential? If Melanie Hellmann received the news 'imposters' were on the *Nancy Lynn*, I shuttered at the possibility.

Answers. I needed answers.

Would Captain Springer retain control for that period of time? I thought he would, though I was less sure since my discussion with Russ. The crew's motive Margo brought on the *Nancy Lynn* held the answer. Having a good time. No problem. Smuggling drugs, gems, or other materials? Captain Springer was smart. He could simply ignore the presence of items snuck aboard util they returned. Bringing aliens onboard or a terrorist attack...problem! As soon as that happened, he'd have to act...and boom. The struggle to control the cruiser would begin.

What would happen if he didn't maintain control of the *Nancy Lynn*? If they contemplated bringing terrorists into the country or wanted it for a terror attack, Springer had to go! Their two alternatives: put a bullet in the Captain's brain, or, put him ashore on an isolated, uninhabited island. The *Nancy Lynn* would likely never return to its berth in Jupiter. A horrifying truth swept into my mind. Getting rid of the Captain was a precursor to those events happening. Reality shook me! The first illegal act was likely to be Springer's murder!

Had I created a problem where one did not exist? I did a prejudice check. Being color blind was a point of personal pride for me. I asked if I used the same standards when I considered the Muslim culture that predominated in the crew of the *Nancy Lynn*. How strongly, I wasn't sure. My last thought answered my question. I'd associated the Marcos with terrorism simply because of their religion. The dilemma...because the majority of terrorists performed their acts in the name of their religion, it was damned hard to keep the issues separated. I'd have to try.

How could I determine when my conjecture became actuality? That line had to come in advance of the action. It made it the most difficult, but critical answer. Wild ideas flew into my head. Dennia could fly me to make visual contact with Springer. I quickly asked, *'What good would that do?'* Send him a telefax? If I tried to communicate with him, a member of the crew would intercept it, one who might know Morse Code. Any answer I got would be suspect. Interpreting the messages he sent my presented the best opportunity. Springer had two different ways he could send clues to me. If his communications *tone* continued in their current mode, it meant he was still in control. His Morse coded messages were his best method to communicate. The brevity made it difficult. No detail or explanations were possible using it. Without these, determining a time to call the Bahamian Police...impossible! The third clue, not from Springer, I saw as the most sinister. A note describing life aboard the *Nancy Lynn* as a family affair, sailing on a sea of milk and honey. My conclusion...A body bag would be required...for Springer. I'd have to contact the authorities to do a search and recovery.

Should I contact Riaffort, or not?

When considering that question, I couldn't remove the fact a plot aboard the *Nancy Lynn* could exist only in my mind. I beloved he should know. The problem?

What if Riaffort called Melanie? The question wasn't if she'd call the Bahamian officials, it was how many minutes it would take to find and dial the phone number. That would make the remaining portion of the trip hell for Springer...it would make Margo's friends miserable and mad. If there was something planned, I doubted it would abort a plot. It would simply forewarn the conspirators. If the deed had been done, the only positive...his body would be less decomposed when recovered. There wasn't a good decision Melanie could be involved in now. Her alternatives evaporated when she agreed to the trip.

Could I inform Riaffort without him contacting Melanie? That was a tough call in light of what I'd just learned. He had his own code of ethics, which he adhered to with unwavering determination. He'd notify her if her daughter's potential involvement or danger was within that code, no matter what promise he made me. My problem, my conscience. Someone besides me should be aware that Margo's friends weren't who they'd represented themselves to be. Riaffort was the logical person to receive this knowledge.

There were many possibilities, other than the dire ones I 'imagined' that could occur.

Damage or loss of the *Nancy Lynn*, or some occurrence that created liability for the Hellmans were more likely than murder. Melanie had deep pockets.

My decision. He needed to know. I'd call him and hold back the most alarming news. At least, state it as conjecture, not fact. And, I'd extract some ironclad promises from Riaffort before my sharing any of what I knew. The toggle switch in my mind kept flipping back and forth on that decision. I was sure he would not call the island police.

Was there anything else that could be done? After exploring several possibilities, I could only think of one that had the potential to succeed. It would be expensive, and its success would depend on if the needed resources were available in a very short period of time.

The answer was a private investigator familiar with the Bahamas, a chartered boat and captain familiar with the waters, with supplies and resources to shadow the *Nancy Lynn* for the remainder of the trip. It meant having weapons and more than one person who could use them on board. The shadowing would have to be done carefully. Tricky! The chance of succeeding without being discovered I assessed as only 50%.

I lifted the handset of my phone and replaced it several times. The calendar caught my eye. The decision had to be made. Dennia would be flying us to Abaco in two days. The Foxxes were on a commercial flight tomorrow. There wasn't sufficient time to call them and get any meaningful information gathered. I reluctantly picked up my phone a final time. I'd call

Riaffort, extract promises, and feel queasy while doing it.

Chapter 36

"That's a hell of a way to open a conversation with a friend. What do I need to know? And about who?" Riaffort asked.

"I'm being coy about this for a reason. I know you feel obligated to keep your clients fully informed regarding anything that can affect them from a legal perspective. My problem is if I share that information with you, and you share it with your client, it could destroy a promise I made."

"You don't have to tell me who it is, Sly. It has to be Melanie Hellmann. I can't promise I won't tell her until I hear what it is."

"Sorry, buddy, that old trick won't work on me." I'd watched Riaffort use that ruse many times. "I have to have your assurance you won't blab this to Melanie. I know how she'd react, and it could cause considerable problems if she does what I think she will."

Riaffort became quiet.

"I know that bit of strategy, too. I'm not going to tell you a damned thing until I get your promise not to call her and repeat what I tell you."

"I can't do that if it could cause a serious effect on her."

"It might have a very serious bad effect on her if you tell her as well," I countered.

I heard him take a deep breath and let it out slowly. He was struggling with his conscience. I let him stew.

Finally, he said, "Alright."

"Alright, what?"

"I'll do what you said."

"And that is?"

"Oh, come on, Sly!"

I cleared my throat to make the point. "Repeat after me...exactly, okay?"

"Okay."

"Repeat... I promise I'm not going to tell Melanie anything that you tell me during this call."

"Is that really necessary?" I knew Riaffort. He was looking for a way around the roadblock. I wasn't having any.

"Yes, it's really necessary. Repeat it."

"Shit...okay...I won't *call* Melanie and repeat anything you tell me in this conversation."

"Full name."

"You didn't say that, but here goes, I won't *call* Melanie Hellmann and repeat anything you tell me in this conversation. Is that all right?"

"Yes."

Riaffort chuckled, "I have to be more careful not to expose my trade's secrets. What do I need to know?"

"The last time we talked you wanted me to calm Melanie down. The last message she got from Adrian lit her fuse, remember. Well, I told you I'd call her to put out the fire. I figured the best way to do that was to check on the Runnells couple, get a glowing report, and pass it on to her. When I had that couple checked on, I found that Houston has a problem. How big I'm not sure."

"The couple that she hadn't met, correct? Weren't they the ones with the executive jobs in Washington and New York?"

"Yes, the Runnells, Diane, and Hall. I checked them out. Hall Runnells is a high ranking engineer with Grumman. Diane Fanatti-Runnells is an interpreter for the United Nations. Nice person. *I talked to her*. Our problem is they aren't the ones on the cruise with Margo and Captain Springer."

"Holy shit! If they aren't on the *Nancy Lynn*, who is?"

"I haven't the foggiest." I paused as I anticipated Riaffort's next question. "Worse,

I can't think of any conceivable way to find out who they are. If you have any suggestions, I'd love to hear them."

The phone was quiet. I knew he was thinking what the ramifications having imposters on the *Nancy Lynn* could create. His first words were, "This could cause a world of legal problems. I don't like this one bit." He hesitated then asked, “Didn’t you tell me these people all went to school together?”

“Yes, at Columbia.”

“Do you think there might be some connection from there? It seems reasonable they would be people who know the real Runnells couple. They’d have to know how to answer questions that came up, that kind of thing.”

I thought about what Riaffort said. It made sense. It was a starting point, and it was better than the zero I had in mind. “It’s worth looking into. Look, you know Melanie better than me. If you get her involved, she’s liable to start something none of us can stop.

Remember your promise.”

“Yes.”

I wasn’t comfortable with the simple, ‘yes.’ “You’re not going to call her, right?”

“You want to hear it again? I’ll repeat exactly what I promised...I even wrote it down. I won’t call Melanie Hellmann and repeat anything you tell me on this call. Is that correct?” he asked.

“Yes.” I relaxed. Riaffort was a lawyer and tricky, but I felt sure he’d keep his word.

# # # # #

Chapter 37

Excitement surrounding the trip to Abaco replaced the dread and worry regarding Captain Springer and the *Nancy Lynn*. The Captain's next scheduled message would be in two days. Tuesday. Dennia was flying us to Marsh Harbor tomorrow. I told myself I'd be in a better position to help Springer if I was in the islands. In reality, that salved my worries more than anything else. Being closer, in the Bahamas, didn't make assisting the Captain any easier.

When packing my suitcase, I slipped my 9mm Hellcat in with my undershorts. The discovery of the body and the attempt that was made to steal our anchor was still fresh in my mind. Finding the *Nancy Lynn* never entered my thoughts when I selected my protection. Picking the final few items of clothes from my bedroom closet, had me oblivious of someone walking up behind me. Fingers tapping my shoulder made me jump.

"Didn't mean to scare you," Trotter's grin told me otherwise.

"What's the problem?" Trotter wouldn't have interrupted me if there wasn't one.

"Yes, we do. The compressor on the beef cooler is leaking coolant. Our serviceman says he can keep it cool enough to keep the meat from thawing by refilling the gas after it leaks out. A replacement for the compressor won't arrive until Wednesday."

"One of us has to be here." "That would be me."

"Nice of you to volunteer."

"It makes sense. Lily won't leave until next week. I'll oversee the compressor replacement. Go visit Lily. Fly down with her."

I grinned. "Things still going well with you two?"

"Like peas and carrots," Trotter dis his best Forrest Gump imitation.

"When do you plan to drive to LaBelle?"

"Wednesday night—Thursday morning."

"I'll call Wednesday afternoon. Don't leave until I do. If I forgot anything or we need something we didn't anticipate, it will give me another chance to get it hauled down. Besides, the *Nancy Lynn* thing has gotten more complicated. Two of the people on board aren't who they claim to be. I might need you to make some calls for me about that."

He nodded his head and said, "Bummer. What do you plan to do?"

"Nothing until I get to Abaco."

"Okay. Me not going tomorrow. That's going to leave you and Dennia to handle the boat. The Foxxes won't be much help until they been on board a few days. You gonna be okay?"

"I think so. If Sallar is available, I can hire him." Trotter's question prompted my decision. Having Sallar on board was a great safety factor combined with providing an experienced fishing guide/shallow water pilot. I decided it would be the second call I'd make when Trotter left.

~ ~ ~ ~ ~ ~

"We'll have one less passenger, Monday," I told Dennia.

"Trotter's not going?" I could hear her surprise come through the speaker.

"He's going, just not on Monday. We have an emergency. The beef cooler in the barn has problems. There are four sides of beef in there, and a lot of other things that would spoil. The repairman tells us he can get replacement parts installed by Wednesday.

Trotter will fly down with Lily, if that's okay."

"I imagine he'll drive down early."

"That's his plan. Is that okay?" I didn't hear an objection in her tone, but...... "Yes."

"If you have concerns about that..."

"Come on...Sly, I don't have any illusions about Lily and Trotter. They are two healthy, normal humans. They are going to do what they are going to do. I just want to be sure Lily picks up her prescriptions." Dennia made sure I understood something else.

"She's not normally taking pills."

What a difference between Margo and Lily. I shook my head but said nothing to Dennia. My first thought...she was lucky. Second thought...she parented her way to her 'luck.'

Dennia suggested, "We could take the Foxxes if they haven't left yet for the airport."

"They have. Besides, I saw all the photographic gear, electronic devices, drones, and several suitcases...it would take you a couple of trips to haul that to Abaco."

"That's no big deal. If we ever need to make an extra trip, it's just one tank of gas.

I love flying my Cessna, and that is a great excuse."

I thought for a few seconds. "How far can you fly on one fill-up?" The distance from Marsh Harbor to Matthew Town on Inagua Island was 430 miles. That's where the *Nancy Lynn* would be for ten or more days.

"The man that sold the plane to me said it would go 640 miles on a tank. I'm a coward. I try to keep my flights at 500 or less miles. I did do one hop of 570 miles. The only problem was I developed a sore neck from looking at the gas gage so much. Why did you ask?"

"Captain Springer and the *Nancy Lynn* are supposed to be moored at one of the islands at the southern end of the Bahamas. I thought we might do a sight-seeing flight down that way if it gets too windy for the *El Gato Gordo* to venture away from the dock. It's a long way down there. Over 400 miles."

"I had the same thought, Sly. I'd really like to fly down. There is a small airport on Great Exuma Island where I can refill my gas tank. It's halfway down. If I refill there going down and coming back, we'd have 150 miles worth of gas to wander over the whole southern area."

"Sounds like a plan. We'll do it if we get an excuse."

~ ~ ~ ~ ~ ~

"*The Sleepy Dolphin*, a cheery hello from Abaco," said Shepard Coloton's friendly voice.

"Hello to you, too. It's SJ Harrell."

"So good to hear from you, monn. Are you still planning to arrive here on Monday?"

"Yes. Unfortunately, Trotter won't come until next week."

"He will be coming then?"

"Yes, and he'll have his girlfriend with him."

"That will be good. Would you be our guests for a meal when he arrives?"

"I could never turn down an invitation for eating the best food in the Bahamas."

"Good, good, good. Is there anything else I can do for you?"

"Two things. Take good care of my friends the Foxxes. They will be there his afternoon."

"They are as good as taken care of. Remember Ollie the cab driver? He will meet them at the airport and bring them here. Mr. Russ and Mrs. Valerie will dine with us tonight as our guests."

"Excellent! I owe you. But...I have one more thing to ask. The Foxxes aren't boating people. With Trotter not arriving when I do, I thought it might be good to see if Sallar would be available to help me with the boat. Could you see if he'd be willing?"

Shepard laughed his hearty laugh, "He will be a most happy fellow. His family needs the money. But more than that, he likes you and your lady, Miss Dennia. And Trotter. Will you need him for one week or two?"

"Two."

"The man will be ecstatic!"

# # # # #

Chapter 38

The Lycoming engine and the Cessna's propeller hummed background for Dennia and my conversation. We flew over the Atlantic, 8,000 feet below. Whitecaps and rolling swells were visual proof of strong winds on the earth's surface. West Palm Beach fell behind us and Grand Bahama Island sat in the sparkling sea in our front.

"Why would you want to use an alias for a pleasure trip? It doesn't make sense." Dennia checked the altimeter and ground speed. "We are going to get there fast today. We have a 45 mph tailwind." She smiled at me. "Where were we?"

"You were saying you couldn't understand why the couple on the *Nancy Lynn* used aliases."

"Yes! If you're going for a pleasure trip. Why make something up?"

"Those are my thoughts, exactly. That's what increases my concern about Captain Springer and Margo. Why use a fake name unless you're trying to hide something about your real name? I have trouble getting past that."

Dennia nodded. "Don't you wonder how the people selected the two names they chose?"

"I figure they have some association with them. The common thread for the Marcos, Margo, and Gino, is their classes at Columbia. There's probably some sort of connection there."

Dennia remained quiet for several seconds. "If you were going to steal an identity, would you pick a name that was a kind of mini-celebrity? Why not pick someone nobody ever heard of before? You're taking more of a risk of someone identifying you as a phony if you pick someone who is known."

That made sense to me. I wondered aloud, "Particularly picking individuals that have skills that you probably don't own. A linguist? A rocket scientist?" I hesitated for several seconds before saying, "Unless there are connections. Probably professional connections."

There was a confused look on Dennia's face. She remained quiet.

"Think of one or both having the same skills. They'd function as a proxy. Maybe that's too far-fetched, but I'm going to check it out anyway. They might be part of the same group."

"Or, by posing as them, they could threaten to destroy the real person's reputation in some way."

"That's interesting." I hadn't thought about that possibility. Dennia's remark opened a whole new line of thinking. If the imposters aboard the *Nancy Lynn* were contemplating performing an act that would destroy someone's reputation, it would have to be newsworthy. Headline, newsworthy. Logically, if that was the object, it followed that the *Nancy Lynn* and the people aboard her were prominent pieces in the possible plot. Why else go to the trouble of establishing a position to commandeer the boat? Farfetched? Yes! But worth examining further? Definitely!

"We're really getting a push from the tailwind," Dennia said and pointed to a cruise liner passing into the waters south of Grand Bahama. "Look at the waves that sucker is contending with. I'm glad I'm not on that ship! I bet there are a lot of green faces down there."

"Yes. The only person that's happy on that ship is the guy that owns the Dramamine concession." I heard the engine change speed. "You beginning to drop her down?"

"Yes, I'll go to 4,000 feet, so we can see better. Also, dropping my engine speed into the economy operating range saves some gas. With the wind we have following us, we'll still get there earlier than we expected."

I nodded and said, "That makes sense. We're not going anywhere in these winds, anyway. It's howling down there. If it stays as windy as it is now, we may be using *El Gato Gordo* as a floating motel."

Dennia said, "Look, they have the roof on that hotel they're building. They were just starting to work on it last time."

The recovery work being done on the islands below captured our attention. However, Dennia's thought was stored in my mind. Was the concept wildly out of the box thinking? It sure was. But it would make many of the pieces of the bizarre puzzle raised by the cruise aboard the *Nancy Lynn* make some sense. *If she was right.*

# # # # #

Chapter 39

"Sallar is entertaining the Foxxes." Coloton's perpetual smile and good nature accompanied us as Dennia and I walked the shell path leading to the dock behind the *Sleepy Dolphin*.

"How's that?" I asked.

"We have a neighbor who feeds his pets this time of day. Sallar found out that your friends are dedicated photographers. He is giving them a chance to use their cameras. Would you like to see? We can leave your luggage here. I'll have one of my people put them on the boat. It's only a hundred meters away." Shepard pointed to Russ and Val standing with a group of three more people aiming cameras at the waters around the dock.

"I'd like to," Dennia said, as she fished her cell phone from her purse and slipped it into her pocket. "I like taking snapshots, too."

We traveled the backyard sands of the *Sleepy Dolphin's* neighbor's homes. As we neared the pier, Russ spotted us and called, "Come on out here, you got to see this!"

The wide dock had a "T" shaped end where the group of people stood. They were huddled around a man who was holding a rope that was hanging into the water. Suddenly, the water thrashed sending splashes skyward. Aww's and Ohhh's came from the group.

"Look at the size of these!" Russ was busy taking video of the milling fish swarming around the dock.

"Oh, there must fifteen of them," Dennia said as we came to a stop next to the group staring at the water. Gray torpedoes glided around the pilings with dorsal and pectoral fins that screamed, 'shark,' at first glimpse.

The man conducting the spectacle had large fish, Bonitas, tied to the end of the rope. He played take away with the eating machines and their toothy grins that cruised below. They lunged at the fish as he constantly moved the ever-decreasing sized meal in a figure eight. Every few seconds another hunk would be bitten away, many times accompanied by a spectacular splash. The sharks were from five to eight feet long. They swam in agitated circles, occasionally brushing one of their brethren aside.

Russ and Val were mesmerized, Russ being so captivated he'd moved within an inch of the edge of the pier, which lacked a rail. I saw, rather than heard, Sallar caution him. Russ shuffled back a half-step.

Dennia tapped me on my arm to get my attention. "Do you know what type of sharks those are?"

I squinted through my polaroid sunglasses. There were three species I identified immediately. "Bull sharks, reef sharks, and the ones hanging around the bottom are nurse sharks."

"They look aggressive. Is it safe to swim here?" Dennia asked.

"Oh, yes, ma'am. Herbert actually swims off this very dock at other times. This is his pier, and when the bull sharks are not around, he gets in the water and feeds them." Shepard was soothing any fears Dennia might have developed. "The water around the beaches is very safe. I would not swim while there are people fishing from your boat. But most any other time it is alright."

"That is all folks." Herbert, the man who had been feeding the sharks, coiled his ropes which the gray ghosts swimming below picked clean. He grinned at Shepard as he passed us. "Good day, my friend. I hope the show pleased your guests."

"As always!" Shepard said.

Herbert's motel guests followed him back to a ring of chairs clustered under a coconut palm. It left the six of us chatting and enjoying our reunion. Russ was already planning a way to film the 'feeding frenzy,' underwater. Val told Dennia about a quaint little clothing store she'd found, where all the clothes were hand-tailored to fit. Sallar, Shepard, and I discussed fishing, weather, and supper, always popular male topics. The sun's dipping to the horizon called us back to the *Sleepy Dolphin*. We walked and talked bathed in the brilliant reds, pinks, oranges, blues, and violets of the tropical sunset

# # # # #

Chapter 40

Sallar said goodbye as we finished our last cocktail of the evening. I was amazed by how much our second stay on the *El Gato Gordo* felt like coming home. Dennia and Val were sprawled out in loungers placed on the bow deck. They gazed into a night filled with millions of stars made brighter by the absence of the moon.

Russ and I were alone inside the salon enjoying the last swallows of our mint juleps. We discussed the upcoming days. High winds were going to be a fact, not a threat. We made plans accordingly. Russ was full of suggestions. It is one of the things I love about the man. He sees possibilities in everything. It's said people can be categorized into two groups: Glass half empty types and glass half full types. Russ is a third class...one where the glass is always full and in danger of spilling over.

"The winds will be out of the west-northwest." Russ squinted, visualizing something. "Shouldn't that allow us to fish on the east shore? I looked at a chart for the ocean around Abaco. It's deep right up to the beach there if I remember right. We could stay in the island's lee. Shouldn't we be able to catch snapper and grouper there?"

"You're right about catching fish just where the drop-off is, but we have to be able to get our anchor to hold. In deepening water, with 20 mph winds, that's going to be hard if not impossible. Drift fishing is out. We'd move so fast fish would need water skis to catch us."

"That's not a big deal. We can leave the *Gato Gordo* tied up. We can rent a car. There's got to be places to go all over this island." Russ moved his hands pushing water aside as he simulated snorkeling. "There have to be places galore to use our fins and masks, I noticed there are historic sites scattered around, Shepard told me about some cool bars and restaurants, we can toss in our fishing poles and wade, hell, it will be great just to beachcomb." He stretched his arms in the air as if he implored a higher power. "The winds will die down. We'll probably be out cruising in two days."

"How do you know? Do you have a built-in weather prediction system in your body? An arthritic knee? Something like that?"

"No. Something much better. The Coloton's have a great setup for using the Internet. They have hotspots set up. I can use my laptops or their big computer. Shepard introduced me to his wife. She's the computer genius in the family. It's in the lounge attached to the *Sleepy Dolphin's* office." Russ reached into his pants pocket and removed a key. He waved it at me and said, "Seven days a week, twenty-four-hour access."

"All the comforts of home."

"I'm short a few of my customized bells and whistles, but pretty much so. I can use it to find all the places we can go on Abaco, get directions, all kinds of things besides the weather."

Dennia and my conversation while flying, thrust its way into my thinking. "You have full access to the Internet?"

"The Internet is the Internet."

"Then if I wanted you and Val to do some more checking for me on say, one of the crew on the *Nancy Lynn,* you could do it?"

"Sure."

"Or, if I wanted you to check on something new, it wouldn't be a problem?"

"Not at all. At least, not the computer part of it. You'd have to give me enough good information to do the job." He smiled. "You have something in mind, don't you? That's great with me. Fun after dark...what can I say." He leaned forward. "You want to find out more about the people your friend Captain Springer is babysitting."

"Yes. I want to widen it some. I want to look into the crew's relatives and friends. I believe I can give you reasonable places to start."

Russ' skepticism showed.

I smiled, "The Internet means I have access to Trotter and Riaffort. They can check on a few things I have in mind. I can pass those along to you."

"What do you want to know?"

"Like info on the brothers and sisters of the Runnells and Marcos couples. Particularly, the Runnells. Parents. Work associates. Neighbors. Things like that. I want to find out more about something you haven't been told about. I used the background checks you did. Made a few calls. The work you did was all accurate. Problem is, two of the people I asked you to investigate aren't on the boat. Imposters are."

"No shit!" Russ' rolled his eyes. "I didn't see that coming. Let Val and I know what you need. I'm sure we can help." He tapped his fingers on the arm of the chair he sat in. "Let us get a start before you bother Trotter and your lawyer. I got the idea. We're good at being nosey."

# # # # #

Chapter 41

"We aren't going out on the ocean today," Russ delivered the news when he was halfway to the *Gato Gordo* on the *Sleepy Dolphin's* dock. "Eighteen to twenty-five with gusts up to thirty-five." That wasn't a great revelation. There were tiny whitecaps in the cove that sheltered a number of Marsh Harbor's fishing resorts and private homes.

"Where's Val and Dennia?" I asked.

"I figured having a car would be nice. They have them at the airport, so I reserved one for a week. Shepard said he'd ferry us around, but that wouldn't be fair. Shepard's driving Val and Dennia over there to pick it up now."

"You've been on the Internet. That's where the weather report came from."

Russ stepped down into the boat and bowed. "At your service."

"While you were on your computer, did you look for some things to do?"

"Yes, I found some neat things, but the one that sounds most interesting is the Wyannie Malone Museum. The problem is, it's in Hope Town and Sallar told me that's a boat trip. A short one, but unless you want to swim, that's the only way. He's looking for a cousin who he tells me has a small boat he can borrow and take us out there. Sallar told me that there's a lot of history about people that made a living off wrecked ships in the 1800s. I know that would interest you."

I asked, "You want anything to drink? I've got a cooler full of iced tea, soft drinks, and water."

Russ shook his head and sat down next to me. "I had a little time this morning. I found some interesting information on Hall Runnells family. He has a brother that's fourteen months younger than him that will interest you. I wasn't able to get into any depth past this. His name is Harold, he has followed in his brother's footsteps. Same schools and same majors as Hall. I'd just started trying to find out information about what he does, if he's married, all the detail. Want me to stick around here? You can ferry the girls around and let them have some fun."

It was tempting to nod. I didn't believe asking Russ to give up the day would be important. I told him, "No. Save it for this evening. Captain Springer is due to send another check-in note today. Let's wait and see how that goes."

"Sounds good. I'm anxious to look around."

The clouds skidded past confirming the high velocity of the wind. "You know, Russ, we might have several days of these winds. We don't want to use up all our possible activities on one trip."

"We can pace ourselves. If all else fails, we come back and fish for the sharks off the docks." His smirk told me he was kidding.

"I don't think that would be a good idea. Herbert's likely to tie a rope to your legs and dangle you in the water. His pets would probably love to have you for dinner."

# # # # #

Chapter 42

"Mrs. Coloton asked me to bring this to you," Sallar handed me two pieces of paper.

They were a cover note from Trotter and I immediately recognized the lines Captain Springer had adopted as a means to convey a clandestine message to us if required. I set the papers aside. Sallar knew places to fish where we could 'hide' from the wind, according to Shepard. Before he could leave, I asked, "Got a minute?"

"For you Mr. Sly, certainly, always."

"Shepard says you know spots that are close where we catch a few grouper or snapper. Eating fish. Is there any place where you can take us where we can anchor the boat securely, and not have the winds scare Dennia and Val?"

"The fish will not be like this," he held his hands three feet apart, "they will be like this," Sallar closed his hands so there was a foot between them.

"As long as they taste good, I don't care."

"I do know spots we can go. You must fish them at certain times."

"Tides have to be right."

"Exactly, precisely!" Sallar grinned.

"Fishing inshore anywhere in saltwater most always depends on fishing the tides."

"New moon is tomorrow," Sallar did a mental schedule of when to be where to catch fish. "You be ready at 8:30 tomorrow morning. We will be catching snapper so quick!"

"No rough patches of water?" I asked.

"No, no, no." Sallar smiled, held his hand out, palm up, then put his other hand a foot-and-a-half above it. "No bigger waves than this."

"Good."

"You don't worry about Miss Dennia or Mrs. Val. They are not scary type ladies. I am sure they will laugh at the waves."

Grinning, I said, "I guess I should worry more about me and Russ."

Sallar laughed heartily, "Exactly, precisely."

"Do I need to buy some bait?"

"No, no, no. I take care of that." He pinched his eyes shut thinking about what we'd need. "If you are going to fish with light equipment, bring plenty of hooks. Where we go there many places for the fish to cut off your line." Sallar's smile returned, "What else can I do?"

I thought for several seconds, then asked, "How well do you know Inagua? If you have time, I'd like to ask you some questions."

"My time is yours. Happily. It is my enjoyment. Yes, I know Inagua and that area. Of course, not like Abaco and the northern islands, but I go there two or three times a year. I have a relative in Matthew Town." He sat down beside me. "What would you like to know?"

"Did I tell you that I have friends that are visiting down there?"

"I believe you might. I do remember we talked about taking the *El Gato Gordo* there."

"My friend is an experienced sea captain. He's been there several times before, but his passengers haven't as far as I know. I'm not worried about danger to them when they're floating. My concern is when they are in port. They are scheduled to be berthed in Mathew Town for ten days. I've wondered if they'd be okay."

"Do you know where they are staying, the marina or hotel?"

"It's written down somewhere. I'll have to find it. It was a marina...I'm pretty sure of that."

"As we discussed before, the southern islands are...more isolated. People use those islands for many things. Some very good things. Some are very bad and bad people do these things. I told you if you stay in the towns where tourists go, mostly you are safe. Short stays are safer than long stays."

"Why is that?"

"People there find out things about you. What you have on your boat. If you have lots of money. Those are things the bad fish find out, and..." Sallar looked at me as if trying to determine to add to his warning. He decided, "What kind of people are those who are on the trip with your captain friend?"

"Three women and three men. Captain Springer is a man."

"No, no, no. What color are they?"

"Three are white, two are Filipino...I guess you'd say brown, two I'm not sure of but I'd guess white."

I could see Sallar was working on his phrasing. "If you can contact your friends, I would give them this advice. There are more people who live and visit that island who do not care for Americans and whites. Some hate them. Even our Conchy Joe's are more careful in the south. I would tell them, the bars are not good places for them. Some eating places and stores could want to cheat them. I would tell them, Matthew Town streets are not always safe after dark for strangers. Staying on the boat is a good thing. Also, the police in the area have to live there. In cases of questions, your friends will be doubted."

"Would you have advised them to go there for a base for a dive trip?"

"No, no, no. If they want to go diving, the Turks and Caicos Islands are a better and safer base. They are about the same distance. Good diving in the Turks is fifty miles away from Mathew Town."

I thought for several seconds, before asking, "Sallar, do you think your relative would mind looking up my friend's boat? It's a white 42′ cruiser named the *Nancy Lynn*. Jupiter is its home port and that's printed on the transom. They wouldn't have to talk to the folks on the boat, in fact, I'd prefer they didn't. I wouldn't want them thinking I'm checking on them."

"Ohhhhh, I understand. My cousin works in a metal shop and does welding. Much of what does is at the docks, so he knows what is going on there. I'm sure he will look and tell me what he finds."

"One last thing?"

"Most assuredly."

"You said you'd get the bait. I have a cast-net and I can catch bait to save you time."

"No, no, no. There is bait and there is bait. I want a certain kind of small fish. It is like candy for snapper and grouper. It is best to catch them at night. I will do this easily.

It would be more difficult for you. Let me do it."

"Okay, but anytime you want help, please ask."

"No problem."

"See you tomorrow."

"Exactly, precisely!" Sallar waved and I watched him walk the dock in the late afternoon sun. He waved to Dennia, Russ, and Val as they relaxed from our day of swimming on the beautiful Abaco beaches. I glanced at the memos, then at my friends sipping drinks from a coconut in the shade of the *Sleepy Dolphin's* cabana. I mumbled, "These can wait until later." I left the boat to join Dennia and the Foxxes.

Chapter 43

Quiet. It was the first time since we'd left for our car ride around Abaco, and our mid-day swim, something hadn't been going on, someone hadn't been talking, some noise hadn't served as a distraction. I relaxed in the *Gato Gordo's* salon letting my T-bone, baked potatoes, and broccoli mix. Val and Dennia had finished clinking the dishes and disappeared. Russ was in the *Sleepy Dolphin's* computer room, and I thought about the Captain's 'check-in message' for the first time since Sallar delivered it to me.

My conscience tapped my shoulder, and guilt made me retrieve the papers from the coffee table ten feet away. The sunburn I'd foolishly suffered made getting up and walking a major ordeal. I deposited my angry-pink body on the sofa, picked up the message, and read what Trotter had relayed to me.

..--..--..--..--..--..--..--..-- ..--..--..--..--..--..--..--..-- ..-
-..--..--..--..--..--..--..-- ..--..--..--..--..--..-..--..--

Report number 4

Melanie and SJ,

We made the trip from Exuma to Matthew Town after having to stay anchored an extra day at the island cove where we sheltered from the wind.-- Peaceful there. All had a good time... Winds were still a problem when we made the crossing to Inagua.. Trouble with our berth at the Marina.-. Not big enough. We had to rent two spaces--. Work is being done to the subs? Hall is adding stuff to them--- Guidance system.. We are to go on the first of our dives tomorrow. The dive cylinders take a lot of space--. Problems mostly are gone-..- I have one concern--. The winds from one direction could be harmful.. To strong. I hope they'll stay down while we are here--- I don't know what to expect. Hall runs the group. We are to dive most days for the rest of our stay in Matthew Town.-.-.- Margo is okay-.. So are the Marcos.-. Galang uses his drone..- Diane is not seasick-. Margo, not seasick either-.- Things are no worse than could be expected... Next message will be on Friday---

Adrian

-------------------………………------------------------

………………--------------------………………..

On my first reading, it was difficult for me to decipher any alarms Springer had built into the wording. The first couple of sentences sounded like he was simply reporting what had happened. The first sentence I thought might contain a clue was, *Work is being done to the subs?* I asked, why the question mark after subs? Was Adrian trying to tell us something? Was he unsure of himself? I went to the next clue. The Captain had isolated something I thought could be a clue. It was, *Guidance system*. I couldn't figure that one out either. You would have to be able to guide the sub to use it. One of the most important clues, *dive cylinders take a lot of space,* I missed completely. Two statements he made led me to believe things were either improving or at least weren't threatening. *Problems mostly are gone,* and *Things are no worse than could be expected,* conveyed that. The strongest clue I detected was his statements, *I have one concern. The winds from one direction could be harmful.* That told me one particular person or thing was a major concern for him. Hall? Gino? What was it? The rest looked like gibberish...until I observed how the short choppy sentences ended. Morse Code!

I found a pen and turned Trotter's cover note over and began converting the code to letters. W, E, S, I, R, E, G, ?, O, I, E, G, X, G, I, N, O, E, period, D, R, U, N, K, S, O was the sequence of letters. After looking at the letters further and where they appeared in the telefax,

I concluded the captain told me Gino was his major concern and he had drunks he was concerned with. Who, I couldn't be sure. Things weren't dire. That was good news.

I turned over Trotter's cover letter and read it.

Hey Boss,

Captain Springer's report is sent with this note. The serviceman got the compressor for the beef cooler. He says he'll have it up and running again by noon tomorrow. Call as soon as possible, so I can round up what you want me to haul. I want to get to LaBelle as soon as I can.

Trotter-

PS- Riaffort said for you to call but no hurry.

Strange, I thought. Normally, everything Riaffort Richards associated himself with he considered critical and requiring immediate action. Very strange.

# # # # #

Chapter 44

Sallar was as good as advertised. He piloted the *Gato Gordo* from Marsh Harbor across the sound to a hole located between Whale Cay and Treasure Cay. The fish weren't large but were excellent eating size. We kept ten, enough for two meals, but caught ten times that number. The sun wasn't straight overhead...we were back at the dock by 11:30.

Val and Dennia were sipping drinks under the cabana, Sallar was teaching Russ the proper way to fillet fish, and I was on my way to the *Sleepy Dolphin's* office to make two phone calls. One to Trotter; one to Riaffort.

"Good morning, Mimi," I said to Shepard's wife.

"Ah-ha, good morning, Mr. Sly. I see the fish gods were smiling today."

"We'll eat very well for a couple of meals." I unfolded Trotter's note on which I'd written both phone numbers I wanted to call. "Your husband said I could use the phone and he volunteered you. He said you know the operator."

She smiled and took the note from me. "Yes, the long-distance operator is my 2nd aunt on my father's side. You don't speak Bahamas English...I do. If you talk to her, you could end up speaking to Fiji, not Florida."

Mimi hummed as she made the first call. When she reached the operator, I quickly learned the truth in what she said. I only understood half the words they exchanged. After several more seconds, she smiled and handed me a handset from the old phone. "Mr. Trotter will answer...I hope."

"Lazy H ranch, Ken Bass speaking."

"What are you doing answering the phone," I asked. "Cindy is supposed to answer."

"Nothing in the receptionist job description says I have to have tits to answer the phone. Cindy had to run into Wilson's store for something. I can walk and chew gum at the same time."

"You said call early. Is the beef cooler fixed?"

Trotter purposely let me stew for a few seconds before saying, "She's fixed. She's running so smooth she sounds like a kitten purring." I could hear him opening drawers in the background. "You packing?" I asked.

"Sure am. You need anything hauled?"

"Nothing."

"Good. I'll be ready to be out of here within twenty minutes. When Cindy returns, I'm gone."

"Did you hear anything from Clareen?"

"She said everything was going smooth. I gave her the *Sleepy Dolphin's* telephone number just in case."

Trotter paused and added, "Don't forget to phone Riaffort."

"I was just about to call him. Do you know what he wants?"

Trotter cleared his throat, a habit he had before delivering bad news. "It has to do with Melanie Hellmann and the *Nancy Lynn* business. Ahhhh...He wants to hire us to find the *Nancy Lynn*. I told him you wouldn't be interested, but he was insistent that you call him."

Trotter was right. I didn't want any more involvement with the cruise of the *Nancy Lynn* than I was already involved with. Riaffort Richards had studied the situation and arrived at the same conclusion that I had. The only reasonable course to follow was to find someone to shadow the remaining portion of the *Nancy Lynn's* voyage and intercede immediately at the first sign of trouble. He decided that should be me. I had already decided that it would not.

~ ~ ~ ~ ~ ~

"No, Riaffort, there is no way. I'm completely unprepared to do that." Past hello, the first words from Riaffort were his intention to hire me to perform a private investigator's function...tail the *Nancy Lynn*. "That' not my business."

"That's not true. You find things; that is one of the things PIs do. Consider this for a second. I'm not asking you to be Rambo and go to the rescue, guns blazing. I want you to find them and observe what's going on. If you suspect something is wrong, you call the authorities."

I snorted. "Think about what you just asked. How am I going to know something is wrong? See a body tossed overboard? Guess what? That's too, fucking, late! If I get close enough to learn what's happening before a calamity, I'll damned near have to be close enough to shake hands. You think they won't recognize me if I put on a fake beard and mustache? And, oh yes, we have no idea what kind of weaponry they have. Remember, they loaded crates on at the marina in Melbourne. Trotter and I saw .50 caliber machine guns sitting at that shop. I have my 9mm. I can use, that and I can throw knives at them.

Those aren't even odds."

"I understand the conditions aren't ideal—"

I cut him off. "Ideal? The conditions are impossible! This isn't even something law enforcement can handle. If it's before they commit a crime, one which we don't know what is or even if they have in a crime in mind, a visit by the police only will make them ten times more careful. If it's after the crime, what good does it do? If they end up killing someone, do you think they'll stow the bodies on board? It will be hard as hell to even prove a crime was committed. About all I could be is a sympathetic bystander."

"Sly, my friend, the conditions aren't ideal, but think. Who else is in a position to help? You know the situation. You're in the Bahamas and already have a boat. As long as you just observe, you won't alarm them. After all, you were the one who tried to convince Melanie Hellmann that she shouldn't approve the trip."

My fuse was burning so I took a few seconds before making a response I'd regret. After a half-minute, I said, "Yes, I did tell her I thought letting a daughter that has major behavioral and emotional problems have control of the vessel was stupid. I'll repeat that...stupid, stupid, stupid. She chose to ignore my warning. First off, you said you'd hire me. With whose money? Yours? Hers? How do you know she'd even want me involved?"

"I've talked to her. Melanie told me you can name your own figure."

"That boat has sailed. Look, it's not like I'm here on business. I have Dennia, and the Foxxes with me now. Trotter and Lily will be here next week. I don't have anything we can defend ourselves with. My Hellcat is the equivalent to a pea shooter compared to what they *probably* have on board. Finding them is one thing. Trying to get close enough to observe, Mission Impossible."

"You're forgetting you have a friend on board. Captain Springer could be an innocent victim in all this."

"Riaffort, buddy, if you're trying to spark my conscience, you'll fail miserably on that. I told Adrian that it was a mistake to let Margo and crew sail off with the *Nancy Lynn*. In fact, he begged me to tell Melanie *not* to let the trip go on as planned. He told me under no conditions would he be part of it. I did. Guess what? Fifty thousand bucks later, he's sitting in the captain's seat." I made a slushing sound to imitate water running. "What you hear is me washing my hands of the whole thing. Look. About the only practical situation, now, is to not poke the hornet's nest and hope like all hell, we're worrying about nothing." I paused for a second then added, "The report I received yesterday from Adrian was encouraging. He indicated things weren't any worse, I read into what he wrote things weren't that bad. The Captain's biggest problem is Gino from what he wrote in code. That's good news considering what we know."

Riaffort knows when to give up on an argument, though he never abandons one. My lawyer friend is a winner. The conversation turned pleasant. We hung up...and the seed he'd planted in my conscience began to grow and irritate. The man knows me too well.

# # # # #

Chapter 45

Even paradise can lose some of its luster after a few days enjoying its splendor. Winds died for the two days after the Captain's fourth message, and we took full advantage. Sallar suggested the short voyage to Eleuthera. The forecast predicted winds would increase on Friday. We had Wednesday and Thursday to make the three-hour trip over and back. Russ and Val were excited. It would be their first night at sea aboard a boat smaller than a cruise liner.

The trip went very well. Fish were cooperative, eating any bait we threw into the water. Snorkeling at the secluded spot Sallar knew and anchored us at, provided spectacular varieties of colorful fish and a new world to explore. The breezes were so light that the ocean's surface looked like that of a pond. And, Eleuthera was as spectacularly beautiful as Abaco, maybe even more so, in that each had its unique images to offer. When we tied up to the *Sleepy Dolphin's* dock Friday at last light, the *El Gato Gordo's* crew were exhausted as they crawled into their berths.

Sunlight streamed through the porthole of Dennia's and my cabin Friday morning. As sleep left and my senses began functioning, my bunkmate was missing. The smell of bacon drifted through our open door. I quickly slipped into shorts and followed my nostrils to where Dennia was finishing eggs-over-easy. She looked over her shoulder and said, "Good morning sleepy head."

"What is the chef making?"

"Bacon, eggs, grits, and toast. I made you a fresh pot of coffee." Dennia put bacon strips on plates.

"Where's everyone else?"

"It's late. Sallar went home to check on his family. I told him we'd call him if we needed him. He said he'd check with us either way in the afternoon. Val and Russ went to the computer room to check for messages and what's going on in the world. I told them I would send you to get them when I finished breakfast."

Dennia wore a filmy cover over her bra and panties. I bent over and kissed her neck.

"That does feel good." She leaned back against me. "I think after we make a mess of this breakfast, we go make a mess of the sheets."

"Everybody decent?" Val's voice announced her presence, before creating an embarrassing situation.

"Give me a minute," Dennia called out. She pushed her butt against me and whispered, "Keep that thought." She slipped her arms into one of my fishing shirts and covered Victoria's Secret with Bass Pro. "Val, is Russ with you?"

"Heavens no! Once he gets his ass behind a keyboard it's guaranteed not to move for an hour. He told me ten minutes. I'd start looking for him in thirty. Can I come in?

The bugs are out."

"Sure. I'm a little short on clothes and I didn't want to put on a show for Russ."

Val entered the galley, sniffing like a bird dog. "It sure smells good."

"It's just bacon and eggs. Should I put Russ' meal on a plate or leave it in the skillet to keep it warm?" Dennia held a spatula loaded with an egg a few inches above a plate. "Put it back in the skillet. My bet is he'll be an hour, at least." Val eyed me. "Russ found more information on that couple you were interested in. The one that's on the *Nancy Lynn*. He had that look in his eye." She sat at the table. "I'm famished. Let's eat."

~ ~ ~ ~ ~ ~

Russ didn't make it back to the *El Gato Gordo* for two hours. When he stepped off the dock and into the boat, he did so with a Cheshire Cat grin.

I said, "You found something?"

He nodded, "Big."

"Well?"

"Can I tell you while I eat? I should have waited for breakfast before I went to the computer room. I'm starved." Russ led me into the galley. Dennia was warming his breakfast in the microwave when we arrived. Russ hunched over the plate when Dennia slid it in front of him. He said, “Thanks,” around a mouthful of eggs.

“So, I gather you found something important.”

Russ nodded, “More by accident than by plan.” He looked up at me and bobbed his head. “That theory about someone wanting to discredit the Runnells may be right on target.” Russ took a hurried sip of coffee. Something went awry; coffee and eggs exited his nose and mouth as a mix-up between the esophagus and windpipe erupted.

“Don’t try to speak and eat,” I said. “We’ll talk when you finish.”

I watched Russ make his breakfast disappear in record time. We went to the rear deck and settled in for the discussion.

Russ started by saying, “You know the old saying, I’d rather be lucky than good?

Well, it worked out that way this morning. I was looking at a site advertising interpreting and mediating international issues that was mentioned in the UN portal. I hit a key by accident and a whole bio statement rolled onto my screen about Diane Fanatti-Runnells.”

“Is it part of the UN’s Services?”

“No. It is a not for profit group. The introductory write up describes the organization as one that promotes harmony between the Middle East and Western cultures. It does a number of different functions. Everything from assisting in arranging business deals to helping find displaced persons. Guess what? Diane and Hall are both key cogs in the group. There were long glowing reports about both of their contributions to the organization's efforts. There's an article written by Diane that extolls the virtue of the two cultures working together, how there isn't as much difference between the two sides, and how stupid it is to be constantly quarreling. It was well written. Hell...by the time I finished reading it, I was humming Kumbaya. Sounds good. But she had some real haters respond. Particularly on the Muslim side."

"Any specific persons or groups?" I asked.

"I looked for that and didn't see anyone or thing that stood out. I didn't see any familiar names like Al Qaeda. It looked like many were made up. The Sword Protector of Allah. Infidel Extermination Society. Ali Big. Stuff like that. There were two posts that claimed to be Arian Nation, but they looked fake to me. It is amazing how some people try to make shit out of sugar. As near as I can tell, the Runnells have busted butt for the last four years trying to be a two-person peace corp."

"Her husband is heavily involved, too?"

"Definitely! Hall has done volunteer engineering projects for the Syrians, Jordanians, Filipinos, Indonesians, and the Israelis. Boy, he caught flak about the last one. He uses his vacations and sick leave to work on them. Diane's the mouthpiece and Hall is the worker bee."

"Did you see anything that would leave you to believe they were putting on this super goody-goody front for a sleeper operation to follow?"

"Not at all." Russ took a breath and paused for a few seconds. "They're the recipients of equal parts glorious praise for their work and death threats. There are a lot of folks who didn't like the bridges they are trying to build. I'd say a lot of people would like to discredit them and dry up the money their organization is attracting."

"That's a hell of a good job, Russ." I got up to leave.

"There's a lot more," he said. His words bent my knees and my rear hit the couch cushion hard.

"What else did you find out?"

"Nothing about the woman imposter, but I think I've identified who the male imposter is. I believe he's Hall's brother, Harold. In fact, I discovered some interesting history regarding the whole Runnells family." Russ held up a flash drive. "I put details on here."

"I take it this fills the void in Hall's early life," I said.

"Yes and no. I wasn't able to find a lot of details about Hall's individual history. A few, not many important items. I did find out about his family. Where they were. What they did. What happened to his parents. Why the information on them was difficult to uncover." Russ handed me the flash drive. "Would you like a quick summary?"

"I sure would."

Russ grinned. "You know me. Once I found an open window, I crawled inside real quick. Some files in the article on Diane gave me something to trace back, did some sleuthing, did some guessing, and walla, I found the buried bones. I finally got to the point where I discovered hidden files on the Runnells family. I unmasked them."

"Why the cloak and dagger?"

They, mom and dad, were involved in some things our government would like to forget and don't want Joe citizen to know about."

"What group were they working for?" I asked.

"CIA."

"Fill me in.

Russ folded his arms and his smile disappeared. "Sometimes when you do things like exhuming the Runnells family history, you learn shit you wish you hadn't. Governments have some built in cesspools. It's made me lose faith in a lot of it." He took a breath.

"Hall's father was a chemist. His mother and her parents were refugees from Belarus. Seems that family, the Voltenko's, got involved with intrigues that a politburo friend had a part. They ended up on the losing side. I don't know why. The CIA helped them out of Russia and into the US. The father ended up as a professor. One of his students, Mark Runnells, married his daughter. Long story short: When Gorbachev came to power, the faction the parents had backed were swept into favor. The Voltenko family returned. Mark Runnels and Voltenko's daughter, Daryna, went back with the family. They took their children with them. Hall, his brothers, and his sisters, spent their childhood in Minsk." Russ paused and held his hands out, palms up. "What I'm telling you now is light on hard evidence and heavy on my conjecture. Best I can figure, the Voltenko family and Runnells and his wife were involved in some type of espionage gathering for the CIA. They got caught. They disappeared. The Runnells children, five of them, just appeared in the US, living with an aunt. That's where the story I found out before starts. However, I found out some interesting stuff about Hall's younger brother, Harold. Like I told you, I believe he is the male imposter on the *Nancy Lynn*."

"What do you have on him?" I asked.

"The aunt was married to a muslin. Very devout. Naturally, all the children were impacted by their foster parents' religion. I told you that Harold tried patterning his life after Hall's. When Hall left for MIT, all was fine between the brothers. That changed as Hall began to move away from Islam, at least the strict fundamentalist brand his uncle practiced. Relations between the two brothers became strained, then ruptured. On Harold's website, he refers to Hall as an 'infidel puppet of the true Satan.' He also stated that his brother travels a lot doing fake good deeds and he hopes a plane crashes while Hall is on it." Russ held up four fingers. "He has all the skill sets his brother has."

One finger came down. "They look alike. I checked the driver's license photos. They can pass for each other, no problem." The second finger dropped. "Harold would love to discredit or even kill Hall." Number three folded. "Last, the way things are set up on the *Nancy Lynn*, as far as anyone knows, Hall would get the blame for anything bad that happened there." Russ' fist remained.

I nodded, trying to grasp all that had been told me, and what its ramifications could be.

"One last thing. On a post in the last two days, there was a notification that Diane would be on vacation from April 24th until the 29th. That's too much of a coincidence for me." Russ shook his head. "Does that leave you as far behind the eight-ball as I think it does?" "To be honest Russ, I don't know. The only thing I can conjecture is it isn't good. The information you gave me opens doors to all kinds of possibilities and closes none."

# # # # #

Chapter 46

The charts stretched out on the salon table in front of me were a stack of enticing invitations clamoring for me to choose one. Dennia, Val, and Russ were off shopping in Marsh Harbor. Sallar was at his home fixing a stubborn sink drain. It left me alone with little to do but daydream.

Those charts tempted me much like a youngster is tempted when in a candy shop. The dollar in your hand allows you to choose one. What a difficult choice! Each destination insisted it was the best. Grand Bahama with Freeport beckoned. It offered all kinds of fascinating activities for the women. Moores Island was close and the gateway to a frontier of flats to explore. Dennia had asked we postpone visiting New Providence and Nassau until Lily arrived. Eleuthera and the northern Exuma's almost demanded a return trip. So did Andros. That big island whispered in my ear making promises of all sorts.

The winds would be light. According to the forecasts, winds would die in the afternoon. We'd have Friday afternoon, all Saturday, and most of Sunday to explore. Dennia would have to make the flight to Clewiston to pick up Lily and Trotter Monday. That ended our planning period. Forecasts were too fickle any farther out in time. I'd narrowed our destination to either Andros or the Exumas when Mimi Coloton's voice entered the cabin.

"Mr. Sly, are you aboard?"

"I'm in the salon."

"I have something for you. It is another two messages from Mr. Trotter and the Captain."

I heard her feet shuffling on the rear deck. "I bring it to you, okay?"

"Come on in."

Her colorful dress and bright smile lit the salon. She clutched two pieces of paper in one hand. "Good day on you, Mr. Sly."

"Good day to you. How are you?"

"Most good. The sun is shining. My monn is working hard. The mango trees have a heavy bloom. We have you as our most good guests. God is smiling on the *Sleepy Dolphin*." She placed the telefaxes on top of the charts. "I hope they are all good news!"

We exchanged goodbyes and before she'd left the *El Gato Gordo*, I realized the news wasn't good. Putting Trotter's note to one side, I read Captain Springers report first. The line Adrian started the report with was alarming. It repeated SOS in Morse Code for the width of the paper.

...---......---......---......---......---......---......---......---
......---......---......---......---......---...

From Matthew Town, Inagua

Slydell and Melanie,

This is my report on conditions onboard the Nancy Lynn number five- This is our 6th day here. Things have changed.-. The diving subs look like rockets but they work.-. They occupy the crew full time--- I don't know how long we will be here.-. We've mounted brackets on the Nancy Lynn to launch the subs.. They work fine.., We don't fish much- I do...Other things of interest.- Not much damage to this area- Hurricane missed most of it- It hasn't hurt the tourist business.- The biggest thing is the Cruise Lines-.-. No damage to the Cruise Line docks-.- Me and the Nancy Lynn will turn gray over this trip..--.. If I were to move here when I retire, I would fear the possibility of what I just said. I wouldn't be sure I want to move here... Margo is okay--- I'm okay... Margo and I don't like the local food/we could get sick/We are talking possibilities/

Adrian

…---……---……---……---……---……---……---……---
……---……---……---……---……---…

I found a piece of paper and translated the Morse Code. – was T, . was E, .-. was R, another .-. was R, --- was O, .-. again was another R, .. was I, ... was S, and – was another T, ... an S. Terrorists! I mumbled, "Oh shit," as I continued. .- was A, - was T, - was another T,

.- another A, -.-. was C, -.- was K. Attack...Terrorists Attack! I moved on to the next symbol. ..--.. that was the code for the question mark. What did that mean? He didn't know if there would be an attack but he suspected it? He didn't how it would be made? It was clear he was trying to tell us he didn't know something critical. But what?

I continued decoding, . was E, ...was S, --- was O, and ... was another S. SOS! The international distress signal. That was the end of the Morse coded portion of the letter.

I turned my attention to gleaning any other messages he'd try to send us.

The first sentence was different than how he'd started his previous reports. The only significance I read into that was this report was to have a different importance. I saw no message in telling us it was the sixth day in Inagua. "Things have changed," definitely did.

Four of the next five sentences were comments on the diving subs. He was trying to tell us was there was something important about the subs, but what? 'Look like rockets,' got my attention. I took, "I don't know how long we will be here," at face value. The next two brief sentences told me a lot. He'd been separated from the crew in some way!

The next six lines were hard for me to extract meaning from, though I was sure there was one. I knew it had to do with tourists or the tourist business and probably had possibly something tied into Cruise Ships and more specifically their docks. I decided I needed to ask Sallar about that. One item I was sure I'd figured out was turning Gray. I figured the boat had been painted. The why was alarming. The next two sentences indicated he had some doubt about what he'd just told us. The last part of the letter completely confused me. The only thing I could think of symbolically was that he and Margo had come together...or really had a problem with the local food. More likely it was where they were staying.

After finishing and reflecting, I faced a real dilemma. I was becoming increasingly concerned that the *Nancy Lynn*, her captain, and possibly Margo were in very real danger. The question was what type of peril? That would tell me if, when, and how, I must act. For the present, there was little I could do.

# # # # #

Chapter 47

The attention and concern Captain Adrian Springer could not garner from Melanie prior to the *Nancy Lynn's* voyage, came easily now. Easily and swiftly.

The *El Gato Gordo's* engine was warming when Shepard Coloton came running down the pier, portable telephone in one hand. He waved frantically with the other. "Mr.

Sly, I have an urgent call for you!" Without him telling me, I knew it was Riaffort.

I confirmed, "Who is it?"

"Your lawyer."

I nodded and reached for the phone. It hadn't taken long for the Captain's message to knot up Melanie's panties.

~ ~ ~ ~ ~ ~

"Reading it again isn't going accomplish a damned thing," I rubbed my forehead with my fingers. Convincing Riaffort we'd extracted every bit of decipherable information from Captain Springer's message was proving impossible. I hated uttering the following words, "It is what it is," but that exactly fit the situation.

The phone speaker barked. "I have a frantic client. She's wringing her hands and threatening to do all sorts of crazy things."

"Like what?"

"She's threatened to call an old friend of her husband's that worked at NASA. Years ago he mentioned that the agency had the use of a large seaplane. I don't know if she's done it, but Melanie was planning to call this guy up and get him to arrange for her to fly down and pick up Margo. She's impulsive and impatient enough to do crazy stuff like that." I could imagine panic and anger reflecting from Riaffort's face. "Shit, Sly, she doesn't know about the Morse Code messages imbedded in the damned telefax. If she knew that..."

"Thanks for keeping *your promise*," I reminded him.

"Have you decoded that part?"

"The Morse Code? Yes. You haven't?"

There was silence, before he finally said, "I saw the obvious SOS repeated across the top of the page."

"You haven't trans—"

He interrupted, "No, I figured you would."

It was my turn to remain quiet. Finally, I asked, "Did you look for it in the telefax?"

"Kind of. I'm not familiar with it. There were lots of periods and single dashes I figured were meaningless."

"Wrong, the reason I thought you were so upset was you'd converted the code to

letters."

"You mean it's worse?!"

"I'm afraid so."

"What in the Hell does it say?"

I took a deep breath, "Remember what you promised me about not calling her about the Morse stuff? You need to reaffirm that for me."

"Damn it, Sly!" He was more mad than panicked.

"I got to hear it."

Riaffort made it a point to clearly enunciate: "I promise not to call Melanie to tell her about the codes you interpret from the Captain's letters."

Strategizing a way to soften the content didn't work, so I dropped it on him. "You got the SOS message from the heading line. The next word was terrorists. The last word was attack. SOS was repeated to end the coded part of the letter."

Riaffort remained quiet for at least a full minute. His voice was calm and controlled when he did speak. "You indicated that he is telling us things are changing...for the worse. They changed the boat's color, why do that unless you want to hide it. He tells you he thinks the people on the boat are terrorists and they're planning an attack. Hell, Sly, we should be sending in the fucking Marines!"

"I also told you he walked the whole thing back in the last third of the letter. Adrian's excitable and he over-reacts. The fact he sent the telefax and he's still at least in figurehead control of the *Nancy Lynn* means nothing disastrous has happened. If we go in there with the Marines, guns blazing, I don't think it will accomplish anything. It will do one thing, notify them they have to be concerned about us. I'm convinced, whatever they're planning is not cancellable. The only thing that will happen is Margo and Captain will go from being in deep trouble to being in a world of shit. Unless the crew has done something that is illegal already, there's more danger for Adrian and Margo if we wade in there before we know what they're planning."

Riaffort considered my words. "We can't do anything. So, sending the Marines isn't right...yet. What can we do to find out what's happening?"

I'd thought of one thing, was remembering another, and hatching a third. "I'll get Dennia to fly us down there. I'll check it out. Cautiously." I paused and organized my thoughts as I talked. "We have a man here that has acted as a mate on the boat and works for the resort owner. I asked him if he knew anyone in Matthew Town. He has a relative in Inagua and he said he'd ask him to check on the *Nancy Lynn*. Before we fly down, I'll get our man to contact his relative. I can go with a plan and a purpose that way. I have an idea to have Russ work on. There is this possibility that the couple that we were told would be on the boat may have a part to play in this. They are going on a trip the middle of next week. If I'm right, nothing will happen until then. I'm sure of that." No lightning bolt hit me, so my lie got passed.

"Will you call me as soon as you find out anything? Anything at all?"

"Will you keep your mouth shut until I do?"

"Yes."

"Deal!" I hoped I really had one.

# # # # #

Chapter 48

Déjà vu! An hour later we were untying the *El Gato Gordo,* again, when Mimi raced down the dock, phone in hand. "Mr. Sly, Mr. Sly, I have a call for you."

Sallar cut the engines as I took the phone from Mrs. Coloton. "Who is it," I asked?

"Mr. Trotter."

"I hope this is important," were my opening words to him.

"I guess it depends."

"On what?"

"Two things. First, Raiffort called. This was after he talked to you. I just got off the phone with him a few minutes ago. He says the Hellmann woman is going nuts. He wants you to call her or contact her somehow to try to calm her down. Quoting him, 'throw her a bone.' I know Riaffort well enough to know he's plenty worried. Can I do anything from here?"

Platitudes and plans were all I could offer at this point. I wouldn't lie to her. "Okay, I want you to do this. Call her. Tell her that I'm working on a plan to fly down to Inagua to be sure things are alright. I'll call her on Monday with what I'm going to do. Be sure to tell her if she does something rash, it could put her daughter and the Captain in more, not less, danger."

"What if she asks—"

"Just cut her off. Tell her that's all you know, and she'll be best off by waiting until I call her on Monday." I took a breath. "What's number two?"

"You had a guy named Arlen Harris call and asked you to call him. The man said you knew him from the DOJ. He wants to know who Russ Foxx is and what he was doing trying to get into the Grumman Company files. I told him you were out of town, but I could tell him about why Foxx was looking at files. I explained you had him checking backgrounds. He seemed satisfied but wants you to call him when you get back. Oh yeah, he said you shouldn't have Russ do that again."

"That it?"

"Yes. Is Lily and my trip still on?" Trotter asked.

"Yes. I'm taking the boat out this weekend. I'll think things out then. While Dennia is picking you two up, I'll deal with Melanie. And, one other thing. Bring two of the ARs and three loaded magazines for them. Pickup my spare Hellcat 9mm and you bring your .45. Don't forget ammo. We don't know what we might run into if... One other thing, we don't want to be crosswise with the Bahama officials. One of the forms is the Declaration of Possession of Firearms, number 16. Go on-line and process any paperwork we need, to have them on the boat. I'll see you Monday afternoon."

When I handed the phone back to Mimi, the fun I had anticipated at my 'parade' was drenched by at least an inch of rain. The diesels roar as we left the pier, was an overture to worries, not relaxation.

# # # # #

Chapter 49

Hungry bonefish and mahi-mahi are great medicine for a troubled mind. They can dull the problems presence, but not eliminate their nagging existence. Our trip to northern Exuma was filled with beautiful scenes, snorkeling adventures, sumptuous fish dinners, and the omnipresent Sword of Damocles that hovered over me.

Often, I found myself distracted, one time to the point I carelessly came close to running aground on a reef. There were so many pieces to put together involving the *Nancy Lynn* and her voyage, the permutations were endless as far as I could tell. I hoped that Trotter had been able to smooth Melanie's fears. The affair was complex enough without adding another layer of problems over it.

Saturday evening came and my apprehensions drove me away from the cheer and drinks Dennia, Val, Russ, and Sallar shared. I picked up my most reliable computer, a yellow, lined, legal pad, and sought the solitude of our cabin. My intent was to isolate the critical from the incidental, the actionable from the distractions. Where to start? That was the first problem

I had to solve. When that was answered, how could I divide it into manageable parts? I worked on a starting point.

Since my meeting at Hellmann's mansion is where my first contact with some of the key individuals occurred, it became my ground zero. I headed a sheet and divided it with vertical lines creating columns for observations about the individuals' style and personal characteristics, information about their pasts, and one for notes and miscellaneous thoughts. I quickly decided to spend no time on Melanie. She had no control over what happened on the *Nancy Lynn*. I had little or no control over her ability to make the problem worse.

After filling a page with my scrawl about the meeting, I realized the only information of value to me was that which helped determine what the crew and trip's objective was. What had I written that would allow me to invent a strategy to influence its outcome? Or prevent it? Or extract Adrian and Margo? When I used those criteria for writing down information, the lists became shorter and more valuable.

Critical questions to be answered emerged. The problem: I'd made no progress— replay.

**Was there some sort of sinister plot in process? What was that objective?*

**Would Captain Springer and possibly Margo become an impediment to the group's objective? If so, would it require their removal or death? Was there a* *way to stop what was happening without endangering Springer and Margo?*

**Were the real Diane and Hall involved or potential victims?*

**When would all this come about? Where would the plot culminate?*

**How could it be stopped?*

**What could I do to help?*

If I could answer those questions, I felt I could save the *Nancy Lynn*, and those aboard her. I began sifting through the lined yellow pages. Slowly, some of the answers came.

# # # # #

Chapter 50

Sunday morning taught me a lesson I won't forget. Winds were out of the northeast and maintained a steady 16 mph. That posed no danger to the sturdy *El Gato Gordo*, but it did to my stomach. I made the error of trying to read and write notes regarding my nagging involvement with the *Nancy Lynn* and her crew. Normally, I'm the one comforting seasick shipmates. I realized my mistake too late. I fed the fish my breakfast and was a rail bird for two hours. A combination of traveling in the lee of an island and dried ginger cloves allowed me to get rid of the miseries the waves had installed in my stomach. We ate lunch in the shelter of Eleuthera before making the final leg of our trip back to Marsh Harbor.

I took advantage of the hour Sallar recommended we remain at anchor to allow our lunch to settle, to pull out my yellow pad, wipe the last remnants of breakfast from it, and try to reach some conclusions about the *Nancy Lynn*. I decided I had to look at the situation as though it was a worst-case scenario. That was the *Nancy Lynn* was going to be used in a terrorist activity of some type. I felt confident, short of that, smuggling drugs or something else would raise the Captain's fins but that he'd be smart enough to "let things happen' and let the authorities take care of the problem after the *Nancy Lynn* was safely back in its boathouse. A terrorist plot of the type I could visualize, smuggling terrorist agents and/or weapons back to the US would be something the Captain would be compelled to resist. Would he survive that? I doubted it.

Would Margo? If she were part of it, Yes. If she wasn't, and I leaned toward that conclusion, probably not. Margo wasn't the sharpest marble in the sack, even when she was sober. That wasn't often. I didn't see any emotional connection to any of her shipmates, not even one to Gino. My observation was he was performing stud service. That gave his group access to the *Nancy Lynn*. He didn't hide his disdain for Margo very well.

My guess was she'd feed the fish a few feet from Springer.

One thing I'd deduced was that whatever the plan, it was scheduled very specifically for Friday, the 26th of April. It was apparent to me the journey to the backwater town and island of Inagua was tied to preparation for what would happen on that day. The group's insistence that the *Nancy Lynn* be on the briny that day and in a specific location was what I had to concentrate on. I believed that held the key to the solution. Galang's and Harold's connection with electronics, drones, and guidance systems, left me with a strong suspicion. Could they be planning to bring down one or more of the airline planes that flew over that patch of water? If one of the larger planes was scheduled for that day... I wrote a note to check.

As Sallar lifted the anchor, I placed my notes into my briefcase and took the case to a drawer in the cabin. As quickly as I could, I was back on deck. Staying below was an invitation for seasickness to return. No replays of green cheeks and jettisoned meals, please.

The hour after lunch was well spent. I'd decided the only eventuality I needed to plan for was the scenario for a sinister event. In that situation, Springer and Margo would be in mortal danger if the event couldn't be halted. How to do that remained. I'd determined where and when the plot was to take place. What and how were at best, a guess. A low probability one at that.

"Are you ready to get underway, Mr. Sly?" Sallar asked.

"Let's do it." I climbed the ladder to the flying bridge right behind him.

Sallar eased the boat into gear as the two diesels murmured and the exhaust coughed. He spun the wheel to point the bow at a small passage in the reef that allowed us to anchor comfortably. When we cleared the coral, deep, blue water beckoned.

"Do you want the wheel?" Sallar asked.

"Yes, I'll play captain for a while."

"Keep it on course. With the wind, cheat a couple of points to starboard. Steer 355.˚

At the speed we're running we'll need to change in four hours plus a little."

I exchanged places with him and settled in for the five hours of sailing left. Sallar relaxed in the seat next to me. I wouldn't have a better opportunity to ask. "Sallar, you remember me speaking to you about your cousin in Matthew Town?"

"Exactly, precisely."

"I want to know if the *Nancy Lynn* is still in Matthew Town. If he can ask around and find out when they are scheduled to leave, that would be great. If any work has been done to the boat. Any gossip."

"You want to know all there is about your friend and his boat, right?"

"Yes."

"I will call tonight after we return." Sallar looked at me questioningly.

"If the *Nancy Lynn* is still docked there, I'm considering having Dennia fly us down. You think your cousin can get me close enough for me to see what's going on without being spotted?"

"You want a sneaky look?"

"Yes, that's pretty much it."

"Exactly, precisely! My cousin is just the man for that. He does sneaky well."

Shouts and a scream came from the transom. Russ yelled, "I have some type of big assed fish, he's headed for Spain, and I need help."

"I will go see," Sallar said. He was down the ladder before I could cut the engines back to idle. There was some excited conversation followed by "Ahhhhhhhh" in unison.

Sallar was sitting next to me within two minutes. I asked, "What was going on back there?"

"Mr. Russ, he did hook a big fish, but it broke off. I told him we didn't have time to fish any more. They are watching waves now." Sallar's smile told me there was more.

"And?"

"I told him it was a shark."

"Was it?"

"No...big blue marlin...400 pounds, maybe." Sallar looked serious. "You don't tell him, okay?"

I used my fingers to close an invisible zipper, lock my lips with an invisible key, and through it into the blue waves.

# # # # #

Chapter 51

I'm not sure what woke me up. Maybe it was the waves of a passing boat that gently bumped the hull of the *Gato Gordo* against the pier pilings. Maybe the smell of frying bacon invading my nostrils. Maybe it was the lack of the now familiar feel of Dennia's body against mine. Whatever did it, caused me to blink like an owl when the sunlight told me I'd overslept.

Dennia was flying to pick-up Trotter and Lily today, and I' hadn't convinced her to let me accompany her on the trip. I swung my legs out of our bed, pulled on some shorts, and headed for the galley.

Russ and Val were seated at the table and were disposing of pancakes Dennia had loaded on their plates. She was fully dressed, hair and make-up in place, her purse at the ready. Dennia was ready to travel. "Hey, sleepyhead, grab a plate. I have a half-dozen or so of these left." She removed a tray from the microwave that kept them warm.

I sat down. Russ slid maple syrup and butter at me. "They're so fluffy and light you need to weight them down with that stuff to keep them from floating away."

Val picked up her empty plate and placed it in the sink. She tapped Dennia on the shoulder as she passed. "Those were delicious!" She punched Russ in the shoulder playfully, and said, "Come on. Push the last couple bites down and come with me. I'm going up to see if I can get into the computer room before that idiot from Chicago gets parked behind the keyboard for the rest of the day."

Russ inhaled the last two forkfuls before following Val out of the cabin. He said,

"Have a nice flight," as he disappeared.

"I'll hurry," I said as I attacked the breakfast.

"Why? You don't need to." She tried to say no nicely.

"I'm going with you, aren't I?"

"We discussed this the other day, dear. You'd just be excess weight. I fly this far or farther all the time." Dennia's smile, was strained...but offered.

I made a last attempt. "I thought since you'd be flying over the ocean you might want me for company."

"I fly to New Orleans frequently. The Gulf of Mexico isn't any less wet than the Atlantic." She shook her head. "Really, think about it. What could you do if I had a problem? You can't fly a plane. The only thing you could do is be company. I sure wouldn't want that. Let's face it. All you'd be is ballast. My Cessna doesn't need any."

Shrugging my shoulders, I pouted a bit and looked foolish enough to make her laugh. "It's three hours over and three hours back. If Lily is on time for the first time in her life, I'll be back in seven to eight hours. It's seven o'clock now...I'll see you at four this afternoon."

A hug and kiss later, she had gone.

~ ~ ~ ~ ~ ~

To my surprise, I heard Russ and Val say goodbye to Dennia as she walked down the pier. I found them seated on the *Gato Gordo's* rear deck when I emerged from the cabin. "I thought you two were going to the *Sleepy Dolphin's* computer room?"

"Privacy," Val winked as she nodded.

"Thank you!" I responded.

Russ stood, "Excuse me. I'm going to do what you asked me to the other day. I doubt anybody will be in the *Sleepy Dolphin's* office at this time on a Monday morning." He grinned. "Where should I start? You want me to look at Hall and Diane or the brother first?"

"Do Harold. He's in the position to do harm, the others aren't."

"Doing harm." Val nodded. "You know that might be something to concentrate on.

See what skills or talents he has that he could use against whomever he wants to attack. We can see if we have access to things to neutralize them." She stood up to leave with

Russ. "I'm going with him. We can cover everything twice as fast."

I watched them chatter to each other as they walked to the office. If the information on Harold's potential weapons could be found on the Internet, they'd find them.

It took a minute to realize I was alone with nothing planned to keep me occupied. Guilt crept into the back of my mind. If my friends were off doing my errands, I should be busy doing something to contribute to my own project. I decided to re-examine the Captain's telefaxes for any clues I might have missed. There were always things. I decided to find them.

# # # # #

Chapter 52

"You busy?" Val stood in front of me staring down at Captain Springer's messages. I'd been concentrating on the papers to the point my mind barred everything else from registering. It had been three hours since Dennia left and the Foxxes went to the *Sleepy Dolphin's* computer room to do the research I'd requested. It seemed like minutes.

"Never so busy to not have time for you." I motioned for her to have a seat.

Val, not one for superfluous chatting, went straight to her reason. "Russ is finding a lot of information on Harold Runnells and Galang Marcos. The more I hear, the more I see the two of them as part of a task team, not a couple of friends working for a cause.

Russ found they didn't even know each other until they were all united in that class at Columbia. Both couples, the Runnells and the Marcos moved to New York City less than four months before that class. You know me, I don't believe in coincidence."

I leaned back in my seat. What Val was telling me was crucial. The fact they might be supported by a major, well-funded effort like Al Qaeda had been just a possibility. Val's information changed that from possibility to probability. If they were part of an organized terrorist group, that meant they'd have access to materials and resources I hadn't considered. It made anything in their plans more potent. I told her, "I believe you're right."

"Russ has all the details. They have the skills to develop a sophisticated weapon.

One knows how to build missiles, bombs, delivery systems of all kinds. That's the Harold guy. The other one is the electronics half. He's an expert on guidance...things like flying drones. You know a drone could be made large enough to act as a bomb."

"If they have those types of capabilities, I wouldn't limit it to drones. Hell, they could come up with a guided missile as well. If they can figure a way to make the *Nancy Lynn* stable enough to act as a platform, they can launch from it." My mind raced. There were all kinds of delivery systems they could produce. It also expanded their probable target past aircraft. Conceivably, they could craft a missile to attack Nassau or even Miami!

Val nodded as I talked, and she was obviously anxious to add to the conversation. As soon as I stopped talking, she emphasized her next words, "Russ was telling me that he knew as much about the electronic guidance systems as that the Galang fellow does. Those are things Russ works on constantly. Russ said he believes his theory on jamming signals and capturing control of a drone, or missile if that's what it turns out to be, *could* be used to screw up their plans. You need to remember that. He may not mention it since he's not sure it will work."

I nodded as I added that potential to a geometrically increasing set of complications. "Thanks, Val. That's all very important information."

She stood to leave. "I'm going back to the computer room." She hesitated. "Promise you won't forget."

"I promise I won't."

# # # # #

Chapter 53

My notes on my review of the messages Captain Springer sent were a rehash of what I'd already gleaned from them. The primary two things I theorized were items I already knew. They were the importance of the *Nancy Lynn* in whatever plot the people aboard had concocted, and the belief I knew the time and place it would occur. Whatever would happen would be initiated from the *Nancy Lynn* and would be in a defined five square mile area of sea.

My debate with myself on whether another pass through the documents would net anything was aborted by Russ and Val's return to the *Gato Gordo's* salon.

Russ' usual smile wasn't visible. He suggested, "I think you're going to want to hear what I found as quickly as possible. It will take time. You want me to start while Val makes us something to eat?" He carried his laptop in one hand and flash drives in the other.

"Sure." A quick check of the clock shocked me. It was nearly one o'clock. Another three hours were gone without my realizing it. I flipped over pages on my legal pad until I uncovered one without my scribbles on it. "Where do you want to begin?"

"I think I should go over what I found out about Harold Runnells first. But, I need to weave in some of the things I found on the Marcos and the woman with Harold...I think putting things together is important. This is like a jigsaw puzzle. You have to see the adjoining pieces to get a better picture."

"Fine. Whatever you think covers what you learned best." I grinned and waved my legal pad. "I have my computer ready."

Russ nodded, opened his laptop, inserted a flash drive, and brushed the keys until what he wanted appeared on the screen. He took a deep breath. "I finally got a way to find out what jobs Harold Runnells worked at after he graduated. He's had several. His employers have a unanimous opinion of the man. Very brilliant. Very, very troubled. The type of jobs he's held aren't the hamburger flipping variety. You'll be very familiar with most of the company names. Raytheon, General Dynamics, Lockheed-Martin, Cochin Shipyard in India. For three months he worked for Northup-Grumman. Evidently, some things he did there helped end him and his brother's relationship."

I asked, "Did you find what kind of items he worked on?"

"Lots of different things. Surface to air anti-aircraft missiles. Anti-personnel rockets. Diving equipment. Plus, lots more. Most all of it was in a parts design capacity. He was in some type of a classified program at Raytheon in a group design team. He got fired five months into that. That's enough to scare you shitless, considering what we suspect. Harold lost the Raytheon job...some major questions about his security status. He took the job in India after that. Lasted two years there. Came back and worked for GE in their consumer products group. He quit that six months ago. No work since then." I started to say something, but he held up his hand indicating he wanted to continue. "His security problems started four years ago. He married an Indonesian woman. She was a member of a number of Muslim and communist organizations. His tilt in that political direction became a full lean over. He didn't play well with others. That's why he got canned most of the time. His adoption of his wife's political views magnified the problem."

"What did you find out about his wife?"

He shook his head. "I still have more on Harold. This ties in the Marcos couple. Everything that Harold Runnells has done on these weapon systems has to do with building and propelling them. He's never had a thing to do with the guidance systems. I believe that's where Galang Marcos fits. That's pretty much all he knows. Electronics. Guidance and Control systems. Galang has worked for a subcontractor for Raytheon for three years and designed electronic games for two years before that. He's good at what he does and gets along well where lives and works. The man is supremely confident in what he does. He brags about his development of drone controls."

Russ stopped, looked at me, and lifted his eyebrows. I rolled my hands indicating he should continue.

"Okay. Besides her strong political leanings, I didn't get much on his wife past her name, Iesha, and that she is an expert on Sharia. She is 5'9" tall. That's big for an Indonesian lady."

"Did you find anything new about the Marcos couple?" I asked.

Russ shook his head. "Nothing that jumped out at me. Dalisay is a graduate of the University of Santo Tomas Electrical Engineering School. She had a job with a microprocessor component company in the Philippines. Galang, he's a dude. He flew a drone outside the women's dorm and took some pictures of the co-eds au natural. Got in trouble when he sold some of them. He has this whole theory about guidance and maintaining control of his vehicles he claims as tamper-proof. I don't agree."

"If the situation arises, say he tries shooting down an airliner, would you like a shot at proving he's wrong?"

"I'm not 100% sure what I'm thinking would work...would," Russ shook his head.

"I wouldn't want to take a chance of making things worse."

Slapping him on the shoulder, I said, "Consider this. If I ask you to try to gain control of whatever they're planning, the alternative is nothing to stop them."

"In that case, I'd love to take my shot."

"Lunch," Val said as she shoved plates with sandwiches and chips in front of us.

~ ~ ~ ~ ~ ~

I read the last line on my legal pad. "We left off where you were telling me you'd be willing to try breaking Galang's control over whatever they are planning."

Russ nodded. He removed one flash drive and inserted another. Within a few seconds, he had a new file on his computer screen. His eyes left it long enough to engage mine. "You've got all the most important stuff on the Runnells and the Marcos. There's more details on this." He held up the flash drive he'd just removed from his laptop. "The one I have in now is one with information on the real Diane and Hall Runnells. It's important. I think it will force you to make a decision after you learn about it." His eyes returned to the screen.

"I take it you found out something that leads you to confirm that the real Diane and Hall are being set up for something." My pen rested on the pad.

Russ remained silent. Finally, he said, "You aren't going to write a great deal. I don't know how many ways you can write, the two of them are being set up to be killed."

"Killed?" I repeated.

"Killed. This took a lot of time to research. The bad part of this is it appears that someone high up in the UN or the US government is assisting in getting them assassinated. It's complicated and simple at the same time. You've said whatever is going to occur will be on the 26th. So I figured: if the real Runnells couple, Diane and Hall, were being set up for something they would have to be close to here on that day. I made calls to the numbers in your file...their offices. Both were to be on leave for five days. The assistant you told me about at the UN is snarky but not very smart. I tricked the whole thing out of him. Where they're going, dates, everything. Diane and Hall are going to a meeting with a rich philanthropist in Vera Cruz to discuss building a water and sewage plant for a small village down there. Or at least, that's what they think. I'm guessing they'll go and never return."

"How'd you come to that conclusion?" I asked.

"It didn't meet my smell test. When I did some checking, here are some of the things I found. Diane's assistant told me the UN was involved informally but wasn't sponsoring it. That sounded strange. When I pressed for details, I found the guy's name. I recognized it from the news. That so-called philanthropist is a Venezuelan drug cartel leader. The meeting place in Vera Cruz is a hotel owned by him. There was some rubber stamping done by the US State Department. I'm not sure if it's part of the setup or incompetence."

I interrupted, "I doubt anybody checked it out. That's a ho-hum group of bureaucrats in State. I'll give you ten to one on incompetence."

Russ nodded, "I was curious about the meeting. The Runnells were to be there, a named three-person delegation representing Macias, that's the cartel boss, and a delegation of town officials. No names for them. Fishy. They gave the town name, so I called around. I began to see where things were going when I talked to the town constable. He is pretty much the government of Verde San Salvador. He never heard of the meeting and he assured me he would know about it and would probably attend as the town leader...if it was real. Sound the buzzer. It doesn't compute that the place to be helped isn't aware of what's in the offing."

I whistled and Russ continued.

"I checked the hotel. Rooms for the Runnels are reserved. No meeting room. No rooms for city officials. I hacked airline reservations lists. There are round-trip tickets for Diane, from and to New York and Hall, from and to San Diego. Guess what? I also found one-way tickets to Nassau on the 25th for the two of them. The round-trip ticket reservations were made by the UN travel office and Hall's assistant. The one-way tickets were reserved by the hotel people. Get the drift?"

"I sure do."

"One other important thing. When I was in the airline files, I saw two coffins were scheduled to be on the flight. That got me thinking. I weaseled into the hotel purchase order file. There are two caskets that were purchased and are at the hotel now. I rest my case. There's lots more on the flash drive, but I think that's what you need to know." Russ turned off his laptop and closed it.

"You're right about needing to take action. I'll have to figure out what." It would take me time to sort things into an order where I knew what to do. And...there were parts still missing.

# # # # #

Chapter 54

Sallar told me he'd speak to his relative in Matthew Town early in the morning. I'd expected to see him by noon. My pocket watch's old fashion hands pointed to two and to thirty. The information Russ uncovered created an urgency that didn't exist before I heard it.

I considered calling him. As I started pushing numbers on my cell phone, Sallar's voice became audible as he walked the dock. Mimi and he were chattering and laughing about something. From my seat on the flying bridge, I waved to them and they waved back. Sallar climbed on board when they arrived. Mimi waved and asked, "Mr. Sly, do you want anything from the store? Missy Dennia called. She says, she'll be on the ground in less than an hour. She has to stop and wants to know what you want?"

"Tell her I don't need a thing."

Sallar climbed the stairs, said, "Hello," and sat next to me. He smiled and waited for me to speak.

"Did you have a good morning?" I asked.

"Very good, very good. Another set of my relatives moved into their new homes. I helped them move their things. My wife and I have more space...we can breathe again!"

"That's good. Is that the final group?"

"That leaves only my sister-in-law. She will leave eventually, I guess. When...I don't know." Sallar's smile was ear to ear.

"You look like a happy man," I observed.

"Exactly, precisely."

"Did you have a chance to call your relative in Inagua?"

"Oh, yes! I called him last evening. We talked. Then this morning he called me back with more news." Sallar stuck his fingers in his shirt pocket and removed a folded piece of paper. He waggled it in the air. "I have learned from you."

"Your cousin knew about them?"

"Yes, yes, yes! He was on the *Nancy Lynn* and did work. He knew very much. That's why I wrote stuff down. So, I wouldn't forget." He unfolded the paper, smoothed it with his palm, and said, "Should I tell you what he said, or do you want to ask questions?"

"Tell me what you have written. I'll ask questions if I need to."

Sallar nodded. "My cousin says the *Nancy Lynn* is tied up just 150 meters from the shop where he works. In the last week, he did work on the boat. He welded brackets together and installed them just three days ago. He says the boss man is nice but is a friend of Burton Dahl. Burton Dahl is a very bad monn. He is known as a thug and gangster. No matter, he is one of the most powerful people in Inagua. The local officials live in his billfold. He is involved in all things bad in Matthew Town. Smuggling. Prostitution. All those things. If you want to get something that is illegal to have, he is the one who can get it. If you want someone to disappear... As I said, Burton Dahl is a very bad monn."

Sallar stopped and stared at me. I motioned for him to continue.

"The one called Hall and Burton talk a lot. Usually, they do that away from the boat. That's because the little man is always mad when they talk on the *Nancy Lynn*. My cousin says, the first week the people on the boat get along fine. The boat is supposed to go diving, but he says not so much. Some of the crew are always drunk. The little man is the captain. He yells. They say yes. They do as they please. They go out and dive three days and test a submarine diving vehicle. There is one for all six who say they are divers. Edwardo, that's my cousin, says the subs are shaped like long cigars. The Hall man likes them very much. Anyway, the brackets my cousin made are to hold the dive subs over the water and to store them when they aren't used."

Sallar stopped. I rolled my hands indicating for him to continue.

"Edwardo says, the problems of the people getting mad on the boat started when boss man Hall has the boat painted gray with this special paint. My cousin says it is the same paint Burton Dahl paints his boats he uses for smuggling. Something about making them invisible to radar. The little man is very angry. Hall and the captain, they scream at each other. Only one person on the boat is the captain's friend. The white woman Margo...she got very upset too. After that Edwardo says he only sees either of them occasionally. Anyway, the boat is to leave Wednesday afternoon. Edwardo is to fuel it."

I asked, "Did he say the last time he saw the captain and the Margo woman?"

"Yes. He said today. I need to tell you a little more. Remember, I said my cousin called this morning."

"Go ahead." I prompted.

"Edwardo's boss called. He wanted my cousin to bring three dozen batteries to the *Nancy Lynn*. When he got to the boat, big things were happening. The local police were there and had the boat cordoned off. He couldn't get on the cruiser to deliver the batteries. An officer did it for him. Anyway, there was lots of excitement. Edwardo asked what was going on. The police would not tell him anything. He asked if anyone was hurt or in trouble on the *Nancy Lynn*, and the officer said they weren't. The constable told him that someone from Nassau was coming, and his boss wanted to avoid trouble."

"Is that all?" I asked.

"Yes. Edwardo told me the officials and the Burton monn run everyone away."

That convinced me. We had to go to Matthew Town. Dennia and my flight went from observation to rescue.

# # # # #

Chapter 55

I heard them before I could see them. Lily's distinctive laugh, Trotter's baritone came from behind the *Sleepy Dolphin* office building. I sat on the rear deck of the *Gato Gordo* tying leaders to hooks, killing time until they arrived. Lily and Trotter's silhouettes rounded the corner of the building. I waved, and when Lily recognized me, she sprinted through the resort's rear yard and down the pier. Lily squealed like a teenager at a concert as she ran. She jumped into the boat, her momentum almost carrying her over the transom.

"Whoa, girl!" I yelled and grabbed an arm to be sure she didn't go overboard. "You don't want to get hurt the first ten minutes you're here."

Lily threw her arms around me and kissed me on the cheek. Then she pushed me away at arms-length. "I wouldn't get hurt...only wet."

"Before you say that, we'll have to introduce you to some of the local residents."

"They have lots of sharp teeth," Russ added. The noise had flushed him from the salon.

Dennia was just becoming visible from behind the office. Mimi and Shepard Coloton walked next to her. All three carried luggage. Trotter stepped into the *Gato Gordo* saying, "Good to see you, boss man."

Russ eyed the situation. "You don't need me. You've got plenty of strong backs. If you want help, call. I'll be working on a sudoku puzzle in the cabin." He started to disappear below, but stopped and said, "Trotter, you need to walk her down the waterfront and let her watch our neighbor feed his pets." He grinned as he went inside.

Tilting my head toward the three baggage handlers approaching the dock, I said to

Trotter, "You left the help high and dry."

"That's Ms. Boss Man's orders. Dennia gave me child control." Trotter pointed to Lily. "Keeping her under control...It's like lassoing a Brahman bull with spaghetti."

"Bull? Brahman bull? What have you been drinking?" Lily may have had a totty or two on the flight from Clewiston. She thrust her chest forward, displaying her large, God given attraction devices. Pointing to her boobs, she hissed, "You don't find these on bulls."

"How many screwdrivers?" I asked. Those were Lily's drink of choice.

Lily's mock scowl got a shoulder shrug from Trotter. If I'd needed any confirmation, they'd become a couple, that would have been it.

"Give me a hand, please," Dennia said as she and the Colotons stood next to the *Gato Gordo,* their arms loaded with bags. Trotter and I immediately returned from Lala land and took the suitcases they handed down to us. As we stowed the luggage in cabins,

I heard Lily ask, "Any reason I shouldn't jump in?"

Shepard and Mimi responded with a chorus of "No's."

"Many people clean fish here at this time in the afternoon. They throw what is left in the water. It draws sharks. You do not want to have them think you are bait." Shepard was talking as I emerged on the rear deck. He was not concentrating on the waters around the pier. Lily had removed her shorts and shirt. Her Bikini drew his attention...or rather what was in it. He added, "If you keep watching, you can usually see one swim past this time of day."

Lily's eyes began roaming the clear water for a large form.

Mimi spoke to Dennia as she got into the boat. "If you need anything, just yell." She smiled at Lily and said, "Miss Lily, it is nice to know you. I know you will enjoy your stay."

"Thank you. I will."

"Shepard, come. Let's let these people settle." Mimi led her husband away whose intense eyes weren't looking for sharks."

"You have a good flight?" I asked Dennia.

"Yes. Luckily, headwinds become tailwinds when you reverse directions. I clawed my way to Clewiston and soared my way back. To my shock, Lily was waiting. Be still my heart! It is the first time I can remember her being on time for anything. Her Daddy used to say she functioned on 'Lily Time.' It's a good thing she was ready. There is a storm front moving this way. Two hours later and we'd be sitting in Clewiston."

"Did you see what weather we might be having here?"

"Yes, not good for the next thirty-six hours. Rest of the week looks fine." She made a cutting motion with one hand. "The front is moving from southwest to northeast. It will affect the northern Bahamas. That's definitely us. Areas south of Andros won't see much, if any, effects from the front. But, I think we'll be spending tomorrow tied to the dock or close to it."

I asked, "Is the weather going to be flyable?"

"Yes. The bad stuff will pass here around midnight. It's moving fast. We'll have strong winds tomorrow, but the storms will be long gone."

"Good. I want to—"

"There's one! See it!" Lily pointed to an eight-foot-long gray form swimming past with lazy swishes of its tail propelling it.

The rounded nose and fin placement told me, "That's a bull shark. They're maneaters."

Lily laughed, "Good, I was worried it was a woman eater."

# # # # #

Chapter 56

Dennia swung her legs out of bed and reached for her robe to cover her naked body.

"You want something from the galley?"

"It depends," I answered.

She stopped at the cabin door, her hand resting on the handle. "Depends on what?" "Are we looking at a doubleheader?"

"Absolutely! Who knows, the third time might be charming." Her smile was full of promise.

"I'd like a Pepsi, a big one. I'll need the sugar."

Dennia opened the robe exposing her front. "No, you won't." She wrapped the robe closed, tied the sash, and left.

When she returned, she handed me a liter bottle, and removed the robe strip tease style. Dennia read something in my expression I didn't realize was there. She asked, "What do you have on your mind? I don't think it's a starting position."

"You don't miss a damned thing, do you?" I hesitated then said, "I want to talk to you about something but I sure in hell don't want to break the mood."

She sat on the bed a few inches from me. "Tell me the subject and I'll tell you if it will break the mood."

"I want to go flying tomorrow."

She smiled. "I told you flying makes me horny."

"I need to tell you everything. Today, Russ' research into what could be going on with the people on the *Nancy Lynn*...it took a crucial turn. This afternoon, Sallar told me what he found out from his cousin. In my estimation, none of it's good news. I originally talked about just flying down to check on the situation. After hearing what I have today, I want to pick up Captain Springer and Margo and fly them back here. They are in a hell of a lot of danger if I'm correct. I don't want to go into details now. We'll have lots of time to talk if you agree to fly down there."

"Sounds like fun."

"Dennia, this could be dangerous. I'm convinced there is something major planned. I'll talk to Trotter tomorrow and get him to contact the Wilkerson fellow, remember the police sergeant from our Andros trip?"

She nodded.

"Sallar tells me we can't count on the local Inagua police officials. They're all crooked. So, we need to be very careful, and we need to get some outside help if we can.

It could get dicey."

"I'll plan the flight out and set things up so we can get away by eight." She stood, gently pushed my back onto the bed, and...

Chapter 57

By the time the Cessna flew over the halfway mark of the Exuma island chain, the huge white-capped waves wrinkling the Atlantic turned to gentle undulations. When we reached our refueling stop at Great Exuma Cay, the wind had changed from fierce to lamb gentle.

My guilt increased as we took off for the small strip on Inagua and Matthew Town. The level of danger I comprehended we'd face once we landed wasn't infinitesimal. Based on my observation, I'd failed to communicate its seriousness to Dennia. I feared she was expecting a Sunday school picnic and would attend a bar fight. We were two hours from discovery.

The time was ten-fifteen. I calculated ahead. We needed to be back at Marsh Harbor by eight. Deducting the remaining flight time down and the return flight time it would leave us two-and-a-half hours. We'd have to do everything needed to find the *Nancy Lynn*, convince the Captain and hopefully Margo to leave it, and get the Cessna's wheels off the ground. That wasn't much time.

Trotter was not only contacting Sergeant Wilkerson, I'd instructed him to reserve a car at

Matthews Town, contact Sallar, and ask Sallar to have his cousin waiting at the airport. My call to him from the Exuma airfield confirmed the car...however, efforts to connect with Edwardo, Sallar's cousin, weren't successful. Trotter told me Sallar was continuing to try reaching him.

My attempts to instill caution in Dennia's relaxed attitude failed. As we circled our destination, I hoped I wasn't placing my girlfriend in serious danger.

~ ~ ~ ~ ~ ~

The Cessna rolled to a stop next to the FBO office where we intended to pick up the rental car, refuel Dennia's plane, and hopefully meet Edwardo. Sallar had described a short stocky man with a bald head that walked with a limp. The only person who took an interest in our arrival, that we noticed, was a pretty, young black girl, dressed in a brightly colored, hibiscus print shift. When the propeller came to a stop, she trotted to the plane.

Her friendly smile and wave welcomed us.

As Dennia and I opened the aircraft's doors, she asked, "You are Mr. and Mrs. Harrell?"

Dennia returned the girl's smile. "That's close enough." She pointed at the FBO office. Are you from the fixed base operator? I need to get my tanks topped off."

"No, no. I am Edwardo's girlfriend. I have come to take you to him." She stopped smiling and said, "I think you should get your fuel now. Wait and watch them. That's what Edwardo said."

"We don't have much time here and we have a lot to do. They can fuel us up while we're going. I'll go get the rental car—"

"Time is not your problem, Mr. Harrell. You don't need the rental car. Using it would be a bad thing. You come with me. I drive my own vehicle. It is best, few people know you are here. People are waiting to see you when you get the rental car." She held out a graceful hand with slim fingers. "My name is Anita. I will take you in my taxi. No one will think much of that." She hesitated a few seconds then asked. "Do one of you have a credit card that has a last name other than Harrell? It would be best to use that for gas." "I do," Dennia volunteered. She looked at me and said, "You weren't kidding."

~ ~ ~ ~ ~ ~

The ride from Matthew Town Airstrip to Edwardo's house sent me through a time warp. Anita's taxi was a vehicle I was very familiar with from time spent in Asia, specifically Bangkok. Referred to as "Toot-toots," they are motorized carts with a never-ending variety of coverings and configurations. Hers consisted of an old Harley coupled to a cart that could have been a rickshaw in its youth. The top was an aluminum square with taut canvas stretched over it. A mural of bougainvillea blossoms adorned the inside, iridescent red, pink, orange, blue, and green tassels hung from the perimeter and fluttered was we sped along graded sand roads.

Anita kept up a running description of the places we passed. Unfortunately, the Harley's muffler-less motor allowed us to understand a third of what she said. She managed to point out buildings associated with the Morton salt works, a historic general store, and a small gathering of flamingoes wading in a pond. Within ten minutes we were driving on a residential side street and stopped in front of a modest, frame home with a roof that appeared to have been recently replaced.

"Edwardo is inside. You go right on in. I will park my taxi somewhere else. If you need me, I will be here super quick." Anita allowed us to exit before scratching off in a cloud of sand and dust.

A man that fit the description Sallar gave me for his cousin was seated at a table, visible through the screen door. He said, "Welcome, welcome. You are Sallar's friends." It was a question more than a statement.

"Yes. You are Edwardo, right?"

"Yes, yes, yes. I have much to tell you and it must be in a little time. Much has happened yesterday afternoon and today. I will tell you now if you came to see the *Nancy*

Lynn, you will not. The people and the boat left last night after many things went on."

"Left?" I was surprised.

"Oh, yes. When I called Sallar in the morning, I did not know what would explode.

Please come inside and sit."

We entered and joined Edwardo at the table.

"What happened?"

"The police happened. And Burton Dahl happened. I was to do some last-minute welding to reinforce some brackets. Everything was quiet on the boat. Even the old captain was not yelling. Then the police cars come, three of them. There is much excitement. The police, they talk to the one called Hall. It is obvious there are some serious problems.

One officer, he took two cases off of the boat. I heard the police lieutenant say that the *Nancy Lynn* was to be restricted to the dock. That she could not leave the pier. The officials in Nassau were sending officers here to talk to the people on board. There was much shouting. Then Burton Dahl comes. Everything calms down. I see him giving away money like you would pour water. I heard him tell his friends in the police, to meet the officers coming from New Providence. He said to tell them something, but I did not hear that."

"Did the people from Nassau get on the boat before it left?" I asked."

"No, no. Mr. Hall and those people leave super quick. The one woman and the captain, they say they want to get off. Mr. Hall say no. They all went into the cabin and there was much yelling. I was told to fill all the fuel tanks. Burton, he tells my boss to hurry fast. I pumped diesel for twenty minutes. The mooring lines were untied before I finished. They left as I pulled the nozzle from the last tank. When the men from Nassau show up. They are plenty mad when they find out the *Nancy Lynn* has left. But Burton is a smart man. He and the lieutenant tell the boss cop from Nassau that it is a jealous wife that is making trouble for the skipper of the *Nancy Lynn*." Edwardo shook his head. "The Nassau people believe that. They are now more mad, but at the person who called them, not the *Nancy Lynn* people. Burton and his police friends tell the Nassau boss cop that the boat men and women are always drunk. He gave the Nassau man one of the plastic cases. They all left laughing."

"Anything else. Do you have any idea where they went? Or who called"

"No and maybe. I don't know anything more about the trouble and I don't have any idea of where they went except the boat turned north when it got to sea. There was a woman who called from the States and a man called Dick."

I muttered, "Shit," under my breath. Melanie and Riaffort.

"One other thing," Edwardo added, "I heard Burton Dahl tell the Hall man he would send another boat with anything they didn't get aboard. He said, 'to where you stayed coming down.' I don't know what that meant. I do know that they quickly loaded one of Dahl's boats with cartons of stuff that was to go on the *Nancy*

Lynn. Some of it had hazardous material warnings on them."

"Do you have any idea of what was in them?"

"I think explosives. C4 maybe."

I said, "Shit!" this time not under my breath.

"That is all I can tell you about the *Nancy Lynn*, but I have to tell you about what happened this morning. Anita is at the airport a lot. She heard one of Burton's men tell the woman who runs the car rental stand, that if a man named Harrell comes in, to call the police. They want to hold him. I think you should go fast. Do not trust the local government folks. Burton Dahl pays them. I will get Anita to drive you back."

As we climbed into Anita's Toot-toot, Dennia said, "The next time you try to warn me about something, I'll pay a lot closer attention."

~ ~ ~ ~ ~ ~

Anita dropped us at the Cessna's side, wished us a good flight, and implored us, "Please don't tell anyone you spoke to Edwardo." Her words were underlined as we taxied down the runway and our plane's wheels left the ground. The sound of sirens drew our attention to two police cars arriving at the airstrip. Dennia banked the plane hard to the north, opened the throttle, and left Inagua behind us. Whether they were looking for us, we'll never know.

# # # # #

Chapter 58

"You want to see if we can find them?" Dennia looked at the ocean below and a white trawler cruising the waters in front of us. "I can fly a zig-zag pattern over any course you think they might take."

I thought for a few seconds, it was a good idea but what course? "That's fine. They came south bordering the east side of the Exumas. I think, assuming they'd return north the same way, is a good bet. Edwardo's saying that Burton promising to deliver goods where they stopped on the way down confirms that."

Dennia looked at a chart she held on her lap. "Where should we start looking?"

"Let me think for a few seconds." I guessed they left Matthew Town mid-afternoon the previous day. The dashboard clock registered one forty-five. That was over twenty hours. Would they have traveled at night? Was Springer at the helm or someone else? There were all types of questions, none with answers. It would be an educated guess. The cruising speed of the *Nancy Lynn* was 28 mph. In twenty hours, she could be completely north of Abaco and out of the Bahamas completely. I guessed they would keep an experienced captain like Springer at the wheel as long as they could force him. Springer would do it. Staying alive and hoping for rescue was his only chance. Among the charts he'd given me, the one for Acklin Island on which he'd mentioned there was an excellent anchorage that had easy entrance and exit. It was one that he could have reached before dark the previous evening. Guessing he'd be there ten hours, leave near seven AM, that would put the *Nancy Lynn* near Georgetown on Great Exuma where we had to refuel.

"Well?" Dennia prompted.

"I figure they at least have made it to the Exumas. Let's fly straight to there, take on fuel then fly your zig-zag up the spine of the Exuma chain. They could go up either side."

~ ~ ~ ~ ~ ~

"I don't have my binoculars. Darn it!" Dennia snorted. "I took them aboard the *Gato Gordo* so I could use them there."

We looked at a grouping of three boats anchored near a cay seventy miles north of Great Exuma. One of them was painted a blue-gray color that could be the *Nancy Lynn's* new hue. A strange irregular mottled cover was spread over the entire top of the boat. An open fishing boat and a vessel slightly larger than its neighbor were anchored along-side. They flanked the blue-gray suspect. I guessed the large boat was an inter-island freighter based on size and configuration. The small island had no signs of habitation, nor did its neighbors up and down the chain. It was a perfect rendezvous location.

I asked, “How far away are we?”

“A little less than a half-mile.” Dennia banked the plane toward the cluster. “You want me to fly over them?”

“Not directly over them, but close.”

She nodded and turned the nose to a course that would almost do a flyover. “I’m at 4,000 feet. I’m going to cut that in half if it’s okay.”

“Go ahead.”

The Cessna dropped quickly, and we sped toward the boats. I asked, “Do you see any activity? I don’t see anyone on the boats or the beach.”

“None.”

As we neared, the covering on the boat became identifiable. “Damn, that’s camouflage netting.” It effectively made what was under it impossible to positively identify.

However, the outline and what I could see strongly suggested we were looking at the *Nancy Lynn*. We zoomed past.

“Do you want to make another pass?”

I hesitated. Was the possibility of observing some bit of valuable information worth raising suspicions on the boats below? “Let’s do it. Go down the opposite side.”

Dennia made a wide loop with the Cessna. When she completed her 180, we flew a straight line that would take us over the line of islands and within a hundred yards of the boats. There were no structures on any of the islands as far as we could see in either direction. The spot was in complete isolation.

As we neared, two men appeared on the deck of the freighter. They pointed at us. One went into the cabin and reappeared with a gun of some variety. He kept it trained on us as we passed by. That fact we weren't welcome was all we learned. The camouflage net did its job.

"What now? We can make another pass...if you want." Obvious doubt clouded Dennia's words.

"No. Take her back to Marsh Harbor. My best guess is we found the *Nancy Lynn*. Those bastards that have her know we've seen her. By the time anyone gets here to prove it, all will be long gone."

~ ~ ~ ~ ~ ~

Sun rays were close to horizontal when Dennia lightly touched the Cessna's tires on the Marsh Harbor runway. Neither Trotter, nor the rental car, were where we had agreed to meet. Something was wrong. What was familiar was Ollie and his cab. His taxi was parked at the place where the car was supposed to be. Ollie leaned against the vehicle, his ever-present smile in place. Dennia eased the aircraft into it's reserved parking spot and we opened the doors to get out. As we did, Ollie trotted toward us, waving as he came.

"Welcome, friends. As you see, I am here for you. I will explain. Do you have any guns with you or on the plane?"

I answered, "No."

"That is good. I will tell you as we go. There have been big things happening at the *Sleepy Dolphin* this afternoon. Trotter wanted to stay at the boat to watch. The police have been visitors. They are waiting for you as we speak."

My head swiveled. Halfway around I saw a police cruiser parked at the edge of the exit road. We'd have company on the road home.

~ ~ ~ ~ ~ ~

"The Coloton's say you are good people. Sallar, who I know well, says you are good people. My fellow officer, Sergeant Wilkerson, at Andros, tells me he knows you and believes you good. That is enough for me. But you must remember I have my responsibilities. Sometimes good people break the law and are not aware of it. I know that you were not directly involved with the circus in Matthew Town. You see I have a boss in Nassau. As you American's say, he stuck his neck out. Way out. When he sent a squad to investigate a kidnapping and found out what created his actions was a jealous wife...well, he is very, very angry. And...embarrassed. He is not happy with the woman. He is not happy with her lawyer. When the only thing the local authorities found as an infraction of

Bahamian law was an unpermitted gun that belongs to you...I think you can understand.

He is not happy with you. I need to search the *Gato Gordo*." Captain Anton Caprees of the Royal Bahamian Police seemed an eminently reasonable and intelligent individual. The man had a warm smile and steel in his eyes.

I looked at Trotter. His faint grin told me he'd done what I asked. I nodded to the Captain and said, "No problem. Before you start, I can tell you that we have weapons on board. Guns. We also have current Bahamian permits for them. You've met Mr. Bass, he has the permits in his possession. Everyone calls him Trotter." I looked at him. "Would you get the permits for Captain Caprees?"

"I can bring the guns back, too." Trotter was already walking.

"No, you can tell him where to find them. I believe he'd be more comfortable if his men found them."

The Captain smiled and tilted his head. "Good. You have made a good faith effort to obey our laws. You are cooperative. We do not wish to be intrusive."

"Form number 17 or something like that," Trotter answered.

"Very good. If you show me the permits and tell me those are the guns you have, I am alright with that." The looked back and forth at Dennia and me. "I must ask a few questions. Informally, of course."

"Certainly," I responded.

"I understand you flew to Inagua today. Is that correct?"

I answered, "Yes."

"Are you the pilot?"

"No, I am," Dennia answered.

"And the plane belongs to you?"

"Yes. It's a Cessna with—" Dennia was interrupted by Caprees.

"That is not necessary. We know which is your plane. I would ask you if we may search your plane, Mrs. Hays. Not now. Only if it should become necessary. You are Dennia Hays, correct?"

"I don't object, as long as...if you break it, you fix it."

The Captain laughed, "I can see you are a woman with starch!" He turned to me. "May I ask why you made the trip today?"

"Sure," I said and nodded. I paused to organize my thoughts. How I answered his question was important. The creditability I established, good or bad, would be critical in how we were viewed and treated. More important, it would determine if we could expect any help from the authorities if the *Nancy Lynn* had been converted from a pleasure cruiser to a terror ship. "In part, because I was trying to determine the degree of truth in the woman's concerns who called your boss in Nassau. Is that how I became associated with this? Her phone call?"

"*In part*, yes. The woman and lawyer both said you were in the islands both on vacation and to investigate." The Captain's smile faded, and a serious caste replaced it. He leaned toward me. "The discovery of your automatic on the boat made the connection more serious. Would you explain how the man," he removed a little notebook from his shirt pocket and read, "Captain Adrian Springer came to possess the 9mm?"

"It's very simple. I loaned him the gun roughly a month ago. Springer didn't have a firearm. He was concerned about some of the places he was to visit."

"These were?"

"Matthew Town specifically."

"How did you come to loan the gun to him? Is he a close friend?" The Captain was good.

"I knew him well enough to be confident he wouldn't miss use it." I decided to direct the conversation. "Captain Springer is an employee of a friend, a friend of the lawyer who called, and he is also my friend. The lawyer is also my lawyer. I've been on a sail with Springer. His character and judgment are excellent." I paused then finished, "That's why

I was comfortable loaning the gun to him. I didn't foresee his neglecting to get a permit."

The Captain smiled and nodded. "May we return to the reason you flew to Inagua today?"

"Okay, what would you like to know?" I wanted to answer specific questions, not a general one.

Caprees stared at me. He knew exactly what I was doing. I thought I might have made a mistake. He phrased his question carefully and asked it slowly. "Why did you choose to visit Inagua today, and what did you do when you were there?"

"I have been receiving communications from Captain Springer. He is not the husband of the woman who called your boss. He works for her. The woman would be Melanie Hellmann." I saw the recognition in Caprees eyes. "The *Nancy Lynn* belongs to her. She loaned it to her daughter for a dive trip. But there is a lot of doubt that this is what the boat is being used for. Captain Springer has concerns about that and the individuals on board. The reason for the messages are those concerns. His last note indicated things were bad. Our trip there was to give him the option of returning to Abaco with us."

Some of the skepticism that invaded his features when I mentioned Melanie's name faded. "And...did you meet with them today?"

"I'm quite sure you know I didn't. The *Nancy Lynn* left yesterday evening. I believe that it was before your officers from Nassau arrived."

The Captain nodded but didn't smile. "You did what when you arrived there?"

"We intended to meet with Captain Springer, but a friend informed us about the incident the previous day. He told me about the misinformation a man named Dahl and your local constables passed on to the officers from Nassau. We were advised the Burton Dahl man was a dangerous person. We left and returned within an hour."

Caprees nodded. "A vile man, but a very clever one. He is harder to catch than a crab in the rocks." He seemed to be easing closer to believing me. The Captain scratched his cheek. I interpreted it as his decision process being in the balance. He might be precisely the ally we'd need if... Caprees asked, "What concerned your friend, Springer, so much, you decided to go to his rescue? Had Burton Dahl tried to use the boat for smuggling?" Caprees interest was peaking.

"Not smuggling. Springer believed that the boat was being prepared to use in some sort of terrorist plan, shooting an airliner down, maybe firing a missile at a city." To my disappointment, instead of elevating his desire to learn more, I could see the switch turn off in his eyes.

"Ha. Your captain might make me believe Burton Dahl would use the boat to smuggle something, maybe drugs, maybe agents, you name it. He does that...both in and out of Cuba and the States. He is a swine. But he is also too smart to involve himself in something like that. Dahl knows we'd find a way to crush him." Captain Caprees smiled and stood. As he readied himself to leave, he said, "I think your friend, Springer, pulls your leg, correct? We don't do terrorism in the Bahamas. Have a good time for the rest of your stay."

# # # # #

Chapter 59

"I didn't intend for any of this to happen, but our beach and fishing excursion has turned into an international mess I've unintentionally committed myself to preventing." I looked at my friends who were gathered around the table in the salon. With the exception of Trotter, these were friends, not operatives. Not in the reality we faced. "My blundering...agreeing to place my nose in a situation my intuition told me it had no place, has put you all in the position where what was supposed to be a holiday for you is now anything but." I paused and tried to read the expressions on my friends' faces. They seemed amused more than concerned. "About all I can do is apologize. I thought I could simply call the authorities down here to extricate myself. That isn't happening...you all saw that."

"I don't know what you have to apologize for? Russ and I are having a great time,"

Val offered. Russ nodded his agreement.

Lily laughed. "I think it's exciting and I just got here. What's the problem? This is paradise and we get to laze around while you sweat. No one is sailing up in a galleon and threatening us with walking the plank. Stop worrying."

"Problem is," I hesitated for a couple seconds trying to figure out a way to ask for help that might endanger them, "I have a lot to do and not enough time to do it. I need help. That means I'm going to ask you. Say no...please! You shouldn't be involved. I don't have an alternative. If I do..." No other circumstance seemed reasonable. "We're on our own."

Russ slapped his hand on the table. "I'm in. I know what you're trying to do. Well, sort of. Let's go for it."

Val chuckled, "Husband, you sound like a game show host." She placed her hand on top of Russ.'

"I go where you go and I do what you do, that's whether your boss or not," Trotter said.

"I'm with him," Lily cooed as she and Trotter placed their hands on the pile.

Dennia said nothing. She put her hand on top to make it unanimous.

~ ~ ~ ~ ~ ~

"That's it. We have this evening, Wednesday, and Thursday, to stop whatever is planned to happen on Friday. We don't know what that is, but I believe it is big...and bad. Right now, we know where, but not the exact time. We know two people's lives, Diane and

Hall, are probably in danger and they don't have a clue. We know Captain Springer and

Margo's chances of staying alive are as bad or worse. Here's the help I need." I looked at Russ and said, "I need to get some kind of clue to what's planned by our terrorist friends. Russ can you find out about what Galang Marcos and Harold Runnells have been doing on the Internet. If you can get into what TV programs they've watched, movies...anything that might help me connect the dots."

"I can do that. I'll see if I can get in phone records, too."

"Val, I'd like you to do two things for me to be sure we contact the real Diane and Hall Runnells. First, see if you can find a way to contact them directly. I'll write a note that explains what they could be walking into. Second, I'll give you my old boss's email address at Justice. Send the note to him and tell him those two will likely end up dead if somebody doesn't stop them from going to Vera Cruz and crawling into coffins. If you don't get him, his assistant will get it done. Her name is Mary Ann. She'd probably be given the job anyway."

Val nodded. "It's only a little after eight. Come on Russ, let's go up to the computer room and get started." They left the cabin, laptops in hand.

Lily volunteered, "I do a lot of commercial flying. I'll take my computer and use the *Sleepy Dolphin's* wifi to get on the net just like the Foxxes do. I can pull up all the airline schedules for that Friday and record them. When I finish that, I'll stick around to see if I can help Val and Russ." She went to her cabin to retrieve her computer.

"That leaves you and me," Dennia blew me a kiss. "Let's get started on?"

"Looking through my notes and the flash drives Russ made to see if we can find something I've missed. Hopefully, that will tell us what they're planning."

She nodded. "While you pull everything together, I'll make coffee. It's going to be a long night."

# # # # #

Chapter 60

Glum. That's the way I have to describe the beginning of our Wednesday, April the 24th. All worked deep into the night. All found little or nothing in their feverish searches. Heads drooped while most sat around the salon table. In the galley, Dennia and Lily put finishing touches on breakfast. Smells from sizzling sausage and frying eggs went unnoticed. The few words we exchanged centered on what we hadn't accomplished.

"It's like sitting in front of the TV with a DVD player recycling the same movie over and over," Russ said. He took a sip of reheated yesterday's coffee, winced, and added, "You think you found something different, but it always turns out the same."

Val frowned. "My experience trying to reach Diane Runnells taught me something. If I ever became a powerful politician or a celebrity, which I won't, I'm going to be sure there is always some way to contact me. Someone may want to save my life. Surrounding yourself with systems and people that are programmed to blow-off everyone who wants to get information to you, sucks."

Trotter just shook his head.

"I know it's there. It's staring at me and I can't see it," I took another sip of coffee, the last in the cup. It came with a sprinkling of grounds...that usually comes with the final serving from the pot. "Yuck!" I put my cup down and shuddered. "That was bad."

"My problem is I'm running out of places to look." Russ leaned back into the soft cushions of the settee. "Social media accounts, telephone records, credit card transactions...nothing. I got into Galang's computer. There isn't anything that we don't know about. Oh, I found a few references to 'project SL,' whatever that might be. I never found anything to identify it." He shook his head. "Same with Harold. I haven't broken his security, so I haven't gotten to his correspondence and that kind of thing. That's my starting point for today."

I asked, "Val, have you tried to get a message to my old boss?"

"Not yet. That will be the first thing I do today."

"If he wants to talk to me about it, get a number where I can get straight through. In fact, tell him I'd like to talk to him about the whole thing. He'll think something is weird if I don't. If you can't get him, ask to speak to Mary Ann. She's his assistant. Tell her the same thing. She'll know how to reach him."

Val nodded as she wrote.

"What do you want me to do? I'll feel useless if you can't find me something," Trotter look liked a wild animal on its first day in a cage.

I thought for a few seconds. Several items came to mind immediately. "Okay, we're going to have to be ready for anything. Make sure the guns are all in the best condition they can be."

Trotter interjected, "They are."

"Good. Get with Sallar. Find out what he thinks of Captain Caprees. See if we can change his mind about this being a jealous woman's stunt to get vengeance on her husband. See if Riaffort can get a hold of one of his friends in law enforcement to call Caprees and attest to what we told him. If he does...tell him it will help tremendously. So, you contact Riaffort and get things started. Also, ask Sallar to sort through all the nautical chats and select the ones we're likely to need. And while you're doing that, feel him out about accompanying us if we have to pursue the *Nancy Lynn*. Find out if there is a price."

Trotter nodded. "Anything else?"

"Just get the fuel topped, triple check the radar, make sure we have extra life jackets on board. Anything you can think of to make this fishing boat more like a destroyer, go ahead and do it."

"It will get done. How about Shepard and Mimi? What are they going to think about you taking their source of income for a possible one-way voyage?"

"I'll talk to them."

Dennia and Lily entered the cabin carrying our breakfasts on trays. They placed them in front of us. Lily sat down while Dennia returned for a fresh pot of coffee. Lily said, "I heard you talking. I have news. Good, I guess. I made a list of every commercial flight and dedicated resort flight for that Friday. If they are out there to bring down an airliner, you have the complete schedules. Most of the flights are small commuters. I wondered why those kooks on the *Nancy Lynn* would be interested in such small potatoes. I'd think a terrorist would be looking for 747, something like that. But I did have one idea. What if someone important was on one of those planes? Passenger lists? Can one of you do that?" "Yes," Val said. "I'll show you how to get into the files and you can copy them."

"Coffee?" Dennia closed our conversation.

~ ~ ~ ~ ~ ~

"I'm truly sorry," I could tell from the sound in Riaffort's voice he was. "I did not call her, she called me. When she received Springer's last message, she went bonkers. She said she intended to call the authorities in Nassau. I thought I could persuade her *not* to call if I shared some of what you told me. I'm afraid that set her off worse."

The fact that I was in the *Sleepy Dolphin's* office, speaking on their phone, tempered the anger in my voice and my vocabulary. It was strong, none-the-less. "You thought wrong. I won't waste time on details. I'll cover them the next time I'm close enough to get my hands on your neck. And...do not tell me that you didn't call down here too."

"I thought I could walk back some of the damage she did. Evidently, I wasn't successful." Riaffort sounded contrite.

"That's the world's biggest understatement. Thanks to whatever you said, and some skillful maneuvering by some of their local allies in Matthew Town, the Bahamian authorities, including the el chafe, think this is a plot hatched by a jealous wife to get back at her husband. They don't believe a damned thing I tell them. The end game is: I can't expect one shred of help from the government officials in forty-eight hours when the shit hits the fan. I'm stuck choosing between sitting back and allowing some kind of disaster that will destroy Springer and probably Margo or...or jumping into something, I'm not sure what, and play-acting I'm a cavalry troop from a John Wayne movie."

"What can I do?"

"You can get on the phone and contact your friends in both governments, ours and theirs, convince them the sky is falling, and get me help on Friday. Get on the phone with Melanie and make sure she makes NO more calls down here. Tell her she's paying my bills...and if anything happens to my people—"

Riaffort finished more charitably than I would have, "You'll come hunting her."

~ ~ ~ ~ ~ ~

Lunch came quickly. Progress came slowly. Val was unable to personally contact either Diane or Hall. Both were in the air and their phones shut down intentionally or by poor transmission. Val decided against leaving messages for the couple at the hotel for the management there was obviously part of the plot. She did get through to my old boss' office, talked to Mary Ann, who assured Val she'd get messages to the two potential murder victims through the airlines. I crossed my fingers.

Russ managed to find how to peek into Harold's computer right before lunch. It would be late afternoon before we got what we could from his files.

Sallar stopped by with more bad news. His cousin Edwardo had been questioned and had to reluctantly confirm that Dennia and I had made the trip to Inagua. Sallar said both Edwardo and his girlfriend were frightened, but to that time, nothing more had happened to them. They implored Sallar to tell us to be careful. The police Captain, there, and

Burton Dahl knew all about us and had a concern. The concern: we were living.

I thought things couldn't get worse, then night closed over the *El Gato Gordo*.

# # # # #

Chapter 61

We stood around the transom of the *Gato Gordo* and watched. It was only the third night since Lily arrived, but she'd already established a dinner stop for the freeloading sharks. She dumped scraps from our meals in at sunset and watched the swirling competition for tidbits the first night she was there. Since her activities were confined to the boat she fished for and caught all types from the menagerie living around the docks. Lily added them to the evening buffet. By Wednesday evening her dinner quests grew from three to eight...including three large bull sharks. This evening she had twenty plus angelfish, tang, and other species on the menu.

Our late supper made for low light conditions...the sun was completely below the horizon. The savage crew vied for each entre. Free lunches kept the eating machines in the area. We all agreed, it was not a place for a night swim, or in the day for that matter. Anything thrown in the water was likely to be engulfed in a toothy grin by a previously unseen shark. Lily rinsed the bucket and poured the water overboard. It elicited blind charges from the gray ghosts circling the pier and boat. It was a curtain call for the actors in an ironic comic distraction.

The shark feeding ended our 'break' for supper. The Foxxes, Lily, and Trotter returned to the Sleepy Dolphin computer room and Dennia and I settled back into our chairs behind my laptop and files in the salon. I continued to go back through the mountain of material that Russ, Val, and Captain Springer had provided. Dennia and I worked separately, hoping we'd find something the other missed. Einstein nagged me. We were repeating the same thing over and over and expected a different result. I could hear the old boy laughing from his grave. What alternative did I have? It would be another long evening.

~ ~ ~ ~ ~ ~

Dennia rose from her chair, put her arms over her head, and arched her back, stretching at the same time. She glanced at the clock on the cabin wall. "Unbelievable! It's almost midnight. I wonder if the Foxxes, Trotter, and Lily know that? I bet they're working away." She walked to the cabin window. "Oh, one of them is coming now."

I continued to work with my head down, paying little attention to her until she said, "Sly, I don't think it's one of our crew. Whoever it is, appears to be sneaking around, going from one hiding spot to another."

That got my attention. "Sneaking? Why do you say that?"

"When I first saw him, he was up close to the office and he was walking upright. As he got closer to the dock, he's hunched over and stops behind a tree or anything convenient to hide behind."

That got me out of my chair and next to her. We both peered through the window. The person was partially hidden behind a coconut palm. From the partial silhouette visible on either side of the tree trunk, the man was large, Trotter's size or bigger. I guessed 6'6" and 250 pounds. He'd stopped at a tree that was only feet from the beginning of the pier. We watched and waited for what seemed an eternity.

Dennia asked, "He's waiting for something, but what?"

"Our standing at the window with the cabin light on means he can see us. If his intent has anything to do with us, he won't move until we move away from the window and the light goes off. Let's leave the window, turn off the lights, then sneak back and see what happens." We walked away.

When we returned a few minutes later, the man became more visible, the lights from the *Sleepy Dolphin's* office illumination being more effective without backlighting.

Dennia saw his first move. "He's getting down on his knees."

Soon he was stretched out on the ground and he belly-crawled to the pier. There were two boats tied to the dock, the *El Gato Gordo* being the only one occupied. If his purpose was not good, we had to be the target. I told Dennia, "I'm going to get my automatic. It's in Trotter's cabin. Keep watch on the bastard."

Even in the pitch-black darkness, it only took a few seconds to get to Trotter's cabin door...and the shock that came with it. The door was locked. I knew why immediately. It was one of the procedures I'd established to be a responsible gun owner. My own rule was about to bite me in the ass. I reached in my pants pocket and removed my cell phone and thanked God the designers had the foresight to backlight the keyboard. I hoped like hell, Trotter had his cell with him. His phone rang once...twice...three times...four...five...I listened for his ringtone, but Dixie wasn't playing...six. He answered, "You need something from up here, Sly?"

"Yes, the key to your cabin. Some man is sneaking onto the pier. I'd prefer not to take him on with a kitchen knife."

"Be right there!" Click.

Grabbing a convenient knife from the holding block in the galley, I returned to

Dennia's side. The man had moved. I asked, "Where is he?"

"He's behind the storage box."

Halfway down the length of the pier, next to the other boat, a large storage box effectively removed him from our sight.

Dennia added, "He crawled on his stomach the whole distance. What do you think he wants?"

"It's not to invite us to a party." Blinking didn't help my vision for the container was large enough to hide him completely from our view. I wondered aloud, "Why doesn't

Trotter turn the pier lights on?"

"Maybe he doesn't want to scare him away."

I put my hand on her neck. "That's really what we want. The last thing we need now is to explain a fight or possibly a corpse to the police."

At that moment, the man rose from his hiding place and began creeping the remaining fifty feet to our boat's transom...the logical place to come aboard unseen. I pushed against Dennia's neck and told her, "Go to our cabin, lock the door, and don't open it for anybody but me or Trotter."

"I don't want to leave you."

"Do it. I'll be worrying about you if I don't know you're safe. That will make me less effective in a fight if I have to get in one."

"I'm gone," she said, hesitated, kissed me, added, "Be careful!" and disappeared into the black.

I returned my concentration to the intruder. He was now parallel to the *Gato Gordo's* bow, still, on his stomach...and he was close enough to see clearly. He had a large Bowie knife clutched in one hand. Light from the moon reflected off of it. I glanced at the kitchen knife I held. It became a children's toy by comparison.

If I had to, where was the best place to take him on? He wouldn't have the element of surprise he expected. But the man was large, physical looking. Not someone I could count on overpowering. The hatch giving access from the front deck was locked. He'd have to come inside the boat from the rear deck, down the stairs to the short passage, then on to the cabins. The knife in his hand made his purpose clear. The best place was just as he reached the passage. I hoped I could launch an effective first blow that would decide the outcome.

I changed my observation position to a porthole that over-looked the rear deck. The man would have to rise to get into the boat. As soon as he rose and stepped on the rear deck, I'd race to the passageway door. My knuckles tighten on the knife, my eyes strained. Perspiration drenched my face and body.

A hand stealthily appeared on one of the gunwales at the rear of the *Gato Gordo's* transom. My legs tensed as they prepared to make the six frantic steps required to reach my intended attack point. A shadow rose as I tensed for his first foot to come aboard. Before I could react, the shadow became a blur over the transom disappearing in the water beyond. Another shadow replaced it on the dock. Trotter!

Loud cursing came from an invisible source for two, maybe three seconds. Then a short piercing scream was followed by a series of splashes. Dinner had been served.

The door to Dennia and my cabin burst open. Her worried voice yelled, "Sly, Sly baby are you okay?"

"I'm fine. It's all over, but the inquest."

# # # # #

Chapter 62

It was as though the intruder never set foot on the *Sleepy Dolphin* property. By the time Trotter and I found flashlights strong enough to do a search, there was nothing to search for. The water wasn't even tinged with red. When Russ ventured back to the boat, he found Dennia, Trotter, and me discussing the last fifteen minutes. How should we handle the event? I had an answer. It never happened.

Val and Lily didn't need to know I explained, at least, not right now. I went through my logic as quickly as I could. No one knew he was on the dock except the people that sent him. That would be the conspirators on the *Nancy Lynn,* probably orchestrated by Burton Dahl. They wouldn't be complaining to authorities that their would-be assassin couldn't be found. If his body was found, there wouldn't be signs of foul play; Trotter had simply shoved him in the water to protect Dennia and I. There'd be no marks or evidence. Besides, it wasn't Trotter's intent to kill him, just foil his plans to kill us. Reporting it to the police would bring further scrutiny to us, scrutiny we didn't need. It would tie us up at the exact time we needed to be free to act. It was apparent there wasn't going to be an option. Though it was the last thing I wanted we would be the cavalry. We all agreed before Lily and Val ventured to the pier to see what was going on.

All of us boarded the boat. Some of us slept. I didn't. Neither did Dennia. Trotter's snoring penetrated his cabin door as did Lily's. I never asked the Foxxes about their evening.

My sleeplessness had three causes. The event pumped adrenalin through my body. That coupled with a pang of conscience. It was misplaced but still there. There was an element of being a watchman...would they try again? Third, the still unsolved parts of the puzzle swirled in my brain. Time was running out.

I hadn't asked Russ, Val, or Lily if they'd made any progress, though I assumed not. The chaos caused by the potential assassin wiped all other considerations from my mind. Sitting in the salon with my 9mm automatic in one hand, afforded me a few snatches of sleep. Each time I woke with a start, certain that the noise of someone slipping aboard had wakened me. My fears were false. Dennia woke me in the morning with a kiss. It started the new day on a favorable foot. I prayed things would continue as they started.

# # # # #

Chapter 63

"Yes. With all the shit going on last night, I didn't tell you," Russ was salvaging the last couple pieces of bacon from Val's plate before Lily returned it to the galley. I'd asked if he'd had luck finding any information. From the width of his smile, I knew he did.

"Good. What?"

"Let's see. I'll tell you the best news first. I hacked into Galang Marcos' computer to see if anything was going on with him. I noticed a file I hadn't seen before. It was where he'd entered many drone and guided vehicle contests. There were a number of entry forms in there. Most had a requirement that the entrant provides the frequency and channel he'd be using to control his unit. He uses three frequencies over, and over, and over, again. I'll give you twenty to one that if he is the one doing the targeting of a plane or whatever, he'll be using one of those three. I have the equipment to screw that up. If we get in position, I should be able to intercept a rocket or a drone."

"That's great! You sounded like you might have additional info. You have something else?" I asked.

Russ nodded. "Yes. How much they mean...you'll have to decide that. Harold was doing a lot of course calculations. For the boat. He was taking into account currents. Speeds from one point to another. The only problem is the speeds seemed high for the *Nancy Lynn* to achieve. He used forty-two knots in his calculations. Isn't that too fast for that boat?"

"Springer told me the top end was 38 mph. That's close enough to consider. Who knows what was done to the boat at Matthew Town." I thought for a second. "What kind of distances?"

"Three to four miles. But the interesting thing was they were from the same point. At least there was a note that said, 'from the same location.' Anyway, I thought that might mean they might have more than one target. Maybe the missiles they have are limited and they need to be close to under the aircraft to guarantee hitting it."

I thought for several seconds. Maybe the reason for the design of the dive subs was they were to function as launch tubes! Those would greatly increase accuracy for units that had to be designed using less than ideal materials. It made sense. "I think you have something there, Russ."

"You have anything else?"

Russ nodded. "You asked about getting ideas from TV programs and movies about what they might be thinking. I got into the movies that Harold downloaded. One-track mind. They were all war movies. A Bridge too Far. Midway. Lawrence of Arabia.

Run Silent, Run Deep. Platoon. Hunt for Red October. Battle of Britain. Thirty-Seconds over

Tokyo. Victory at Sea. Those aren't comedies or romances."

"He's getting himself ready for battle." I thought for several seconds trying to tell if the titles told me anything else about his plans. They didn't, though I thought they should.

"One last thing. He listed information about night navigation aids, lights, and such, in one file. I'd bet whatever he'll do, it will be at night."

That information caused me to jerk my head. The data that Lily had gathered on airline schedules showed all but a few took place during daylight hours. Most occurred in the middle of the day. If that was true, and the airplanes were the targets, it would narrow them to a few flights. If there were few enough, we might be able to avert the disaster by warning the airlines whose routes were left as possibilities. That nagged my sense of logic. Maybe they just wanted to arrive in position early. Shrugging my shoulders, I asked, "Do you have the information on those lights and intervals? If you do, I might be able to match them to the information on one of my charts. We'd know where they are coming from."

"No, but I can go back into his files and capture it."

"Do it. I'll pull the charts out that Springer gave me. We might be able to intercept them before they get to the square they have staked out south of Grand Bahama. That would screw their plans up." I said the words, but my gut screamed, 'those feathers in your hand are from a wild goose.'

~ ~ ~ ~ ~ ~

Trotter reported. Everything was as ready as we could make it for *something we believed would happen* but weren't sure of. Was it aircraft that were the target? I wished I was sure. My doubts out-weighed my belief the targets were airliners. Fuel tanks full?

Check. Extra life-vests on board? Check. Radio okay? Check. Radar working at its best? Check. Guns and ammo ready for action? Double-check.

Time raced by. The uneasy feeling I was missing something important increased geometrically. There was too much planning and commitment of materials for the shooting down of a couple twenty passenger commuter planes. What was I missing? Marcus Aurelius' advice was to reduce things to their simplest denominators. I was looking for something big in the Bahamas. Dennia was seated next to me, reading Captain Springer's telefaxes one more time.

"Dennia let me ask you something. When I say the word Bahamas, what is the first thing you think about that's connected to it?"

Dennia thought for only a second. "I think of taking a cruise on a liner."

I stiffened. That was it! All the clues were there all along. Run Silent, Run Deep, and the Hunt for Red October. The 'dive subs' were torpedoes. The calculations were for torpedo run times. I couldn't believe I hadn't recognized it before. "You're a genius, babe. Where's Lily?" I looked at the clock at the same time I spoke. It was 6:30 and the sun was racing for the horizon.

"She's fishing off the transom."

"Would you get her? I have a job she can do. She's good at working with schedules.

I need her to make a list of all the cruise ship schedules for the next three days."

Dennia's eyes opened wide. "They wouldn't try that."

"Yes...they would. They aren't going to try to kill forty people on two airplanes. They're going to try to kill 10,000 people on two cruise ships."

# # # # #

Chapter 64

"Holy shit!" I stared at the paper Lily handed me not a minute before. The departure and arrival times of the cruise liners slammed the reality of what we faced firmly into my consciousness. I would have to do some calculation, but one thing was clear, the event I foresaw would not be like I'd imagined it. When I envisioned Friday, April 26th, I saw sunlit skies, not darkness with only stars above. It was clear: the schedules indicated the concentration of ships would be in the area where I knew the attacks would occur in the early hours of the day. Very early!

I glanced at Lily. Her face showed she recognized the seriousness. The clock said

7:45. I'd previously calculated the time it would take to get the *El Gato Gordo* to the area

Springer had said he was sure 'something' would happen, 77° longitude by 25° latitude. That was in the sea lanes between Nassau and the Florida coast. I figured two hours and forty minutes of time to reach the area. It would take an hour to leave. I told Lily, "Get your mom, Trotter, and the Foxxes. We have to discuss this right away!"

While I waited for the rest of my crew, I pulled out the chart for the area. Whatever calculation I made would only be an estimate. The speed and course the cruise ship captains chose were within their discretion. Leaving Thursday evening were four ships. Ships leaving from the Port of Miami and Port Everglades appeared they would reach the area sometime between one and three in the morning. The most important thing was they needed to control their time of arrival at Nassau. They were the most likely candidates.

One liner, *The Party Hardy*, was from the Festival Line. The other, *The Golden Mermaid*, was from Regal Britannica Cruises. According to the statistics Lily copied for me, each carried in excess of 5,000 passengers, plus crew. The loss of life could be horrendous. I grabbed a legal pad and scribbled what had to be done. And prayed.

~ ~ ~ ~ ~ ~

"Sallar?" I asked.

Trotter shook his head. "I couldn't get a hold of him...or he avoided talking to me."

I turned to three very disturbed women. "Ladies, you have the most important job of all of us. I know you've tried before, but double up everything you've done. First, try to get through to the cruise line, again. Maybe you'll get someone to listen this time. If the captains know what's happening, they stand a better chance of avoiding it. Call the police, the President of the Bahamas, call the US Coast Guard, the Navy, hell, call the White House. Get somebody to help us. We'll do what we can to delay them or stop them if we have to."

"I'll go, I'm a hell of a good shot." Lily's sense of adventure was stronger than her common sense.

"We'll be fine with three of us," I lied.

The panicked looks on Val and Dennia's faces told me they had no illusions. Trotter, Russ and I were leaving on a fool's errand at best, mission impossible at worst. The clock told me it was time. Half-past nine. We'd make it to the *Nancy Lynn's* hunting ground at midnight at best. I revved the engines and they growled with false bravado. "You girls...off the boat!" I said sternly. The diesels gladly returned to idle.

They complied. Dennia stood starring at me. Lights from the cabin reflected from the moisture under her eyes. She shouted, "Damn it, Sly, take care of your ass! I don't want to lose you!" Anger and fear shared equal parts in her voice. Trotter gave Lily a parting kiss and she joined Val and Dennia on the dock. It became quiet, tension robbing us all, of our voices.

Trotter and Russ untied the last mooring lines as I climbed into the flying bridge.

I nodded and they tossed the lines up on the dock. I eased the throttle forward and the *El*

Gato Gordo slowly got underway.

"Wait! Wait!"

The voice was familiar. Sallar sprinted down the pier and leaped onto the boat's rear deck. He crashed into the cabin and fell to its flooring. "I am going," he said as he looked up. Relief spread through me. Having a more experienced boatman aboard was a relief. It also meant an extra trigger finger. He climbed the steps to the flying bridge, "I'll take it until we are in deep water...if you want."

I slid over, giving him the wheel. We slowly went from channel marker to channel marker.

Lights and vehicles clustered around a dock a couple of hundred yards away. Sallar pointed, and said, "There, it looks like they're recovering a body." He stared at the group.

"Or what's left of it. They're taking it out of the water in pieces."

The ambulance lights blinked, accusing me of a dastardly deed. "Looks that way."

~ ~ ~ ~ ~ ~

"I didn't figure out what their targets were until late this afternoon." I related my plan to Sallar as the *Gato Gordo* strained to maintain 26 mph as it headed south to the end of Abaco Island. "The group on the *Nancy Lynn* are sure-enough terrorists, Sallar. The real thing. Remember me telling you they had dive subs made?"

"Yes."

"Actually, they are torpedoes. Their plot is to sink cruise liners. Two if they can."

"Holy Mother!"

"Dennia, Val, and Lily are trying to get us help. We have to hope they're successful.

If they aren't, it is up to us to stop this thing."

"How do you intend to do that?"

"We believe they intend guiding the torpedoes with a radio signal. Russ believes he can interrupt it and misdirect the torpedoes. He says he has several tricks he can use. Russ is a genius with electronics. We're going to try to stay between the *Nancy Lynn* and liners.

It gives us the best chance to intercept."

"What if their genius is better than our genius?"

"Hope you can turn the *Gato Gordo* faster than the torpedoes can maneuver and who is guiding them can react."

"If they are terrorists, they will have guns. If they shoot at—"

"We shoot back." I patted Sallar on the shoulder...and sincerely hoped that there were no .50 caliber machine guns on the *Nancy Lynn* like the ones we'd seen at the manufacturing plant in Melbourne.

# # # # #

Chapter 65

According to the GPS and Loran readings, the *El Gato Gordo* had arrived at the north edge of the tract where we expected the attack to take place. Dull lights illuminated the instruments on the dash in front of Sallar and I. Russ sat next to us with his electric control units. He scanned for frequencies he expected our adversaries to use. Trotter sat on the front deck. The two AR-15s were at his side. His MAC 10 rested on his lap. We were as ready as we could be.

The boat moved forward slowly; we were running at ten knots, zig-zagging to cover as much ocean as we could. I had guessed at what ground zero would be. The point chosen was my best guess at where the two liners would be close together as they turned to make their approach to Nassau. I needed...pure luck.

I had Sallar turn off all lights except those illuminating the instruments. We wanted to be as invisible to them as they hoped they would be to the liners. Sallar had his eyes glued to the radar screen.

“What’s the range on the radar?” I asked.

“The mast is eleven feet high. That should give us a radius of eight miles. The boat is fiberglass so that will cut the distance some. I’d guess five miles.”

I didn't say anything about the paint job that was supposed to reduce that farther.

I asked Russ, "How far away can you pick up the radio signals you're looking for?"

"I'm guessing seven miles. You normally get five or so, but you can soup them up

40%. Mine's real powerful. I've had my drone out nine-plus miles. When he turns it on, I'll know. I should be able to get a faint signal at twelve. He'll be on one of the channels on the 2.4 GHz bandwidth. It gives the most range. He'll use one of the two channels. I'll own him."

Russ might have spoken in Latin for some of his explanations. I'd have understood as much. But, if he was correct...the part I understood...according to what I'd calculated, we'd be able to locate the *Nancy Lynn*...if I guessed right.

After a glance at the empty radar screen, I peered into the darkness. The soft breeze barely wrinkled the Atlantic with gentle wavelets. A sliver moon provided a minimum of ambient light. For one not long accustomed to life at sea, nighttime is foreboding. My senses told me of every splash, every creak of the boat, of Sallar's breath. Keen apprehension and tension did that to me. I wasn't a stranger to it...my time at the DOJ placed me in similar circumstances many times. That didn't make it less odious. I checked the instruments. Nothing on radar. The clock display said time was closing. It was 12.25.

"Russ?" I asked.

"Nothing."

The hopeless feeling I had, came from being unable to do anything but wait. Where would the *Nancy Lynn* come from? Probably from the east or south. The *Gato Gordo* needed the advantage of position since the boat was not as fast. How to get that? Both of the targets would approach from the west. I decided to head toward the cruise liners along the course I expected them to take. When we spotted one, we'd reverse course and take the point for our big brothers. I gave Sallar the order.

~ ~ ~ ~ ~ ~

"One of the cruise ships!" Sallar pointed to the radar. "What do you want me to do?"

"Just wait for him to get closer. When he gets within two miles we want to stay ahead at the same speed and on the same course he is."

Sallar adjusted our position as we 'treaded water.' Within minutes the ship's lights became visible.

"It's five minutes after one," Sallar observed.

The climax was hurtling toward us. Or was it?

# # # # #

Chapter 66

I looked at the radar. Nothing but the liner. I nudged Russ with my elbow. He shook his head. We had been on the liner's course for forty-five minutes. The only change was the boat's slowing to time its arrival in Nassau. The first half-hour, tension rose. When I didn't believe it could go higher, it did. Any noise, any imagined movement in the sea around us tightened the bands around our throats. Our eyes strained. It became hard to swallow and our mouths dried.

Then it reached its peak. No sign of the would-be attackers...that planted a seed in our collective minds. Maybe, just maybe, they had given up on their plan. Could the visit from the authorities at Matthew Town have discouraged them? Did the failure of their assassin make them believe we might be able to stop them? Were they worried we had convinced either Bahamian or American government agencies the threat was real and would guard against it? Or...had they just lost their nerve?

"We have company." Sallar's eyes were focused on the radar screen. "Big company." The second cruise ship was catching up with its brethren and us. I turned toward the transom and looked past the stern. Lights from the liner were clearly visible and closing fast.

"Russ, you have anything?" I asked.

"Not a thing."

Were they out there? We would have to chug along and wait for what we hoped wouldn't happen.

~ ~ ~ ~ ~ ~

The only thing worse is when you're in the same situation, alone. Night's black curtain obscures your surroundings. The knowledge that something may be lurking behind that curtain to hurt you...destroy you...changes possibilities to certainties in your mind. It can be in the woods or a city street. It definitely is there on the ocean. The fear of the unknown. I had my friends to lessen it, and I gave thanks for their presence.

The second liner had reduced the distance between the two cruise ships to seven miles. Four miles astern and five miles south. It had slowed its speed to the point it nearly traveled at the same rate we were and changed course to one that paralleled us. The distance to the south is what presented the problem. If the *Nancy Lynn* was going to attack both ships, we weren't in the right position to stop her. I remembered Russ' discovering calculations Galang made from a central point in opposite directions. That was it! They would lie in wait in the gap between the two ship's courses. When it was at its minimum, they would launch an attack on one ship, rotate 180°, and launch their remaining torpedoes at the other.

"Sallar, we need to be on a line between the two liners and be as close to the middle of it as we can be. That's where we'll find the *Nancy Lynn*."

It was 2:16.

~ ~ ~ ~ ~ ~

"I got something!" Russ yelled.

"Anything on the radar?" I asked Sallar.

"No...I don't think so...see that smudge...it is probably a patch of fog...but..." He wasn't sure what was on the screen.

"It's gone. He was just testing his gear," Russ told us.

I looked at the 'smudge' on the radar screen. It didn't move. However, the two cruise ships were almost abreast of each other. If I was correct, hell would break loose in minutes. As we watched the 'smudge' became a sharper image. We needed to be sure. I asked Russ, "Can you track the radio signal back to the boat?"

"I have my direction finder on. If he sends another signal, I'll get a line right to him."

The radar screen confirmed the presence of a boat of the correct size to be the *Nancy Lynn*. Its skipper positioned the boat a third closer to the liner that was farther south. It made sense and confirmed my thinking. He'd spin around the 180° and shoot at the closer liner last, giving it no time to react if the explosions of the torpedoes fired first alerted its captain. Good. We wanted to approach from his stern, the portion of the boat I supposed would be the lightest defended. That would give us the opportunity. The biggest question I had: Was the crew on the *Nancy Lynn* tracking us and did they have a plan to deal with our presence? It was time to act.

"Okay, Sallar head right at him at full speed. Russ, when they launch the first torpedoes, let them run for seventy-five seconds, then gain control of them. They'll be firing the second volley in the opposite direction. You ready for that?" Russ didn't answer. The lights from the instruments barely produced enough light to see exhilaration and fear in his features.

"Russ, you got this?" My words were too sharp.

"Yes, stay the fuck quiet. I'm concentrating. Hold this second control unit; give it to me as soon as I ask for it." He shoved it into my hands.

Scraping noises and the familiar sound of a magazine being inserted into an assault rifle drew my attention to the bow. Trotter was lying on the deck, an AR-15 pointed forward. He was ready.

I glanced at the radar screen. The sharp image of a boat was in front of us and we were approaching it. Fast! I told Russ, "Forget the direction finder. We know right where the *Nancy Lynn* is!"

Each second lengthened geometrically. The radar screen silently screamed. Each second the distance became less and less. Fear that we'd get too close tugged at my elbow. I was about to tell Sallar to cut our speed when......

"I got a signal! They've launched two." Russ began making all types of adjustments before flipping the switch to try to 'steal' the torpedoes and send them to nowhere. "Here goes," he said.

"The boat's doing the one-eighty," Sallar yelled.

I glanced at the radar screen. The *Nancy Lynn* was in the final forty-five degrees of its turn. We'd closed within a half-mile of its position. I asked Russ, "Where are the torpedoes?"

"Coming right next to our boat."

"Have you got control of them?"

"No! Not yet. I'm...I'm...Shit...I'm...I've got them!" Russ screamed, "Yeehaw! Those puppies are on my leash." He handed me the first control. "Point the unit out to sea. Anywhere but at the liners." He watched the second control. "He's using the other channel he usually does." After another few seconds, Russ said, "They just launched the second group. This isn't going to be as easy."

The radar showed us to be three hundred yards away. The other option to alter the torpedoes course was to take out the person controlling them. I yelled to Trotter, "I'm going to turn the spotlight on the *Nancy Lynn's* bridge. Marco will be up high with his controller. He'll be next to whoever is at the wheel. As soon as I find them with the light, put half a clip into him and the rest into the helmsman."

"Gotcha," he answered.

"You got control of the second group, Russ?"

"No. Even if I'm able to get control, it will be close."

That shattering sound of two explosions harmlessly detonated miles away. The first torpedoes were history.

Russ screamed, "We're passing control back and forth. I don't know..."

We were inside of two hundred yards. Aiming the spotlight at where radar said the *Nancy Lynn* was, I yelled to Trotter, "Be ready. I'm turning on the light in three...two...one."

The spotlight's margin caught the gray form of the cruiser. A split-second adjustment of the light illuminated the *Nancy Lynn*. Its captain was in the process of beginning to spin the boat around to face us. It provided a beautiful shot at Galang. Trotter put at least six of his eight shots into the man. The person in the captain's chair took cover denying Trotter a second target.

"The radio signal is dead!" Russ screamed.

"Can you—"

"I'm trying!"

"Dat-dat-dat-dat-dat-dat-dat..." The firing of a heavy machine gun erased any thought of torpedoes. A Browning .50 caliber was spewing fire in our direction. The only thing that saved us was the fact it was mounted on the front deck and it couldn't be trained on our boat. Within a few seconds, the bow would put the gun in a position to shred us. We'd kept the cruise liners from being sunk...at least one of them...but chances are we'd die doing it. I saw a woman feverishly working on one of the two remaining torpedoes. We had one chance.

"Sallar. Try to stay behind the transom of the boat as long as possible. I'm going to help Trotter." He nodded at me. I raced down the steps from the bridge, circled the cabin, snatched up an AR, and took a kneeling firing position next to Trotter.

Trotter shifted his fire from the helmsman on the flying bridge to the machine gunner, but the cabin that provided protection to us also provided cover for him.

I had no interest in either man. The shiny steel tubes were my target. I fired my first shot. The *Nancy Lynn* was winning the maneuvering contest. Machine gun bullets got closer and closer. Within seconds, they wouldn't whiz past. They would rip through the *El Gato Gordo* and us.

I fired at the nose of the torpedo rapidly. The woman disappeared after my first shot.

One...two...three...four... I changed my aim back another foot. The first machine gun bullet struck the side of the *Gato Gordo's* cabin. Five...The thunderous explosion lit the night sky with an orange-red glow My eardrums rang. I saw Trotter's mouth moving but couldn't hear anything. Within seconds burning diesel fuel and a debris field was all that remained in front of us.

Both liners were unharmed. At first, the lone acknowledgment of our presence was for one of them to shine a couple of lights on us. Within a minute, both blew their horns. They finally believed the information Dennia, Val and Lily had transmitted to them. I guess seeing is believing. Sallar cut the throttle, took the boat out of gear, and let us drift. Stunned we were frozen, not thinking about what might be next. Honestly, at that point none of us gave a shit.

# # # # #

Chapter 67

Russ was the first to emerge from the shock-induced trace we had lapsed into. “If I live to be a thousand years old, I don’t want to go through that again.”

Sallar focused the spotlight on the small areas of burning oil and the floating bits and pieces of boat, of luggage, of items that were unidentifiable. And, mixed in, I sighted life jackets. At least three of them were around bodies. Eventually, we found a fourth. Though I didn’t think it possible, we had to look for survivors. I told Sallar, “Crank her up. We need to check and see if any of them are alive.”

The *El Gato Gordo* coughed and started, its engine noise sounded as if our boat had an attack of conscience. If it did, it reflected the emotions of its four human occupants. Taking another life, even in defense is sobering, and leaves a stamp on those who do. Trotter and I had many stamps that woke us at night and at times drove us to irrational thoughts. Only psychopaths avoid the scaring.

I pulled my pocket watch from my pants. It was a quarter until four.

Over the low rumble of the engines, Sallar shouted, “Mr. Sly, someone is trying to reach us on the radio. Should I answer?”

“No. Nobody wanted to talk to us before this all happened. Well, I don’t want to talk to them after it’s over. You agree?”

I imagined that Sallar smiled as he said, “Exactly, precisely!”

Trotter walked past me with a long-handled boathook and a coil of rope. He said, “I been through this before. I’ll check out the bodies.” When he reached the front tip of the bow he looked back at Sallar and said, “Just follow my hand signals.” He looked at me questioningly.

“Bring them on board. I’ll get blankets to wrap them in.” I went into the cabin as the first helicopter appeared. The next portion of our ordeal was about to begin. Facing it made me bitter.

# # # # #

Chapter 68

The government officials asked all their questions several times, tired of the same answers, and allowed us to leave. More aggressive and more insensitive, the media hounded us as we left the government offices, as we returned to the *Sleepy Dolphin*, and they followed us to the dock. The vultures hovered until Shepard, Mimi, and a half-dozen policemen chased them away. I made the sad, short call to Riaffort I knew I must. He understood my promise to call back with more detail. I wasn't up to details. Finally, finally, finally, Russ, Trotter, and I did what we wanted to do most, sleep. Our ladies stood guard.

Sallar became an instant celebrity and a national mini-hero. As captain of the boat that "saved" the cruise liner tourist business, he was revered, lionized, and was already receiving offers to do commercials. He laughed as he told me he'd been asked to do surfboard endorsement. Sallar had never touched a board, much less ridden one.

Most surprising was the Coloton's reaction. I didn't expect either to be happy with our using their assets to conduct an unapproved military maneuver. The opposite was true. Shepard pointed out that the publicity they were receiving was fifty times what they could afford in an advertising budget. They were already getting reservations from new names. Mimi's lament, she hadn't been able to protect her flowers from the trampling feet of the press. That led their list of two concerns...the other being repairs to the *El Gato Gordo* where four fifty cal bullets did some minor damage. Three flats of pansies and periwinkles solved the first and my check for the repairs the second. As Mimi put it, "We are as happy as two crabs in a basket of dead fish."

Initially, my slumber was the sleep which the mini-death exhaustion brings. The adrenalin that peaked mine and my friends' efforts during the long night left us all in a valley. Dreams came later in the cycle. Dennia told me that several times she shook me to free me of demons she visualized streaming through my nightmares. I slept until Saturday morning. It was a dream that began tying the finishing bow on my adventure with the *Nancy Lynn*.

~ ~ ~ ~ ~ ~

My dreams transported me to a world where venues changed instantly and the impossible and grotesque were norm. I sat in Captain Caprees office answering two questions over and over again. He'd ask, "Who was on the *Nancy Lynn*?" I'd respond with the seven names. He would shout, "Why did you only find four bodies?" As the dream progressed his anger increased as he asked the second question.

Without a segway, I stood on the bow of the *Gato Gordo*, helping Trotter find and secure the bodies floating among the debris. I saw the sightless eyes of Galang Marcos, the face of Iesha, a woman I'd never seen, the headless body of a man who could only have been Harold Runnells, and the permanent smirk on Gino's legless corpse. Suddenly, all the dead stood on the deck behind me, thanked us for bringing them aboard...then they laughed. They laughed! The water cleared. I sat on the flying bridge of the *Nancy Lynn*. I was not alone. Captain Springer sat on one side, Margo on the other. For a long period of time, they just looked at me. At last, they spoke in unison, "Why did you leave us, why did you leave us, why did you leave us..."

When I awoke, I'd already sat straight up in bed. My question, why didn't I find at least one of them. The first answer, they were killed and tossed overboard. That *was* logical. My gut wouldn't accept what my mind swore was fact. There was one loose thread to pull and find if it led somewhere.

~ ~ ~ ~ ~ ~

The Cessna glided through the skies over the Exumas as effortlessly as a gull over a school on baitfish. Dennia cradled a chart on her knees as we flew southward. We were pulling my thread, or as Trotter termed it, chasing a wild goose. The message the dream delivered wouldn't be sent away. Whether we found any trace of the *Nancy Lynn's* missing passengers or not, my conscience refused to be silent until I made an effort.

My phone conversation with Melanie reinforced my determination. The guilt in her soul compounded in layers. Her initial approval of the trip. Her failure to listen to those of us who counseled against loaning the *Nancy Lynn* to such a group. Her payment to Adrian Springer to make the sail possible. Her ill-timed and coercive phone call that soured local officials and denied us help. Despite her stupidity, my heart went out to her. She was guilty of trying to please a loved one, then rescue those she placed in danger. Her feelings toward me were apologetic, not hostile, or condemnation. If I could find Margo and Captain Springer's bodies, it might provide some closure.

"I have the key where we saw the three boats anchored marked on this chart. It's

Old Dog Cay. Do you want to start there?"

I took away the binoculars I'd been holding to my face and set them down. The Exuma islands formed a line a little longer than a hundred miles. The location of the island was in the least inhabited portion. They couldn't have traveled far without a boat and I had to assume they didn't have one. However, it might be possible to move to a neighboring island to look for water or something to eat.

"Let's start here," I pointed to a key four islands north of our objective. "I'd like to fly right down the chain directly over the islands. The pass down, say we fly at a thousand feet. After we go four islands past our target, I want to go back north over the same islands as low as you feel comfortable."

"I'll get you close enough for you to pick coconuts."

Dennia banked the Cessna to the east until she was over the middle of an island then turned to the south. The plane bisected the land as we began the first flyover. I scanned the sands looking for any signs of life, alternating between looking through the binoculars or without them to get a wider scope of vision. Seeing anything in the tangle of palm, pines, and underbrush would be near impossible. If they had survived the captain would put some a signal on the beach where it would be most visible. That's where I concentrated my vision.

"We're getting close, Sly. It's the third island from the one we're over. At least, that's the one I marked on the chart." Dennia pointed to it. I recognized the deeper blue water that provided the anchorage for the three boats on our first visit.

"Can you slow down some," I asked.

"Sorry. I'm right over stalling speed."

"Good enough,"

Nature appalls straight lines. The straight line in the white sand got my attention immediately as we neared the island. As we got closer, I focused the binoculars on it. The line consisted of coconuts with spaces between them. "Somebody left a message." I read aloud what I saw. "Three coconuts...space...three nuts...space...three nuts...space...six nuts...space...six nuts..." No reason to look farther. I yelled, "Springer's send us an S.O.S. in Morse Code. Let's get low and circle."

Dennia dropped our altitude to a hundred feet and flew a tight circle around the cay. She saw them first. "Three people. I see three."

When we passed over the beach with the coconut signal laying on it, I recognized Captain Springer, Margo, and Dalisay Marcos standing near the Morse SOS. They were waving wildly. Dennia wiggled the Cessna's wings and we waved out the windows. Springer stopped waving and placed both his cupped hands in front of his mouth while tilting his head back.

"They need something to drink. Is that cooler waterproof. There are bottles of water and cans of soda in it. If we can drop it to them in the water just off the beach. I'll put a note in it that we're sending help."

She nodded, "I'll fly parallel to the beach, about twenty feet offshore and ten feet off the water."

We made the second circle, this time with the water so close I felt I could have reached down and touched it. Dennia is a damned fine pilot.

Our last vision of the stranded trio, before Dennia returned us to Marsh Harbor, was them splashing and crashing into the Caribbean waters to retrieve the cooler.

~ ~ ~ ~ ~ ~

"The airport people at the Georgetown airstrip said the police will have a boat to pick up the Captain, Margo, and Dalisay within three hours." Dennia switched off her microphone. "I can't wait to hear their story."

"It will be something!" I agreed. Mentally, I told my conscience to take a hike. I stretched my legs in front of me. "It will be great to get a full night's sleep."

Dennia put her hand on the inside of my thigh. "Maybe not a full night."

THE END

DL Havlin

"Open Minds – Open Books"

www.DLHavlin.com

DL Havlin is an eclectic author whose rich, varied background mirrors his novels, novellas and short stories. Mr. Havlin packed three lifetimes of experiences into one brim full existence. He believes, "The one big advantage writing at an advanced age provides is that life is what you know and not what you project it might be."

An avid lover of the outdoors and sports enthusiast, his passion for fishing, hunting, and camping are frequently included in his writing. A deep love for nature and especially wild Florida often furnish settings for his work, but his travels make places such as Kiev, Singapore, London, New York, Modena, or Sachsenhausen backgrounds for his stories as well.

His unique combination of vivid imagination and ability to weave intricate plot lines, seasoned by his lifetime exposure to fascinating story possibilities, provides the heartfelt, enjoyable reading his novels provide. DL is dedicated to the theory that readers are thinkers and one of his favorite responses to anyone questioning the assertion is "Open minds, open books."

He answers, "Why do you write?" by saying, "To entertain - that's first, but to provoke thought is a close second. I firmly believe both are done through the heart, for the mind is seldom opened until it is emotionally conditioned to respond."

Titles by DL Havlin

The Grave with Greener Grass

Turtle Point

Out of Italy

Escaping Skeletons

The Bait Man

Bully Route Home

Blue Water Red Blood

The Cross on Cotton Creek

A Place No One Should Go

The Hangin' Oak

September on Echo Creek

Christmas Story Collection

Story Time-R

For information regarding the author contact PRLady2016@gmail.com or 239.283.3975

www.ingramcontent.com/pod-product-compliance
Lightning Source LLC
Chambersburg PA
CBHW070427170726
48291CB00002B/388

* 9 7 8 1 9 3 3 6 7 8 3 3 7 *